THE SOUL FROM THE SUPERNOVA

A.M. HARTE

Copyright © 2025 by A.M. Harte

All rights reserved.

No portion of this book may be reproduced in any form without written permission from the publisher or author, except as permitted by Canadian copyright law.

No part of this book may be used or reproduced in any manner to train artificial intelligence technologies or systems.

FOLLOW THE AUTHOR!

If you enjoy The Soul from the Supernova and are interested in further tales in the years to come, please join A.M. Harte's official newsletter! Every month, free poetry and book news are available to readers.

Join now!
Talesofangela.com

Dear reader,

My heart is always open to yours

CONTENTS

1.	Rubble	1
2.	Dust Settles	10
3.	Hazel	19
4.	Observations and Star Charts	25
5.	Get the Lights	37
6.	A Memory	48
7.	Secrets and Spies	60
8.	Symbols	70
9.	Blackstone	82
10.	Something Lost	88
11.	Precious Trinkets	97
12.	Chickadee River	104
13.	Beach	119
14.	Rescuer	131

15.	Edeyn's Sorrow	142
16.	Trek	149
17.	Something Hissing This Way Comes	158
18.	Scoria Island	170
19.	Tracking	178
20.	Captives	191
21.	Rose Garden	202
22.	Garden Stroll	218
23.	Assassin	224
24.	Supernova	241
25.	The Best Laid Plans	255
26.	Docks	269
27.	Love in Lost Places	278
28.	The Vigil	294
29.	It Isn't What It Looks Like	304
30.	Shifting	313
31.	The Drowned	321
32.	Aftermath	332
33.	Wreckage	342
34.	Palan	351

35. Of Spies and Lies	362
36. Reunion	373
37. Roses for Passion	383
38. Drop Your Weapons	392
39. Repairs	401
40. The Soul from the Supernova	411
Acknowledgements	415
About the author	417

Chapter One

RUBBLE

Nova stepped across the charred beams of what used to be his front porch. The air smoldered, thick with smoke as fires blazed across entire city blocks. Asayouga was decimated. It had taken him an age to find his way home amidst the debris.

Nova's shirt clung to his chest, soaked in sweat. He now stood in what was left of the house he shared with Nayeli. Filled with an unshakable sense of dread, he swore under his breath. The energy of doom hung thick and heavy around him. As he searched, Nova simultaneously hoped and feared he'd find her remains.

The fire had destroyed nearly everything. Nova couldn't avoid stepping on pieces of broken pottery and splintered, burnt-up furniture. He rubbed his eyes to clear his *sight*—his gifted *sense*. Straining to *see* through the heavy smoke, he scanned the ground for clues of her remains, but there were none to be found.

After finding his kitchen buried in rubble, he doubted whether he would be able to access the back rooms of the house on his own. That didn't matter now. He couldn't just leave her. He climbed over collapsed walls and dug his way through piles of fragmented stones, ignoring the pain in his hands as he made contact with glowing orange debris. How could any of this be real?

Nova held his sleeve across his mouth, struggling to breathe through the fiery particles clogging his chest. As he swept aside the remains of a wall clock, a chunk of stone crashed to the floor, stirring up more ash. Pain ripped through his throat as he erupted in a fit of coughing.

Once he caught his breath, Nova tore his sleeve, tying it around his face in a makeshift mask. He hoped it would add a layer of protection between him and the toxic air. Silently, he continued his work. He had to find her.

Knots formed in his stomach as he carried the image of his beloved in his mind. Images of her thick, black curls, or the pretty colored fabrics she loved to wear appeared in his mind over and over again. But when he blinked, the visions evaporated. It was difficult to hold onto his mental reconstruction of her. Nova hoped he would not have to rely solely on memory to see Nayeli again.

He tried to focus his *sight* to see through the smoke, but the effort made his head throb. The disarray of broken furniture, burnt beams, and collapsed exterior walls distorted his perception.

A gleam of silver caught Nova's eye. He crouched low, crawling through the hallway until he scooped the delicate strand into his palms. He fought back a flutter of panic as he recognized Nayeli's favorite accessory: A carved crystal rose on a thin silver chain. She never took it off.

A sudden eruption of shouting broke Nova's concentration. He leaned back against the wall, sliding down and drawing his knees up to his ears as he rubbed his head with his fingertips. He listened to the voices growing louder as they approached, heart sinking as he only heard one—the voice of his friend Palan. Nova closed his eyes in a silent prayer to no one. *Please tell me they found Nayeli alive.*

Nova, Palan, and Fen had arrived from their research on Observation Point to a scene resembling a nightmare. Nova recalled the moment of sobering realization that something was wrong. Catastrophically wrong. One minute, the three friends were joking and laughing, and the next they stood frozen as they caught sight of smoke rising above the trees.

Palan, often more consciously observant than Nova, had been the first to point out the blazing city. He growled as he observed the smoke, black and billowing above the trees. "Fire," he said.

Nova halted, fear like lightning coursing through his body.

"Nova, can you *see* anything?" Palan asked.

Nova tuned in his own enhanced *sight* to catch glimpses of human figures, dressed in black from head to toe, running through the streets of the city. Nova could *see* far into the distance with his gifted *sense*, even through physical barriers like stone walls or trees in the forest.

His head burned when he amplified his *sense* too intensely. The number of obstructions in the distance between him and the city made even his heightened *vision* indistinct. But he *saw* what he *saw*.

Nova's voice shook as he told his friends, "It's the city. I *see* attackers. Thousands of them. An army?" he said in disbelief.

Palan sniffed the air. Everyone was born with one amplified *sense* and Palan's was his *scent*. With a nose like a bloodhound, he could track anything down. All he needed was a *whiff*.

Palan often complained his *sense* was next to useless. He made no secret of feeling jilted by the gods in that regard. Nevertheless, his enhanced *sense* often attuned him to dangers others were unaware of with their regular sense of smell.

Palan shook his head. "I smell burnt flesh. Death," he said with a grim expression.

As Nova stared at the skyline, he could feel himself going numb.

They prepared to enter the city by stealth, but by the time they reached the outskirts the streets had fallen silent. Smoke sizzled from the remains of abandoned, ruined buildings. Only the sound of his own breathing, labored from inhaling ashy air, hummed in Nova's ears.

They split up to look for their loved ones, the city eerie after the attacks. The assailants seemed to have run through everything and disappeared as quickly as they came.

He lost the ability to process anything he heard or saw. All feeling vanished from his fingers as he sat listening to Palan shouting his name. Nova couldn't even choke out a response to indicate he heard him.

Despite Nova's silence, Palan located him a few moments later. Nova couldn't find the strength to lift his gaze to acknowledge him. Instead, he stared at the tops of Palan's soot-covered boots when he approached.

Silence rang out between them.

"We found her," Palan whispered after a moment's pause.

Nova's heart leapt to his throat. "Where?" he croaked as his head shot up to look at his friend.

Palan pressed his lips into a thin line. "Come," he said. He shifted the silent bundle on his hip: his daughter, Melly. She didn't let out a peep; Nova nearly missed seeing her. Her head rested on her father's shoulder as she chewed her fist, eyes wide.

Nova pushed himself up from the ground and swept his hands against his pant legs to remove the ash that coated his palms. The action only seemed to make things worse as black streaks formed on the fabric of his trousers. He looked around at what used to be his home, sniffed, and adjusted the positioning of his sleeve-mask against his nose before nodding. "Yeah. Let's go."

Palan led the way. It was mid-morning, a time when the streets of Asayouga should have been bustling with activity. But there was no one there now, only the crackling of smoke, the shine of glowing embers, and lifeless bodies—many of which were charred beyond recognition. The city had burned impossibly fast.

The three of them made their way slowly to the outskirts of the city. Finally, Palan came to a halt and nodded in a direction a little further ahead of them. He still carried Melly.

Nova could *see* Nayeli's body clearly, lying on the ground among the trees. He steeled himself to go the rest of the distance, squeezing his eyes shut in an extended blink before stepping over sticks and leaves to get to her. Although the earth was soft and springy beneath Nova's feet, every footfall roared like thunder in his ears.

She looked so peaceful. Nayeli's face was still, her chest unmoving, her expression tranquil. Not wanting to accept reality, Nova could almost believe she was simply asleep.

Tears choked Nova as he slowly knelt beside her. His fingers tenderly brushed her hair away from her gentle features. Her black, silky curls clung to her skin, sticky with blood. At that moment, Nova had never experienced anything as painful as looking at Nayeli's motionless body.

"Not you," Nova whispered. "I... need you."

His eyes traced the frame of her body, noting the torn and blood-soaked clothing clinging to her skin where she had been stabbed. A wave of nausea washed over him as he stared at the gaping wound in her abdomen. His gaze reached her hands. A dagger, covered in blood, rested in her palm. Nova didn't recognise the weapon as one of their own. She had clearly removed it from her own stomach.

Nayeli's body lay alone on the forest floor. Whoever killed her was long gone. A pang of anguish shot through Nova as reality sunk in. His beloved held no weapons of her own. She wouldn't have had much chance fighting back while defenseless. He wondered if a killer pursued her as she ran, or if the encounter in the woods was incidental. The city had been wiped out so quickly.

Nova looked up at the sky, darkened with thick smoke from the ruins behind him. He could hardly tell it was still daylight, even with his enhanced *sense* of *sight*. Nova took the dagger in his hand and stared at the deadly, curved blade. It was beautiful in a way, carved out of shimmering black stone. There were symbols etched along the blade and hilt alike in a language Nova could not recognize. He wiped the blade clean and tucked it into his belt.

Nova touched his fingers gently against Nayeli's forehead and closed his eyes. He imagined he could *see* her light appearing in the sky above them shining brighter than the surrounding stars.

Everyone knew souls were connected to starlight. He hoped to see her brightness shining over them that night. The thought of her soul resting safely in the vastness of the outer universe brought Nova a fleeting moment of comfort. He held onto the peaceful thought as he leaned down to kiss Nayeli's face for the last time.

Gingerly, he lifted Nayeli's lifeless arm into his lap. He extracted her silver rose bracelet from his pocket and clasped it onto her wrist before resting her hand over her heart. He lingered as time stood still. Neither Palan nor Melly interrupted Nova's reverence.

"I will find you," Nova whispered, his voice hoarse as he spoke the promise he didn't fully understand.

He sat by her body, hoping he would soon see her again living in the stars.

Chapter Two

DUST SETTLES

Nova sat next to a campfire along the shores of the Chickadee River watching as his neighbor, Sonny Pippit, poked at the coals with a stick. He didn't mind their new living arrangements. The roaring waters of the Chickadee brought a sense of peace, though it would never feel the same as home.

As she nudged the fire, he regarded the frayed hem of Sonny's shirt, noticing every smudge of dirt ground into its coarse fabric. Glancing down at his own dirt-caked fingernails, Nova sighed. There wasn't much time for hygiene after all the energy spent securing their camp.

Asayouga's survivors were homeless and displaced after the city was decimated. The river promised a source of fresh, clean drinking water. Banding together to restore a place to rest, they divided into groups, each assigned to secure a camp with a combination of mundane fortifications and *sensory* illusions. It had taken weeks to fully migrate, and efforts to recover supplies from the destruction continued every day. Nova's research team, along with Sonny, had been assigned to the site of the Great Library.

Nova struggled to feel useful. Creating visual *illusions* with his gifted *sight* had never been his strong suit, so he could not help with camouflaging the campsite. Though he tried his best to focus on recovering books and archives at the Great Library as he was supposed to, his thoughts always wandered to Nayeli. He replayed the Ceremony of the Departed over and over in his mind, recalling the hope he held as he gazed at the stars, only to have it shattered when he could not find her there.

Ancient Asayougan tradition said souls transformed to starlight when they passed away. Likewise, when a star died it was said a human life was born in exchange.

If anyone knew anything about the stars, it was Nova. He had been studying them with his small research team for years, long before he ever met Nayeli. Even as a child, the outer realms held his fascination.

He had always held the legends as established truth. New stars were often recorded after people passed on, though not always. The discrepancy was easy enough to explain as the universe was infinite and a new star could appear anywhere within it. Nova understood he may not be able to observe anything new from his vantage point, but he desperately wished for physical evidence to restore his faith. If Nayeli's soul had not become starlight, there was nothing left for Nova to believe in, and he *needed* to believe in something.

He watched as Melly sat next to the fire, tightly clutching a doll. She hadn't spoken for as long as they'd been at camp. Though they'd never recovered Sapphira's remains, they assumed the little girl's mother perished in the attacks.

A sharp curse word rang out and snapped Nova to attention. He glanced up to see Palan kicking the dirt.

"What's wrong with you?" Nova asked, his voice wary. He felt Palan's tension building daily since the attack. Everyone was on edge, and Nova couldn't prevent himself from noticing everyone else's anxiety on top of his own.

Palan let out a snarl like a wild wolf. "What *isn't* wrong!"

Although Nova agreed, he knew there must be more eating away at his brooding colleague. "Something in particular, though?" Nova asked, unable to keep the impatience from his voice. It wasn't his job to handle Palan's ferocity. He knew that, yet he still felt a familiar tightness growing in his chest.

Palan sat down next to his daughter and handed her a wild strawberry. The gentleness of his action contrasted sharply with his flaring anger.

Melly accepted the strawberry but stared at the fruit in her palms without eating it.

"It's *FENWICK*!"

Nova shrugged. "What has he done?"

"Nothing. That's the whole point, Nova. He's done NOTHING."

"Why should that be any of your concern?"

Palan shot Nova a thunderous look. "He's never where he should be, and when he IS somewhere, he's completely drunk. He's useless."

Nova disagreed silently regarding Fen. He would be drunk as well if his body didn't react so poorly to alcohol. "I think he's just hurting," he replied with a shrug.

Palan growled and changed the subject. "We need to return to The Point. The records may still be there."

Nova considered their years of research. The last time they saw Observation Point was on the day their city burned. Nova was terrified of what they might find when they returned to their observatory. He shuddered at the thought of all their hard work destroyed.

"Then let's go," Nova replied.

Sonny inserted herself into the conversation. "I hope you find something," she stated. "If I have to look at one more burnt tome, I'm going to throw myself into the Chickadee."

As a keeper of records, Sonny was particularly devastated over the ruined Great Library. Thousands of years of knowledge—hers to guard, protect, and disseminate—eliminated in a flash.

Nova nodded. "The star charts are there. I just know it." It was more of a prayer than a knowing, but he hoped if he repeated the phrase enough it would become true.

"Oh yeah? You know it?" Fen's voice drawled behind Nova.

Palan leapt to his feet and grabbed at the energy pistol kept loosely holstered in his belt loop. "Does no one find this suspicious that he shows up now, just as we discuss returning to Observation Point!"

Nova stood and held up his hand as if that could do anything at all to stop an energy blast. "Palan! Leave him alone."

"Ohhh, don't worry about defending me, sweet thing," Fen said, his eyes never leaving Palan's despite his heavy inebriation. "This old fool can't aim true to save his life."

Palan growled and pulled his pistol anyway. Fen spat into the dirt.

Nova created a barrier between his colleagues, holding out his arms in a gesture of surrender. "Put your weapon down, Palan."

"Enough!" Sonny hollered in a voice that froze them all. "You're frightening the child. Although I'm not sure who the children are just now!"

Fen popped open another bottle and swaggered over to the fire. "Excuse me, little lady," he said with an apologetic nod to Melly who sat clutching her doll for dear life, strawberry juice oozing through her fingers.

Palan tossed the pistol into the dirt and growled. He stomped in a circle before sitting down next to Melly again. He pulled the child into his lap in an attempt to comfort her. She hardly moved.

Nova lowered himself back to his seat, still wired for action. As they sat around the fire, Sonny dished out food and they ate in silence. Except for Melly. She crawled out of her father's lap and into their sleeping shelter without a word, leaving her portion of dinner untouched.

"We should go back," Nova said at last, once the food revived him.

"I'm in!" Fen announced in a cheerful voice.

"I'll believe that when I see it," Palan said, adding a few colorful but indistinctive words to the end of his sentence.

Nova leaned back to look up at the sky. The sun's light shone low above the horizon, casting an array of colors everywhere. Even with the remaining daylight, he could already see a faint trace of the stars. He looked for the Castle and the Knight. His two favorite constellations. He routinely found them first and it offered him inexplicable comfort to see them there, always exactly where they were meant to be.

As the night darkened, Nova drifted in and out of sleep where he lay. Somewhere in the middle of the space between consciousness and unconsciousness, a vision appeared above him.

It was her face. She knelt over him, her silvery dress resembling the ceremonial garb traditionally worn during the Ceremony of the Departed. She looked as beautiful as she always did. Her fingers brushed Nova's cheek, feeling as real as ever against his skin.

Nova woke, choking on his own tears. Gasping for breath, he sat up, clinging to the fading vision of his lost love. Only the darkness greeted him and he shivered as the temperature had dropped in the hours since falling asleep.

"Gods above," Nova whispered as agony tore again at his heart. He wondered when this was supposed to get easier, if he could ever just breathe again without the pain of missing her. "Why did it have to be her?"

As Nova's heart rate—racing from his abrupt wake-up—returned to a normal speed, he lifted his gaze to the night sky again. Kelmundy's three moons glowed brightly as they made their way toward their annual super alignment.

Searching for the Castle and the Knight once more to calm his nerves, he paused, staring into the dark sky as an unfamiliar star caught his attention. Nova fixed his gaze at the foot of the Knight constellation where he saw a new speck of light. He couldn't look away, afraid it would turn out to be an illusion created from his own desperation and grief. As long as he stared, the star didn't fade.

His heart leapt, hardly daring to believe his own eyes. He had to be certain.

Nova raced to the supply crate near the sleeping tent and rifled through its contents, pulling out parchment and pen in a hurry. He cleared a space in the dirt, grabbing stones to pin down the corners of the blank page. As he craned his neck to examine the stars again, relief overwhelmed him to the edge of tears. The star was still there! He wasn't imagining it.

With gridlines already pre-sketched on the parchment, Nova only needed to add his observed findings to the correct coordinates. He drew the Knight first for reference before adding his observation. Excitement buzzed within him as he added more and more stars to the chart. It wasn't just one new point but several, forming a full constellation that looked like a fortress of starlight. It looked like Asayouga.

When he finished his drawing and verified it twice more, as was his routine with any discovery, Nova sat back in awe attempting to collect his thoughts. It was her. Not just her. It was all of them. Everyone who was lost in the brutal attack. A tiny glimmer of relief settled into Nova's chest. He felt his breathing ease as a fraction of prolonged tension left his body.

Nova's initial apprehension about returning to Observation Point evaporated. Whether or not their equipment remained standing no longer seemed to matter. What mattered was that his beliefs were still true. Knowing Nayeli was there, shining even after death, restored a modicum of Nova's hope. Maybe his beliefs weren't a lie after all.

He rolled up the parchment and clutched it tightly to his chest. He could hardly wait to show Palan.

Chapter Three
Hazel

Sonny hugged herself as she stood outside her sister's ruined home, the silence of the city pressing in on her. She normally loved peace and quiet, but the stillness of a destroyed Asayouga didn't have the same serenity. Unconsciously, Sonny used her *touch* energy to *feel* for anyone nearby, but there was no one present. Apart from a few small creatures like mice and squirrels, there were no signs of life.

It had been years since she and Hazel connected. Sonny didn't spend much time contemplating her sister's life choices. Instead, she buried herself in the solitude of her work. Record-keeping took all of her attention when she allowed it to. Still, family was family.

When Hazel didn't show up by the Chickadee, Sonny's heart sank. Desperate for closure, she looked for any opportunity to search for her sister's body. She hadn't been found—yet. At last, Sonny found time to venture out on a search of her own.

As she stood on the front porch of her sister's ruined home, she hesitated. She ducked her head, afraid to climb over the wreckage of the collapsed front door. What if she didn't find her? What if she *did*? Desolation sat in her stomach as heavy as a boulder. "You can do this," she whispered to herself.

With a deep breath, she ascended the front steps and, one-by-one, pulling splintered wood aside until she could fight her way over the threshold. Hazel's living room looked eerily untouched despite how the home's exterior appeared.

The ongoing search for survivors left unanswered questions. Sonny felt she needed to take matters into her own hands if she wanted to know for sure. Despite wanting to know one way or another what happened to her sister, she had avoided approaching Hazel's home, afraid of what she would or would not find. She wasn't sure how she would react to finding Hazel's body, but she gathered the courage to push past her worries.

Rubbing her palms together, Sonny called an orb of light to guide her as she took tentative steps up to the second level. Although she knew where she lived, Sonny had never been inside her sister's home. A laugh bubbled up in her throat as she traced along rows and rows of bookshelves lining the hallway. She and Hazel were more alike than either of them had ever acknowledged to each other.

Sonny kept her steps slow, holding her orb of light in her palm as she took in her sister's décor, so similar to her own. She passed an office, covered in a thin layer of ash, but otherwise untouched. The floor was bare except for a white and purple area rug with frayed edges.

She pushed open the wooden door at the end of the hallway to reveal what she assumed was Hazel's bedroom. The room was quiet, like everything else. Her tired, sore feet dragged along the floorboards as she thudded across the room until she reached her sister's neatly-made bed. Sonny rubbed her aching joints, a reminder as to why she chose a lifetime of books and research over a more physical career.

As she allowed herself a moment for the aches to resolve, Sonny closed her fingers around the orb of light in her palm, snuffing it out. Silence pulsed in her ears as a wave of her sister's energy filtered to her awareness like the warmth from a ray of sunshine.

"It's like you're still here. But I can't see you," she whispered.

She scanned the darkened bedroom as her eyes adjusted to the dim. The room was kept neat and tidy. Her gaze fell on a thick notebook resting on the bedside table. She brushed the dust from the cover with her palm as she picked it up and held it in her lap, staring at the cover art.

Guilt held her back for a moment, but she pushed past the feeling and opened the book, leafing through the pages one at a time. It appeared to be a journal, every page filled with perfect, round handwriting. She was afraid to read the words.

Her hand continued turning the pages almost against her will, until a name caught her attention. It was her own. Flattening the journal with her hand, she stared at the writing, her chest constricting with tension. What did her sister have to say about her?

The entry was dated over a year past, but Sonny hadn't spoken to Hazel in at least a decade. Part of her screamed to set the diary aside without reading, letting whatever words her sister had written remain private and unknown to Sonny. But she couldn't stop herself after all.

Hazel's writing was easy to read:

Sometimes I wonder about Sonny. Could we have worked it out? But it's been so long now, I don't want to disturb her. She was always so sensitive. If I make an appearance now, it'll just rattle her. I saw her outside the library, talking to Isara. She always liked the smith, but probably has more affection for her books. Anyway, maybe she made friends, maybe she has someone now. I hope so. I came home and made tea after that. I can't stop thinking about it. But I see Lani tonight. She'll cheer me up.

Sonny read the paragraph several more times. It surprised her. She'd thought of reaching out to Hazel many times, too, but had always thought it best to leave things be. Sighing, she wondered if she and her sister could have repaired their estrangement. She would never know now.

"I hope you made it out," Sonny said, though she knew it couldn't be true. There weren't many places to hide on the island. There was no way of knowing where her sister was when Asayouga fell. If she couldn't find her body in the home, she didn't know where else she could search. The only logical conclusion was that Hazel perished along with everyone else stuck in the city when it was attacked.

Sonny shuddered. It must have been horrifying. Grief threated to choke her as she envisioned those she cared about fleeing and being struck down, others buried under collapsed infrastructure. It was too much to think about. Only a stroke of fortune—whether good or bad—had spared her own life that day. She was out cataloguing plants near Observation Point. It was rare she ever ventured beyond the library. Instead, she preferred to spend as much time with books and records as she could.

Why she had been spared when so many others were not was a puzzle Sonny couldn't work through. The cosmos didn't seem to care one way or another who lived or who died.

Sonny didn't know how much time passed as she sat in silence with Hazel's diary open in her lap. At last, she shut the book and tucked it inside her coat. Maybe she would have the guts to explore it more later. At least she would have something of her sister to carry with her.

She rose, her legs throbbing briefly as they adjusted to her change in posture. Sonny moved slowly through the rest of the home until she was certain Hazel's remains were not there. Accepting the most likely truth was difficult without seeing the evidence with her eyes. Eventually, Sonny returned to the empty city streets and navigated her way back to the ruined library.

Chapter Four
Observations and Star Charts

They returned to Observation Point the next day, fueled by a renewed sense of optimism combined with fresh, astronomical data. Nova stood a moment in reverent silence upon finding the observatory still standing, all of its stonework intact and exactly as they had left it on the morning Asayouga was destroyed. He knew every bump or notch in its stone walls by heart, and everything was the way he remembered.

He could hardly move as relief and gratitude coursed through him. Finding all their work still safe and untouched felt like a miracle.

The site had been deeply protected from the start. *Illusions* were set deep into every brick of the observatory but the ground itself was rumored to be blessed by the gods. It was why the hill was chosen in the first place. Their years of careful study were priceless. To have that information destroyed would have been gut-wrenching. Nova understood Sonny's grief over the library. There were not just physical books that had been lost but centuries of wisdom and memory.

Whether guarded by the grace of the divine or simply by sheer luck, his beloved workspace and sanctuary remained unscathed. The first thing Nova did was run up the narrow spiral staircase to the observatory's upper deck, checking to see whether all his equipment remained properly calibrated. He examined every dial, taking his time with the view finders until he was satisfied. Everything remained in its place.

A sudden shriek pulled Nova's attention to the ground. He leaned forward over the railing to find the source of the noise as a brief moment of panic re-entered his chest. He could do without ever feeling that level of shock again.

There was another shriek, followed by an eruption of bubbling laughter. The moment of puzzled confusion vanished as Nova realized there was no cause for alarm. It was a happy scream. He smiled as he watched Melly collapse onto the ground in a fit of giggles as her father caught up with her. Nova hoped this was a sign the child may regain her voice soon.

The journey back to the hill had brought up complex feelings, but being there again, seeing the open sky and all his bookcases, workbenches, and equipment seemed to break through the haze that hung over his mind since Asayouga burned.

Nova's boots clanked against the metal steps as he ran back down the staircase to join his friends, his mood lifted immeasurably.

A variety of weapons decorated the wall of the observatory entrance. Although, Asayouga was a peaceful city up until the day it was destroyed, it had not always been so. Centuries prior, Asayouga was renowned for its military discipline. Over time, the city had become the sole power on the island.

Many Asayougans still chose to practice the art of weaponry, even though the need for combat readiness had long since passed. Ancient techniques were revered as an art form, and some committed themselves to the discipline entirely. Nova wished that had been enough to defend the city. Asayouga no longer had an army, and though some had fought, the invasion was unexpected, swift, and utterly devastating.

On sudden impulse, Nova grabbed two glaives from their stand, a small smile crossing his lips. He carried them out to the hilltop where Melly and Palan played.

"Heads up!" Nova shouted as he tossed a heavy, double-edged weapon to Palan who caught it with startling ease.

Palan leaned down and ruffled his daughter's hair. Melly still held onto the doll that never seemed to leave her side, but she appeared more relaxed by far than she had in weeks.

Nova assumed his opening stance as Palan whirled his weapon around in his hand, showing off his mastery of it. The two sparred, Nova's footwork still as fast as ever. His friend, however, seemed to have advanced his skill since the last time they practiced.

Nova ducked as Palan's glaive swooshed, the speed at which it flew past his head enough to blow his hair into his face. He found himself rolling and dodging at ground level, struggling to block his opponent's blows and regain his footing.

Finally, an opening appeared. Nova leapt to his feet as Palan swung at him in a grand, sweeping arc. Grabbing Palan's weapon with his free hand, he lunged forward with his glaive, aiming to knock his friend off balance and end the match.

But just as he launched his final strike, Nova fell back with a hard thud, the wind knocked from his lungs. Palan pressed the heavy oak weapon against his throat, pinning Nova to the plush grass beneath him. He stared up at Palan in shock, surprised to see Palan's expression of stone-cold thunder. He wondered when this man had found the time to improve so much.

Nova laughed as he regained his composure. "That was incredible!" he gasped, returning to his feet as Palan retracted his weapon. "When did you learn that?"

Palan's posture relaxed, as he tossed his glaive to the ground. "Asayouga is gone," Palan said, his tone grim. "If we ever find out who's responsible, I'm not going to give them a second opportunity to destroy us."

"Agreed," Nova said. He squinted up at the clear, bright sky. They still had plenty of daylight before he'd have the opportunity to view the stars through his telescopes.

Nova shifted his weight back and forth from one foot to the other. He'd been toying with an idea ever since he discovered the new constellation. It was an idea that had grown quickly into a burning need. Yet, he hesitated to mention it to Palan, knowing how practical his friend was and how terribly impractical Nova's plans could be on first conception. He had a tendency towards impulsivity.

He brushed his hands against his trousers once more and cleared his throat. Despite how incomplete his plans were, now seemed as good a time as any to share them with Palan.

Observation Point stood safe and sound, and he had found Nayeli's energy in the cosmos—it all felt like a good omen.

"Listen," Nova began.

Palan sat down next to Melly in the grass and leaned back on his elbows, staring at the clouds and not at Nova. "Mmm?" he said, acknowledging he was listening.

"I was wondering if..." Nova hesitated. He could anticipate Palan's mockery and nearly lost his nerve. He plunged ahead. He had to get the words out. "I was wondering if you'd ever considered space travel."

Seconds of silence passed as Nova braced himself for any response.

Palan sat all the way up. "You're serious, aren't you?" he asked, keeping his voice low.

The concept was not new. Nova's team had been gathering and studying data from the outer expanse for as long as Observation Point existed. In addition, they devoted time to speculative technology.

Legends told of an ancient race of star travelers who originally founded Asayouga. Nova had studied countless volumes of knowledge about their spacecraft and how it operated, although no tangible remains of those vessels had ever been uncovered.

Regardless, they had at least proven the materials were possible, and they even crafted prototypes of the materials needed to construct the outer hull using technology that would survive the forces of the atmosphere as well as the vacuum of space. They had never constructed a full ship, but pieces of structures existed.

Ancient myths and stories told of spacecraft built to maintain life in space. Many described how a spaceship could be fueled, and detailed the use of *sensory* technology that would provide working systems. Nova had no way of knowing if any of the tales were possible to create in the real world, but he allowed himself to dream they were. Now seemed as good a time as any to find out.

As he admired the new stars each night, charting them, observing celestial patterns, he wondered what it would be like to observe them more closely. Perhaps it wasn't possible to reach the stars, but the thought of being surrounded by them thrilled Nova to his core.

He had the advantage of his enhanced *sight*. All were born with a strengthened *sense*. Some could *see* long distances, create visions, illusions, or *see* through dense substances. That was Nova. While he'd never been very good at visual disguises, he could *see* further than anyone he knew. It was part of what caught his fascination with astronomy so deeply. The wonders of space would surely be even more incredible from beyond Kelmundy's sphere.

Palan Keentrack could follow trails and pick up on the faintest change in weather simply by using his nose. Their partner, Fenwick Greensong, was skilled with the *voice*. He could understand and recreate any language, while using the power of his words to sway his listeners. Any melody Fenwick sung could shift the mood of his audience in an instant.

The three of them combined had three of the five gifted *senses*, a fact which had proved very useful as they worked together on their research. There were legends of some who were born without a physical *sense*, who could perhaps *know* the future, but Nova had never met anyone with such a talent.

"I'm very serious, Palan," Nova said, smiling again. Aside from his natural scientific curiosity, Nova wondered what it would feel like to observe the soul stars up close. Even if Nayeli's energy only existed as a ball of light, the warmth that filled Nova's chest as he imagined being closer to his beloved once more seemed to awaken an innate purpose within him.

"What makes you think that's even possible?" Palan said, his voice betraying his curiosity.

"We've done it before," Nova said, shrugging.

"No. WE have not. Those are tales, Nova," Palan said. He looked at his daughter who was quietly playing with a handful of rocks.

"Many of the tales contain truth," Nova replied. "And we have done some of it. We already know how to build the hull. We haven't solved every potential problem yet, but we've used our *senses* to create technology for centuries. It's possible."

He thought of the new constellations appearing just as his hope had nearly disappeared forever. Some beliefs were worth holding onto if they kept hope alive.

Palan shook his head, dark hair flopping into his eyes. The man was a mess and somehow made the aesthetic work. "I don't know, Nova. It would be a huge undertaking."

"Yeah. But what else were we going to do. Our home is gone. Maybe home never really existed down here."

Melly's laughter rang out and the two men looked up to see what had caught the child's attention.

A dark figure, clad all in black, loosely resembling the marauders who had tried to destroy them, held Melly's hands while dancing with the little girl. Nova focused his *sight* to *see* past the shadow cast by the sunlight behind them. Quickly, he recognized Fen.

Nova smiled and waved his colleague over. "He's here," Nova said softly.

Palan's countenance darkened as Nova acknowledged Fen. "Sure," he muttered under his breath. "You just show up when you please, highness."

Nova pretended not to hear Palan. He witnessed Melly's laughter as Fen twirled her around. Reflecting on all the little girl had seen sent a wave of bittersweet sorrow washing over him. Tears spilled from his eyes before he could stop them. He wiped his face quickly before anyone else could notice. It was good to see her smiling.

"I have arrived," Fen said in a bright voice. He held Melly on his hip as he joined Palan and Nova.

Palan sighed, saying nothing as Fen handed his daughter over to him.

"Look, daddy! Fenny gave me a present!" Melly held up a milky white stone that shimmered faintly in the sunlight.

Nova recognized it as moonstone.

"Did you say thank you?" Palan asked, hiding his animosity better as he spoke to his daughter.

Melly was distracted looking at her rock, holding it at different angles to the light to see how it changed its colors, sometimes catching a flood of luminescent blue. She didn't respond.

Nova grasped his friend's arm in a welcoming greeting. "You're just in time," he said.

"I'm always just in time for the party," Fen said with a throaty laugh.

"We've been discussing space travel," Nova informed him.

"You know I always love a good delusion. What are we doing?" Fen asked.

"*WE* aren't doing anything, yet," Palan said, although his voice gave away his resignation.

"We're building a spaceship," Nova exclaimed, unable to hide his excitement at the idea despite Palan's obvious lack of enthusiasm.

"Great!" Fen exclaimed, "Where is it?"

Nova hesitated a moment before replying, embarrassed. "It's in my head at the moment."

Fen smiled. "We'll be needing to get started, then."

The three of them headed back to the observatory to begin planning. There were more details than Nova originally imagined there would be. Although they had developed some technology already, most of the framework remained theoretical. The task of bringing it all into reality felt daunting.

Every aspect of the design needed to be planned down to the smallest detail. They would have to craft quarters for sleeping, waste disposal, food storage and consumption, and that was before the technology needed to power the ship.

As they entered the observatory, Nova pulled volumes of research from the shelves and stacked them on the table. The critical information was all there, carefully recorded over the years. The sheer amount of data would have been enough to deter Nova in the past from ever beginning such a project.

He wished for Nayeli's wisdom as they began their discussions. She would have pointed out what he would inevitably miss. Yet, Nova knew she would have been just as enthusiastic and excited as he was at the prospect of space travel. He wondered if her soul, in its current form, still supported him and his work. He wondered if she still held memories of their connection, or if she merely existed as a ball of fire.

As they drew out their plans late into the night, Nova allowed himself to slide into the fantasy of being near to her once more.

Chapter Five

GET THE LIGHTS

Sonny Pippit swatted at the night flies annoying her as she gathered her satchels and cookware before dawn. "Damn pests."

She shifted and twisted, attempting to distribute the weight of all her supplies more evenly across her body. With a heavy sigh, Sonny used her *touch* to send comforting energy through her spine, easing the burden of all she carried.

A tiny hiccup drew her attention to the little girl who had been her silent helper over the months camped by the Chickadee River. They had been there so long Sonny could no longer say with confidence that she knew the calendar date. She prided herself on keeping excellent records, but the days since the destruction of their home all blurred together, effectively stealing her anchor to the reality of time. She noted the air had grown heavier as it often did toward the end of the year.

Although the survivors had spent months combing through the ruined city, they made slow progress. They focused their rebuilding efforts on the new site at the Chickadee. Digging through the city would take years of intensive efforts. Sonny held onto hope she would one day see her Great Library again, even if it meant rebuilding it anew along the river. For now, she focused on salvaging all the materials she could from the heaps of shattered stone that had once held more knowledge than she could ever dream of knowing in one lifetime.

A sense of permanent sadness swirled through her as she recalled the only place she ever felt she truly belonged: among rows and rows of books. The library was the closest thing she had to home. She loved her role there, researching information, organizing records, and preserving the knowledge of Asayouga.

Even amidst its current state of ruin, she felt a familiar peace surrounded by the spirits of books, if books had spirits. She didn't really know, but to Sonny, it only seemed natural that they did. Lately, Sonny split her time between recovering materials from the site of the library and aiding Nova with building his spaceship. She had plenty of skills and expertise to lend to his project, and she found it gave her hope to focus on new possibilities instead of ruminating on lost knowledge.

Construction continued along the Chickadee. Sonny had already lent her *touch* to adding protections around the encampment. The survivors combined their gifted *senses* together to create complex illusions that would discourage further surprise attacks in the future.

Sonny felt more drawn to the spacecraft than to rebuilding efforts. As a keeper of knowledge, the new technology fascinated her and she was much more comfortable within that skill set than she was with construction.

She held out a hand to Melly. "Are you ready?" she asked. Melly had stuck by her side traveling back and forth to the hill as often as Sonny herself went.

Melly nodded and stood up. She held onto her doll, never letting it out of her tight grasp. Sonny felt sorry for the little girl who lost her mother along with her home. Although Sapphira's remains had not been uncovered, anyone still missing was now presumed dead.

There were other children who survived, but Melly never seemed interested in engaging with them. Sonny did not press the child to interact, knowing she herself would have a hard time understanding the situation at such a young age.

Most of Sonny's family passed away when she was a child. She had grown up in charge of caring for her sister, and although there were adults around, she couldn't remember a time when she had anyone caring for her aside from herself.

Sonny's sister, Hazel, was the only family she'd ever known, and even that eventually fell apart when Hazel entered adulthood. Sonny preferred keeping to herself after a lifetime of doing so. All she really wanted to do was study. The knowledge she guarded in the library was not only her work but her passion.

Seeing herself in the child's situation, Sonny took it upon herself to look after Melly when her father could not. Palan was heavily involved building Nova's starship, as well as investigating the now-ruined city. He was a natural at the latter, given his powerful tracking skill.

Sonny knelt in front of the child and smiled. "Ready to go see your dad?" she asked as she tried and failed at adjusting Melly's tangled curls.

In response, Melly nodded and hugged her doll close to her chest with both arms.

Together, they traveled to Observation Point. By the time they reached the top of the hill, the sun had risen above the horizon. The seasonal humidity also thickened as daylight arrived, causing Sonny to break into a sweat.

Melly seemed to transform into a different child as soon as she saw the worksite. She broke into a run and didn't stop until she grabbed onto her father's legs, forcing the man to reach down and pick her up.

Sonny followed at a more natural pace until she joined the others. She gladly dumped her burdens onto the ground, planting her hands on her hips as she surveyed their progress.

It was incredible how much they built in such a short time. It was as if Nova had been waiting his whole life to command a mission to space, and the unexpected massacre was somehow a necessary catalyst. It was strange to think that destiny could be born of such despair.

Isara was hard at work crafting metal sheets and panels as the star vessel's construction demanded. Her metal shop in Asayouga was only half standing. Being somewhat fireproof by design, it wasn't left as desecrated as the surrounding buildings.

They took what they could from the old blacksmith shop and brought it closer to the building site, eliminating the need to transport materials back and forth from the ruined city. Salvaging Isara's forge would take more effort than building her a new work space close to the ship. It was easy to integrate changes with Isara close at hand.

Sonny caught herself staring at Isara in open admiration as the blacksmith worked, her muscles rippling visibly as she hammered away at a sheet of metal.

"Come inside and have a look at what we've added," Palan said, at last greeting Sonny.

She broke her gaze away from Isara's work and smiled. "Of course! Yes, show me."

Sonny clomped up the ramp, boots ringing out on the metal surface. She had never been a graceful mover but—in striking paradox—she used her *sense* of *touch* with the elegance of a dancer.

She specialized in healing, cooking, and lightwork. Sometimes she found it ironic that her own body did not move as flexibly as most. But her power was strong when it was turned outward.

Palan gestured at a small room. The vessel was set up with the engine in the middle, twisting through the ship from floor to ceiling, while small, sectioned pods lined the perimeter.

"Will this do for food storage, you think?" Palan asked, sounding like he couldn't care less what Sonny's opinion of the space would be.

Sonny poked her head inside the room anyway. "That'll do," she said, voicing her approval. She found herself wishing she could escape the land along with Nova. An adventure to the stars sounded far better than staying on the ground speculating whether or not her beloved library would ever feel like home again without her books.

"Good," Palan said.

Sonny caught a glimpse of gold beneath Palan's shirt collar. She noticed he wore the chain before, but he always kept it tucked carefully inside the fabric of his clothing. She wondered why he kept it hidden but didn't presume to ask.

"Now, if you don't mind, we actually need help with the lighting," Palan said, always ready to continue working.

"I would absolutely love to take a look at the lighting," Sonny said, eager to do anything besides speak to Palan. The man always made her slightly uncomfortable. He had an edge about him that clashed with her own rough edges.

She and Nova completed the wiring throughout the spaceship's panels, but now the time came for her *touch* to hum throughout the ship, coursing through the vessel like it was a living, breathing being with metal skin.

Just then, Palan's expression hardened. Sonny frowned. She turned to see what had caught Palan's notice and discovered Fen darkening the doorway of the spacecraft.

"Oh, look who decided to grace us with his presence," Palan said grimly.

Sonny could hardly ignore the growing animosity between the two of them. It was becoming difficult to stand in the same room when both Fen and Palan occupied the space.

"You always greet me so warmly!" Fen said with a bright grin, seemingly unbothered by Palan's acerbity.

"That's because you're so bloody charming," Palan said, voice dripping sarcasm.

"I... was just about to get the lights going," Sonny said, quickly cutting in before the two could launch into another round of pointless banter.

"Can I help?" Fen offered.

Palan snorted.

"Yes!" Sonny said, shooting Palan a pointed look. "Yes, you absolutely can help."

Although it was true Fen had frequently been absent from the project, the work he did contribute was invaluable. Nova would not have a hope of launching without Fen's careful calculations. As much as his comings and goings seemed to irritate Palan, he contributed plenty to Nova's team.

Sonny and Fen set to work. He offered stand-by assistance for Sonny as she carefully rubbed her hands together to call in power. She closed her eyes. It felt easier to send her *touch* through the wires when she wasn't looking at the object in front of her. Somehow, observing physical reality impeded her ability to focus on the energy she needed. Instead, she preferred to let her intuition guide her. Although she didn't understand why, she didn't question her process because it worked.

She *felt* through the walls, directing her *sense* through the complicated network of cords and wires, filling them with light. One by one, she electrified them with her *touch.*

It was slow, methodical work requiring her full focus. By the time evening arrived, Sonny was famished. She was so absorbed in her task she had forgotten all about stopping to eat.

It wasn't until Nova entered the spacecraft that she realized how long she'd been working.

"Fen!" Nova said, surprised but seemingly enthused to see his friend.

Sonny wondered how he could have missed the palpable tension between Fen and Palan earlier. To her, it had felt so discernibly loud anyone should have felt it across all the Ersette Isles.

"Nova!" Fen said in his usual boisterous tone.

"I didn't know you were here! When did you get here?" Nova asked.

Sonny shook her head. Nova was always so disconnected from the rest of them. He didn't seem to notice details despite his gifted *sight*. It was as if zooming in close to every detail made everything else in the peripheral fade away.

Fen laughed easily. "I've been here all day, Nova."

Nova looked surprised. "I didn't see you! Why didn't you say hello?"

"You've been very busy," Fen replied, softening his voice a little. "I didn't want to interrupt."

"Does Palan know you're here?" Nova asked.

Sonny realized perhaps Nova noticed a little more than she first thought. "Oh, he always notices Fen," she said.

"That he does," Nova agreed. "That he does."

"I did bring food! It's in the satchels," Sonny announced. She'd made sure their supplies remained cool throughout the day, using her *touch* energy to hold a steady temperature.

The three of them exited the spacecraft and headed for the satchels. Carefully, they spread the food out across a table they dragged out from the observatory. Nova called over Isara and Palan. Before he could join them for the meal, Palan had to chase Melly, who was following a rabbit around the hilltop.

As they ate, Sonny observed Nova gazing at the stars as he often did. She thought part of him lived among the stars already.

"She'll be visible soon," Nova said between mouthfuls of food.

"We know," Palan said, sounding tired.

"And won't that be a sight," Sonny replied. She smiled gently at Nova who did not appear to notice her.

Chapter Six

A Memory

Cheers erupted across the gaming house as dice flew across the tabletop, landing on triple sevens. Palan grinned as Fen gripped his shoulders in a congratulatory gesture. He raised his glass, enjoying the sweet *scent* of apple mingled with spices for a brief moment before gulping the remainder of his drink. With a nod to his friend, he swept his winnings toward himself. The coins added significant weight to his purse.

"Try your luck again!" Lunelle offered, her whole face illuminated with a bright smile.

Palan shook his head with a chuckle as he collected his share of coin. "Not this time, love. Half of luck is knowing when to quit," he said. As he rose from the table, he nodded in thanks to Lunelle for hosting the game. He spotted a table near the back where he could recline in peace.

His lifelong friend and colleague, Fenwick Greensong, followed him across the crowded gaming house to the quieter booth.

"Should have kept it going a little longer," Fen said with a wry smile as he slid onto the bench across from Palan.

Palan laughed, closing his eyes as he took another drink. "I promised Sapphira I would be available at a moment's notice to help with the child."

He had broken promises in the past. It was far too late to repair trust with Sapphira, and she treated him accordingly. Palan could not recover what he had destroyed, but he knew he would never repeat the same mistakes again if he could avoid them. He was careful to honor himself, keeping true to his word as much as he could. He wouldn't make a vow in the first place if he knew he could not complete it. The least he could do was provide support to Sapphira after the birth of their child. She deserved that, and so did their daughter. *Especially* her.

"You can't help if you play a little longer?" Fen questioned.

"Not quickly," Palan replied. "Besides, I've already had my win for the evening."

"Pity," Fen said.

"Why don't you try for yourself?"

"It's much more fun when the risk isn't my own," Fen replied with a smirk as his eyes wandered.

"Charming," Palan said. He could see he had already lost his friend's attention.

"This calls for a song," Fen declared, his gaze landing on the opposite side of the room.

Palan watched as Fen strode confidently across the wooden floor, causing an immediate stir as he slid onto the piano bench and played the first note. Everyone loved Fen's performances. He was incredibly entertaining, using every bit of his skill with his *voice* to enhance his natural musical talents. He could liven any gathering within seconds.

A twinge of jealousy fluttered within Palan as he saw the way his friend pulled in attention seemingly without even trying. He wished he could enchant a room like that, but he did not possess the same magnetism.

It was one reason Palan resented his gifted *sense*. There was no way to draw in a crowd by expertly smelling anything. The *voice* would command him all the social ease he lacked. The *scent*, while useful, seemed boring in comparison to the power of words and song.

Palan waved a server to his table and ordered another drink which he guzzled in a few gulps. His ears buzzed as the alcohol kicked in, drowning out the chorus of voices singing along with Fen.

The thrill of his win already fading, Palan tossed his coin purse in the air and caught it three times, appreciating its weight each time the satchel landed in his palm.

The thought of keeping the money for himself tempted Palan for a brief moment but he knew a guilty conscience would eventually get the best of him. Only one person deserved that money along with all the riches in the world, and that was his daughter. Or for now, his daughter's mother as Melly was still too small to speak for herself or make use of coin on her own.

Palan had few regrets, but Sapphira counted enough for a lifetime.

Instead of dwelling on the mistakes of the past, Palan brooded with jealousy over Fenwick. "You were always magical," he muttered to himself as he sat back, observing Fen's natural charm as he effectively held his audience captive.

Fen's innate charisma was more than just his talent. He also had an ideal figure, standing tall and slender with a muscular physique while his dark hair and memorable eyes held further allure. If there were gods, they had heaped a disproportionate number of blessings onto one particular human.

Palan shook his head, annoyed with himself for dwelling on Fen. He couldn't change his *sense*. Observing Fen's performance once more, Palan's gaze halted on a familiar figure sitting in a booth near the piano. He recognized Sonny's sister, Hazel, leaning forward on her elbows, deep in conversation with a fair-haired woman whose long hair fell lusciously around her shoulders. When Palan focused his *scent* he caught a *whiff* of strawberry that matched perfectly with her red dress.

Jealousy sprang up once more in his chest. To dispel his growing frustration, he rose from the table and slid out the back door of the tavern into the night. A gust of wind blew, causing Palan to snarl in aggravation as the seasonal humidity forced his hair to cling his face.

After fighting with the wind, humidity, and his hair, he paused to observe the night sky. Only two of Kelmundy's three moons were visible as they approached their alignment. The moment of reflection eased some of the tension in his body.

Sapphira's house was not far. A fog of misery enveloped him as all his regrets played themselves on repeat in his mind. He could never change his past faults, and so they would always haunt him—unforgiven and unresolved. Palan raked one hand through his hair and started down the road. The streets were quiet, though he could still hear raucous music coming from inside the gaming house.

Palan rounded a corner, deep in thought. He had first been drawn to Sapphira's strength. She radiated beauty from the inside out. Ultimately, Palan didn't feel he could measure up to her standards. She deserved a better partner than he could ever be for her. Although he recognized the hurt on her face every time he visited, he tried to act as if he'd moved on. He was certain she would have plenty of choices for partners. He couldn't imagine anyone not wanting to be with Sapphira.

As he rounded another corner, he froze, a cold, sharp blade piercing his abdomen. Palan staggered, breathless, slamming forcefully into the stone wall behind him. The streetlight behind his assailant's head nearly blinded him as he tried to focus on the person in front of him. Palan couldn't make out any visual details; his attacker moved like a shadow, indistinct and elusive. He blinked at the blood flowering through his shirt, the dark, shining hilt of a dagger sticking out. The *scent* of his own blood overpowered most of the other smells except for one—the faintest *whiff* of wildflowers.

"You took a good bit of coin tonight," said a slick voice close to Palan's ear. "Hand it over."

Palan cursed under his breath as he remembered he was unarmed. The gaming house no longer allowed anyone to carry weapons inside after a previous violent incident between two patrons. He left his usual armaments at home on gaming nights.

Armed or not, Palan's significant height made him an imposing figure. He realized in that moment he may have made a mistake relying entirely on his own physical stature to ensure his personal safety when walking alone, carrying a pile of coin.

Despite fighting to draw a proper breath, Palan forced enough air into his lungs to swear at his assailant. Fear was only another weapon in his attacker's hands, and he would not allow that to be used against him.

"I'm the one holding the blade," the figure responded, twisting the dark dagger a little harder into Palan's flesh.

As the *scent* of his own insides filled his nostrils, white hot pain seared through him. This angered Palan. He was in no mood to be murdered. Such an undignified death did not become him. His mind raced for a way out of the situation while he stared into the void before him, keeping his gaze cold and unfeeling despite being unable to focus on a face, a head, anything. He couldn't see anything but emptiness.

Nausea prickled through his body. As the initial shock of the stabbing wore off, pain threatened to overtake all his senses.

"Hand over the coin and you can be on your way," the assailant said again.

Palan rallied. He grinned as he tightened his fists, his fingers always well decorated with rings, some with hidden extra features. "I don't think I will," he said, almost enjoying himself when his attacker showed a split second's hesitation.

Palan took his chance and grabbed the assailant's blade-wielding hand, digging his long, manicured fingernails into the fleshy part of the person's wrist. Though he could not see into the cloak, Palan used his *scent* combined with intuition to guide him as he swung his tightened fist upward, connecting with his attacker's throat just under their jaw.

Spikes from Palan's rings sliced through the soft, vulnerable part of his opponent's neck. They fell, convulsing with gushes of blood oozing from their mouth.

Palan gripped the hilt of the dagger that remained embedded in his belly, grimacing as he pulled it out. He groaned in agony, pressing his palm hard against the open wound before leaning down to pull off the assailant's hood. He crumpled the slippery fabric in his free hand, fighting to remain conscious as he examined the dead body.

Palan blinked in confusion at the lifeless man. The hood had veiled his face beyond a typical disguise. It was as if it created an emptiness, a total absence of physicality. Looking at the lifeless body now, he was surprised to see how young the man looked.

Palan opened his palm, trembling as he viewed the hood more closely. "What the hell is this?" he said aloud.

The fabric, unusually opaque, obscured the outline of his hand. He held up the fabric to the dead man's face and then to the stones beneath his feet. Whatever was behind the garment didn't just disappear, it became nothing. Whatever it touched vanished from perception entirely.

Perplexed and fascinated, he pondered the illusion even as the world blurred around him.

He winced as he crouched to peer more closely at the assassin. "And what were you doing going after me, specifically?" he asked the dead man. Palan tilted his head to one side.

The *scent* of metal mixed with the wildflowers he picked up on earlier reached his awareness again. He passed his hands over the body until he found the source of the *scent*—a thick, gold chain tucked under the assailant's shirt.

"Well, isn't that a curious thing for an assassin to have," Palan said. He removed the jewelry from around the dead man's neck and held it up to examine more clearly. A stone pendant, wrapped in a thorny gold cage dangled from a braided chain. As Palan pinched the stone in his fingers, he fell back, startled when his eyesight seemed to zoom in on the scene around him.

Palan blinked, feeling perplexed. Frowning, he lifted his gaze to the stars where it was as if he could see an entire galaxy. The constellations he observed regularly became clearer than ever. It was like being right next to them. Stunned, Palan looked across the street. He could see blocks and blocks ahead where his view would normally be obstructed by buildings, trees or other obstacles.

Sounds around him were amplified as well. Sudden noises roared in his ears, causing an almost instantaneous headache. He dropped the stone and the chaos faded.

"What the..." Palan whispered to himself. Realization dawned on him: he had just experienced *sight* and *sound*. Awestruck, he narrowed his eyes at the locket. He suddenly had access to the gifts of all five *senses*. He marveled at the incredible power he held in his hand.

A powerful twist of pain in his stomach overpowered his amazement of the amulet. He grimaced as he carefully coiled the braided chain into his money pouch, determined to examine it more closely after finding someone to heal his wounds.

Palan staggered forward, trying to recall the location of the nearest healing shop. Before he had a chance to think, two more figures landed in front of him, appearing out of the darkness without warning.

"Shit," he gasped. He felt his legs going numb until he was no longer able to move.

He fumbled as he searched for the weapon he'd pulled from his own gut, but he came up empty. Almost without thinking, Palan jammed the black hood over his face and readied his fists. He could not stand upright anymore, the pain growing more and more unbearable as his wound continued to gush, soaking his shirt with blood. The metallic, earthy *scent* of his insides overwhelmed him.

He took an undisciplined swing at one of the attackers and missed. He swayed backward, recalculating. Mind racing, he hoped his muscles would respond by memory even if he didn't consciously remember how to fight.

Starlight flashed on the black metal blade as it shot toward his shoulder. But the blow never landed. Palan watched in astonishment as both new attackers collapsed at his feet.

Confused once more, Palan raised his head to discover Fen standing in front of him, wielding what appeared to be a tree branch.

Palan let out a strangled croak, unable to force any words to leave his throat.

"Got any gambling debts you haven't paid?" Fen asked, joking even as he still breathed heavily from the exertion.

"Uh...N-no," Palan stammered. Fen's presence did not make sense. He had left him behind, singing, entertaining a crowd. He couldn't have reached Palan in time to save him, and yet his fortuitous appearance suggested otherwise. Paranoia replaced rational thought. Fen must have been following him the whole time.

"Lucky I came along when I did," Fen said cheerfully.

Is it luck? Palan wondered. He was still confused. How could Fen have been there in time? How long had he been there and how much had he seen? Suspicion twisted in Palan's gut...or was it the dagger wound? He touched a palm to his abdomen and staggered forward, his vision blurring.

"Woah there, friend," Fen said, his voice softening as he dropped his makeshift weapon and grabbed Palan under his arm. "Let's get you some healing, shall we?"

Palan slumped and the world went dark.

Chapter Seven

SECRETS AND SPIES

Fenwick carefully transcribed every word filtering through his ears from around the nearby campfire. He'd secretly been observing the sailors for days, ever since he spotted them on the secluded beach. Finally close enough to hear their conversation, he wrote down their words as quickly as he could record them.

For as long as he was a part of Nova's research team, Fen had also been involved with the Rose Network. The Network focused on gathering intelligence to protect Asayouga and the island. It was imperative the work remain unknown to anyone outside their small organization.

Spying kept him away from Observation Point where work continued on Nova's spaceship. It was easy enough to explain his absences when the city was still standing. After the devastating attacks, Fen couldn't easily be so elusive.

It was becoming almost impossible to hide his secret profession from Palan, who was deeply suspicious of him since the mugging not long before the attack on the city. Nova was easier to evade. Nova saw only what he wanted to see in people. Palan saw what he didn't want. It stung to see someone he once enjoyed a friendship with treat him with such open hostility now.

Fen tried to remain nonchalant but he knew he wouldn't be able to keep Palan's frustrations at bay forever. Eventually, their conflict would come to a head. He shifted his attention back to the mission at hand. Whatever Palan thought of him would have to wait.

He was close to understanding who attacked Asayouga. It didn't bode well to see strangers on the beach, their warship anchored and heavily concealed in *sensory* illusions, much like the cloak Fenwick himself wore.

Fen used his *voice* to whisper every syllable the invaders uttered. The repetition aided his *sense* in deciphering what he heard into words he could understand. He hoped the intelligence he gathered would be enough to protect the others this time. It had not stopped their city from being destroyed.

Fen chose his position carefully, not wanting to risk being spotted. His cloak added additional cover, but extra caution couldn't hurt. As he crouched in the thorny bushes, cramped and uncomfortable, he scratched runes onto the pages of his notebook. The runes were his own creation. Fenwick had invented his own cipher decades ago as a way to keep his journal entries safe from his brother's prying eyes. It continued to prove useful well into adulthood as he gathered secret information.

He grew more and more cramped as he crouched among the thorns. In an attempt to drown out his own discomfort, he closed his eyes listening closely to the sailors who camped along the water's edge. Filtering through all the sounds of the wind, waves, and wildlife would be far easier had he been gifted with the *sound*. Fen sighed and continued to listen until sailor voices became the prominent sound again.

"—not what we expected," a voice said.

Fen could only pick up snippets of information. After straining unsuccessfully in an attempt to hear more clearly, he grunted in frustration and shoved his notebook and pens away in his satchel.

He needed to get closer if he was going to pick up anything useful, but opportunities for cover dwindled closer to the shoreline. Fen scanned the area once more, looking for anything at all he could safely use for camouflage. His cloak would help make him less visible, but it wasn't enough. The ship, perhaps, could shield him. He'd still need to find a safe route to get there, though.

Fen hiked up his trousers and removed his boots. If a crewmember were to spot his abandoned footwear, it would alert everyone to an unwelcome presence at their docking site. That was the last thing Fenwick wanted. Looking around for a place to stow them and finding nothing, he decided it was better not to leave them behind at all. Instead, he wrapped and tied the boots through his belt, then tucked the hem of his cloak to get it out of the way.

This looks incredibly stupid, he thought. Fen reassured himself that as long as he did his job and stayed hidden, no one would have an opportunity to judge his fashion. He would be the only person who knew he looked ridiculous.

Fen moved into a crouched position, bracing himself with his hands in the sand like a cheetah ready to take off. He glanced around once more to ensure no one would spot him before running, hunched over, towards the stern of the cloaked ship.

He waded into the water, allowing the edges of his cloak to float around him on the ocean's surface. The warship was intimidating up close. Fen stared at the thorn carvings that covered the prow of the ship. Its hull shimmered with black paint, and gold vine-like emblems. The flag, lowered to reduce visibility, matched the outer decorations—gold thorns on a black backdrop.

After confirming he made it to his new position without detection, Fenwick listened in again. The voices by the fire were much clearer now, so he retrieved his notebook to resume scribbling.

One of the men poked at the fire, sending sparks and soot up from the flames. Another coughed in protest. "Watch what you're doing, you doorknob," the victim of the smoke inhalation said.

"Pathetic," came the reply.

"Not as pathetic as you."

"Quiet," said a third sailor. "It's bad enough having to be back here. I hate it."

"Maybe you'll feel better after we finally finish what we started," the first man said.

Fen wrote furiously, trying his best to keep up with transcribing the sailors' discussion.

His neck prickled when he heard them mention a spaceship and he lowered his pen, forgetting his initial task. Some of the dialogue became distorted, spoken too rapidly for Fen to decipher every word. It was clear they were speaking of space travel.

Concern for Nova's work hampered his ability to understand properly. Only snippets reached his awareness. A name—Lani Gemward—caught his attention, along with a few phrases about an underground research facility. He thought he heard mention of Oleress along with the City of Thorns, but the noise of the wind and the sea drowned out many of the words. Fen lost his focus as his mind raced.

Pages crunched as he hurriedly stowed his notebook inside his cloak. He glanced behind him, hoping the coast was clear to return to the rose bushes. The Network needed to hear what he learned.

As Fen turned, he felt an arm close tightly around his neck, pulling him into a chokehold. Instinctively, he grabbed his surprise assailant's forearm as he was dragged under water. Fen sputtered. He fought against the strong grip. Tucking his legs in, Fen hooked his heels behind his attacker's knee caps and dug in with a sharp thrust. He felt the pressure against his throat loosen just enough in response. In one split second of freedom, he somersaulted free of the headlock.

So much for trying to keep my boots dry, Fen thought as he sloshed and splashed his way out of the water.

His cover was blown. Cloak or no cloak, they knew he was there. In an instant, Fenwick found himself surrounded by sailors. They shouted at each other in their language and Fen closed his eyes again, filtering the strange sounds through the power of his *voice*.

Dragged in front of the fire, Fen found himself shoved to his knees, hands tied behind his back with at least eight weapons pointed in his direction. He looked into the eyes of a strikingly attractive man with shoulder-length black curls.

Fen's captors exchanged more words. They seemed to be addressing the man in front of him as "Captain."

The captain stood with a placid expression until the other sailors quieted. He addressed Fenwick in a cold tone, using a common dialect.

Fenwick fought to find his *voice*. He threw all the charm he could into his inflection and smiled as he answered in perfect reply, "What an honor it is to meet you."

The man looked Fen up and down, clearly assessing what Fen's abilities may or may not be. "Who are you and who has sent you?" he demanded.

Fen swallowed hard. He had to tread carefully, not letting his captors become aware of any *sensory* charms. He answered, slowly pulling in the slightest musical cadence as he responded in the man's native tongue.

"I mean no harm at all. I am only a traveling merchant. I thought I might board your ship in passage, but I did not know how to approach you," Fen said, chancing the smallest of glances to ensure his soothing song had not been noticed. He saw weapons gradually lowering in his peripheral.

"What are you selling?" the captain asked, warily. "I don't see any wares with you."

"No! You wouldn't," Fen replied, easing into more musicality as he spoke, increasing the power of his *voice* as gradually as he could.

"My caravan is far back on the road," he continued, gesturing behind him, always keeping his smile in place. "My wheel is stuck."

Fen watched as the captain blinked slowly. His song was beginning to work. He only needed a few more words exchanged to break free.

"Lead me to your caravan then," said the captain, voice slightly weakened.

"Of course," Fen said, intensifying once more, though hoping he was not too quick. "I would rather walk with my hands untied of course." He allowed his *voice* to burst making it difficult for the sailor to decline.

"That... will not... be..." the captain struggled to speak. Fen heard a thud behind him. To avoid looking suspicious he did not turn around, though he assumed one of the sailors dropped to the ground after falling asleep.

In full song, Fen replied, "That's a shame. I so would love to have my hands free."

The leather straps fell away from his wrists and Fen took his chance. He ran full tilt toward the brush, trusting his cloak would make his direction less obvious, and the hills, when he reached them, would provide further cover.

After successfully making his way back to the Chickadee campsite, Fen sat along the outer edges, leaning against a tree trunk to catch his breath. He unfastened his sopping wet boots and dumped them onto the ground. He had been lucky. He knew that.

The power of his siren song was one as yet unmatched. But had any of them recognized the illusion, he would not have survived. He needed to be more careful in the future.

He looked up and swore as he saw Palan directly in front of him, unexpectedly.

"Gone for a little swim?" Palan asked, raising an eyebrow in skepticism.

"Yes. It's such a fine day!" Fen replied, keeping his tone bright. He could not manipulate Palan. He couldn't reveal his mission, although he wished he could explain. Fenwick fidgeted with the rose emblem on his cloak as a twinge of sadness caught in his throat. He longed for the days mutual trust existed between them. Fen quickly shoved his feelings aside. Things changed. There was nothing he could do to erase the past.

"It is. Though it was better before you arrived to spoil it," Palan replied, though he didn't sound quite as annoyed as he usually did.

"Well, aren't you a ray of sunshine!" Fen said. "By any chance is Sonny around to dry my boots?" Changing the subject was his best chance.

Palan nudged his head in the direction of their campsite. "She's there. Better hurry. Wouldn't want to miss a meal."

Fen chuckled and patted his colleague on the arm. "Thanks for looking out for me." With that, he grabbed his soaked footwear and walked on his tired, aching bare feet to the campsite to join Sonny and the others.

Chapter Eight

SYMBOLS

Nova lay on his back, the night sky alive above him with dancing colors all flashing and bending in a brilliant display. The stars were clearly visible, dotting the blanket of darkness in all directions. It was a perfect night for *seeing*. Instead of appreciating the view, Nova lay turning the deadly blade that killed Nayeli around in his hands; examining it from every angle.

The weapon was a mystery Nova could not release from his mind. The black shimmering stone was impossibly sharp and lethal. He stared at the symbols carved into the blade almost every night, entranced by their horrifying elegance.

Tears burned in Nova's eyes and he set the blade down next to him once more. He focused his *sight* as far as he could, appreciating the rugged beauty surrounding him. He sighed, imagining how it would feel when he finally launched his ship among the stars.

Eventually, Nova gave up on sleep. He rose quietly to his feet, careful not to wake Palan and Melly. At times, they chose to sleep on the hill rather than returning to Chickadee River. They often put in long hours on the construction of the spaceship and it didn't always make sense to travel back and forth to the camp.

Melly didn't want to leave with Sonny. Instead, she slept soundly next to her father whose hand rested against her back.

Nova tucked the dagger back into his belt's holster and wandered inside the observatory. There, he grabbed scrolls and ink, carrying the supplies with him up the staircase to his workspace. He set the items down carefully, taking time to organize them before settling himself into his armchair.

Nova leaned back and lifted his face toward the moonlight, closing his eyes as he drew in a long, deep breath. He had always enjoyed working in the quiet solitude of night. Starlight brought with it a sense of silent company watching over him as he focused on his studies. He stared down at an empty page and smiled, embracing the peace of the moment.

Readjusting himself, he hunched over his parchment and penned his observations about the dagger. He had kept records of all that transpired since the attacks, carefully separating his notebook into sections. He regularly added to Nayeli's section, hoping to keep her memory alive with his words. She would always be in the forefront of his thoughts whether he was awake or asleep.

Before long, Nova's thoughts wandered. His attention drifted as he marveled at the expanse, now filled with dancing lights. He set down his pen and watched the twisting colors fade and flutter above him. Their visibility always heightened at the closing of each year.

He understood the lights to be a phenomenon caused by sun particles interacting with Kelmundy's magnetic field, but Nova entertained the idea the Ancients had of divine beings creating the display. They were called Angel Lights for a reason. Although he understood the mundane explanation for the lights, Nova liked to believe both the magical and scientific explanations were simultaneously correct.

Nova glimpsed a swish of fabric passing between the trees below. The sudden movement drew his attention to the ground. He had been so deeply absorbed in his thoughts he almost missed seeing the dark figure slowly weaving his way up the hill toward the observatory. Nova frowned, setting his instruments and ink down beside him as he stepped forward and leaned over the railing.

He tried to focus his *sight* on the wanderer for a closer look, but he couldn't make out any clear details. Nova drew in a deep breath, closing his eyes before refocusing once more but it didn't seem to make a difference. The figure appeared to be cloaked in darkness matching the night. Only the faintest edges of a human shape were visible to Nova as the breeze moved the edges of fabric against the stealthy figure.

Nova's hands tightened on the railing as he tried to decide whether to wake Melly and Palan or to watch and wait. He couldn't make up his mind. Worried his hesitation would put everyone in more danger, Nova decided almost anything at all was better than simply standing idle. He re-secured the black dagger, grabbed a torch and ran back down the staircase, leaving his work open on the table.

He shut the door behind him and muted the torch before making his way down the hill. It was easy for Nova to remain quiet as he moved. More than once, he'd startled Nayeli by sneaking up on her unintentionally with his noiseless footsteps.

The ability to remain undetected served him well as he hurried down the hill, careful not to alert the lone intruder. Nova ducked behind a tree—listening, watching before making any further moves. He furrowed his brow as he lost *sight* of the shrouded figure.

Nova pressed himself up against a tree, all his senses on alert, especially his enhanced *sight*. His heart raced as he scanned the area, now unable to *see* anything moving in front of him.

The night air wafted against Nova's neck, bringing with it the faintest scent of roses. Goosebumps jumped across his body. He gasped.

A soft chuckle twisted Nova's stomach into knots before the relief of recognition registered in his mind.

"Out for a midnight stroll?" Fen asked in a soft, silky voice.

"Gods!" Nova gasped. "Fenwick!" He breathed deeply to slow his racing heart as his body responded to the recognition of his friend.

"Yes," Fen said. "It is I." He gave nothing away with his voice.

"I saw you from the observatory," Nova said, offering an entirely unnecessary explanation as to why he had been following Fen.

Fen shrugged. "I assumed as much."

Nova recovered his equilibrium. "You startled me. I wasn't expecting you."

Fen chuckled. "No one ever expects me."

"Indeed," Nova said, still frowning. Fen's comings and goings were never predictable, unlike the movement of the planets and luminaries. Nova preferred things to be predictable. But he trusted his friend, even if Palan did not. "Why?" Nova asked.

Fen held a finger to his lips and his other hand in the air, pointing to his side.

Nova's gaze followed the point and landed on the sight of Palan standing nearby, holding a glaive, his hair still tousled from sleep.

"Gods!" Nova exclaimed again. "It's only Fen."

"I can see that now," Palan said with a snarl. "Lurking in the middle of night in a bloody cloak. I wouldn't expect anything less."

Fen brandished his cloak in a flourish and bowed. "Indeed. I've already been introduced."

"Can we please all go back to the observatory?" Nova said. His initial alarm vanished, turning into irritation as the threat of danger faded.

"We can," Palan said. "As soon as Fenwick cares to explain what he's doing creeping around in the middle of the night."

"Was I creeping?" Fen asked mildly. "How interesting. I thought I was just walking."

"You did startle me," Nova said.

"Well," Fen said, voice still soft, "That was never my intention. In fact, I had very much hoped not to alarm you, as it is quite late and I only wanted a place to sleep."

Palan raked his fingers through his hair. "Hm," he grunted.

Nova shook his head. "Let's just go to bed."

"With you? Sure," Fen said with a smirk.

Nova rolled his eyes and started the climb back up to the observatory. He swiped at Palan's weapon on his way past, suddenly overcome with annoyance at his colleague's constant readiness for a fight.

"Hey!" Palan snapped.

"Can you relax for once," Nova said.

"I will," Palan replied, "As soon as Fenwick stops doing these little pop ups." He tucked his weapon under his arm and climbed after Nova. "It's been long enough. Stay and work with us or go on your little adventures and get lost permanently. The rest of us are here, contributing."

To Nova's surprise, Fen did not reply to that statement as they returned to the hilltop where they discovered Melly still asleep, her expression blissful. The three men silently agreed to continue their discussion inside the observatory, away from the child's ears.

Palan placed his weapon back in its mount against the wall.

Nova looked at Fen, unsettled as he noticed how the cloak seemed to dampen his presence. "Please, take that ridiculous cloak off. It's giving me a headache."

"As you desire," Fen said. He twisted the rose clasp in one deft motion and tossed the garment to the ground without any care to where it landed. "Your highness," he added with a flash of a grin directed at Nova.

As the slick fabric fell onto the stone in a heap, Nova caught the slightest glimpse of familiar runes and symbols woven into the interior of the cloak. He tensed as he realized why he recognized them. They matched the ones from the dagger used to murder his love. *Why does Fenwick Greensong have a cloak with those symbols?* Nova wondered.

He drew out the dagger and held it in front of him, resting against his palms. The other two stopped bickering as they beheld the blade.

"Are you planning on killing me for startling you?" Fen asked drily.

"That wouldn't be the motivation to kill you," Palan quipped.

"This dagger—" Nova trailed off a moment, swallowing hard as he remembered "—This dagger is the one that killed Nayeli."

Neither of his companions spoke. They waited for Nova to continue.

Nova looked into Fen's green eyes, which were filled with surprising warmth. "Have you tried to read the symbols before?" he asked, hopeful, but uncertain. He had always been a little envious of Fen's gifted *voice.* He was grateful for his own *sense* of *sight* being so strong, but the *voice* was pure magic in Nova's opinion.

"I haven't," Fen admitted. His usual confidence appeared to slip away from him. It was a long moment before he sighed and took the dagger from Nova's hands.

"Forgive me," Fen said. "I should have asked to look at it sooner."

Nova shrugged. "I've been hanging onto it pretty closely. This is the only intact weapon we have found, and it..." Nova trailed off a moment before continuing "it was important to me to keep it."

Palan made a noise in his throat. Nova turned, expecting Palan to add a comment. Instead, the man straddled a bench near the bookcases and fixed his attention on Fenwick.

Fen stared at the carved symbols in silence, moving his mouth wordlessly as he gazed. No one spoke as they waited for Fen to piece together what information he could from his *voice*.

Fen spoke at last. "I'm not sure but..." he trailed off, shaking his head. "It doesn't make any sense."

"What does it say?" Nova asked, his curiosity heightened.

"I think it's—" Fen stopped himself. "No. I don't know. I'm sorry I couldn't translate it."

Nova felt his heart sink as Fen shuffled to the door.

Palan's voice broke through and seemed to freeze Fen's hand to the door lever, mid turn. "You know what it says, don't you?"

Confused, Nova glanced back and forth between his two colleagues. He shifted uncomfortably on his feet as thick tension hung in the air between them. Doubt crept into his mind as he wondered why Fen would hide the meaning from him if he understood it.

Fen stood as still as a statue.

Palan smirked and rose to his full height. "You've seen those symbols before, haven't you? I wonder how you came by that information?" He mused.

Fen adjusted himself. "I don't know," he said.

"You do know," Palan replied, voice dripping acid.

Nova had to interject. "I don't understand. Fenwick. Do you know what the symbols mean?" he asked again, desperate for answers.

Fen turned to Nova. His voice, usually nonchalant, serious now as he spoke. "I'm sorry, Nova. I don't know for certain."

Nova tilted his head, glancing at the weapon in his hand again before shooting a quizzical glance at Fen.

Fen slumped. "It says, 'I love you.' At least, I think it does. And there are some other symbols—maybe a name. It's hard to know for certain. That's all my *sense* could pick up. I'm sorry. I don't know what it means."

Nova blinked in confusion. "I don't understand. The blade says 'I love you?'" he asked. He could not imagine a reason for carving such gentle words into a weapon of death.

"Why?"

"It's impossible to know the smith's intentions," Fen said with a shrug. "Perhaps it was crafted as a gift to a lover," he offered as a possible explanation.

Palan snorted. "Funny you would come up with that suggestion, Fenwick."

Nova shook his head at Palan. "I wish you would explain to me what happened between you two," he said, weary of their silent feud. "You used to be best friends."

Palan stared at Fenwick with an icy expression. "You should be careful who you assume is a friend, Nova." He shoved Fen aside and exited the observatory without another word.

Nova looked at Fen who returned his look with a wan smile.

"I'm sorry I couldn't decipher it further, Nova," he whispered. He retrieved his cloak from the floor and nodded goodnight before following Palan's example and leaving the observatory.

Chapter Nine

BLACKSTONE

Sonny sat perched on a tall stool watching Isara Blackstone hammer a sheet of metal into submission. The makeshift smithy on Observation Point was open to the air, though a metal awning covered the top to prevent rainy weather from ruining any of its operations.

Even though the main structure of the spaceship was finished, the ship's interior was not. Isara worked tirelessly to provide the project with all the building materials they could need. If there were extra parts leftover, they could be used to repair the ship if anything malfunctioned.

Isara sniffed, standing back to wipe sweat from her forehead before hurling another curved, metal panel onto a pile. Her muscles rippled as she threw the piece effortlessly.

Awed by the woman's strength, Sonny took the opportunity to make Isara aware of her presence. "Do your arms not get tired from all that?" she asked.

Isara flashed her a wide grin. "When did you get here?" she exclaimed.

"I've not been here long," Sonny lied. She didn't want to let on how long she'd been observing.

"Do me a favor and grab me that sheet mould will you?" She waved vaguely next to her workbench.

Sonny approached the forge cautiously. Hot perspiration trickled down her neck, her arms immediately prickling with heat. She'd never fared well in hot summer weather and she was silently grateful she didn't lead the life of a blacksmith. As she examined the array of items arranged neatly around the workspace, she couldn't tell what Isara wanted but didn't want to let on how clueless she was.

"It's this one."

Sonny jumped as she looked up at Isara, surprised to find her standing next to her. "I'm sorry! I honestly couldn't tell," she replied with a sheepish chuckle.

Isara winked and heaved the heavy, stone caste into her arms. Sonny would never have been able to lift it even if she'd known what to look for.

Sonny returned to her perch and watched in awe as Isara prepared the next metal sheet for the forge fire. Her muscles rippled and she completed every step so easily, an onlooker wouldn't be able to tell how heavy everything actually was.

The hissing of the forge and clanging of metal mesmerized her. Hours passed, escaping her awareness as she allowed the sights and sounds to keep her entranced.

Finally, Isara pulled a lever next to the forge to cool it before turning back to Sonny with another beaming grin. She untied a black band from around her head, freeing her tightly-spiraled curls. Her appearance was wild and untamed. "Did you bring Melly? I've got something she might like," she asked as she shielded her eyes with her hand, seemingly scanning for the child's presence on the hill.

"Oh, she's around here somewhere," Sonny responded, though she didn't know where. She wasn't keeping a close eye on the little girl who mostly followed her father or played near the observatory.

Holding up one finger, Isara nodded before rummaging through a pack stowed under a table. Before long, she produced two pairs of matching bracers, and sauntered to Sonny, presenting them with a proud grin.

"I made her and that doll matching ones. You think she'll like them?" she asked, her eyebrows furrowed with uncertainty.

Sonny *felt* peace and generosity surrounding Isara's offering. As she took the tiny, matching gear pieces from Isara's hands she smiled in reassurance. "I know she'll love them!"

"Good, good." They stood smiling at each other until the silence became awkward.

Sonny stood as if she were looking for the child as she racked her brain for something to say. She wished she were better at making conversation, but words eluded her.

To her surprise, Isara followed her around the forge. Before she spotted Melly, she forced herself to say *something*, anxious about the continued silence. "Sapphira would have been impressed."

"Ah, Sapphira wasn't that easily impressed as I recall," Isara replied with a loud laugh that rang out across the hill.

"Well, she *should* be impressed, I think. I am."

Isara's cheek dimpled as one corner of her mouth turned up in a smile. "Thanks," she replied. Her gaze drifted to the distance and silence once again filled the space between them. Eventually she shrugged and resumed speaking. "It's a shame we couldn't find their remains."

Sonny nodded, *sensing* the woman's intent in her words. There were so many left unfound. The city's destruction had been swift and absolute. They'd recovered some bodies during extensive searches, but many survivors still didn't know where their loved ones passed.

It was a comfort to look at the newly discovered constellation each evening and connect in a different form. She was grateful to have the opportunity to name one of the points after Hazel. "I know. I wanted to find my sister," she offered.

"I didn't know you had a sister?" Isara said, her eyebrows raised in surprise.

"Yeah. Hazel." She turned her head to look away and saw Melly running across the hill. The sun was low in the sky. It would soon be time to return to the Chickadee. Traveling in the dark wasn't advisable.

Isara's brow crinkled with concern. "Did something happen between you?" she asked.

As much as Sonny appreciated Isara's intuitive question, she wasn't certain how much of it she could put into words. She and Hazel never had a falling out. They drifted apart as their lives went in different directions. There were some hard feelings, but those feelings remained unaddressed. Now there wouldn't be another opportunity to reunite.

With a wan smile, Sonny replied, "We didn't talk much I guess."

"I know what that's like," Isara said with a sympathetic nod as she jammed her hands into her pockets and shrugged.

"I'm sorry to hear that."

"Don't be," Isara replied.

Sonny gathered her belongings from the corner of the workshop, contemplative as she did.

"Heading home?" Isara questioned.

Sonny tilted her head as she paused. Was the river her home now? It didn't feel like it. Nothing ever did except for books.

Isara quickly corrected her words. "I'm sorry. I meant—"

Sonny interrupted, "No. It's ok. I'm heading back to the river. I'll give these to Melly once we're at camp."

"Good," Isara responded, her lips upturned in a gentle smile. "I'll see you later, then."

Sonny raised her palm in response before hoisting her pack onto her shoulders. She craned her neck to look at the spaceship standing tall and shining in the waning daylight. It wouldn't be long before they could launch.

Chapter Ten

SOMETHING LOST

P alan tuned his sharpened *scent* to the layers of dirt beneath the ruined library. As much as he wished he'd been born with any other *sense*, he had to admit his particular ability proved useful now. When he was not actively working on Nova's spaceship, he devoted his time to rescue and recovery efforts.

Months of exploration yielded limited results, although they salvaged what they could from the wreckage.

Palan was able to locate bodies using his *scent*. As grisly as that was, Palan felt the satisfaction in knowing neighbors, friends, colleagues, and lovers alike could gain closure from their discovery. But Palan wasn't only there looking for bodies. There was something else just as precious to him buried somewhere below the rubble.

His secret secondary objective was his alone to know, and Palan intended to keep the information to himself forever, if possible. The only person who could possibly ruin it for him was Fenwick, but Palan hoped the secrets he knew about his colleague would, in turn, deter Fen from talking about him.

With that thought, he glanced at his long-term friend and colleague, Nova Nightfall, who was busy examining a partially-burnt document with his monocular magnifier.

Palan chuckled to himself. It was ironic that Nova would magnify his *sight* even further when he was already so gifted. *Sight* was the most common of the *sensory* abilities, but Palan had never met anyone else whose visual *sense* was as powerful as Nova's.

He hoped Nova would recover all the information they needed for their celestial mission.

Palan had to admit he was impressed by the progress they made on the vessel's construction in such a short time. He was skeptical of their success in the beginning, despite all the years of research they had already done investigating potential future technologies. After Isara Blackstone agreed to help them smith a new metal alloy to withstand the ship's transit into space, Palan believed it might be possible after all. It was exciting to think about exploring a whole galaxy, especially now that their earth-bound home had been destroyed.

A *whiff* caught Palan's attention and he turned his head, looking down streets filled with rubble and ruin. The stones of a collapsed tavern and gaming house scattered in all directions, distinctive in their rich, red color, cleverly designed to stand out from the other buildings.

"Nova!" Palan shouted across the site of the library.

Nova lowered his monocle and document, his voice sounding detached as he answered, "Yeah?"

"I'm heading up the street," Palan said. His instinct combined with his *scent* tracking told him where he needed to search next, and Nova could not be permitted to follow. He hoped his friend's intense focus would keep him tethered to the library exploration for as long as Palan needed privacy.

"Okay," Nova called back, already turning back to his document.

Perfect. Palan strode confidently across the road, climbing nimbly over debris as needed, his long legs making easy work of most of the obstacles he encountered. He locked his *scent* onto the *whiff* he had picked up earlier. The trail became visible to Palan's mind's eye, guiding him in the direction he needed to go.

Before long, Palan reached the wreckage of Fenwick Greensong's estate. The place was enormous, and Palan had to admit Fen took excellent care of its upkeep. It was a shame to see the beautifully carved columns now collapsed in the front entrance.

Traces of musical illusions still hung in the air around Fen's old home. Garbled-sounding lyrics and half-measures floated up to his ears. As Palan stepped over floorboards, the notes triggered like traps by the weight of his footsteps.

As he made his way through the debris, Palan pulled away fallen support beams and pushed aside a colorful blanket. The disturbed dust caught in his throat, sending him into a fit of coughing that forced him to stop. There was no way he'd be able to continue without taking a moment to sit back and recover his breath.

Palan whispered an expletive to himself. "Gods assured; I do not have time for lung rot." His throat burned as he swallowed hard several times to clear the particles.

"Ok," Palan sighed at last. "Back to work." He talked to himself in a low volume whenever he was alone. It was a habit he developed so long ago he could not recall its beginning.

He tracked the *whiff* to the base of the stairs. His innate tracking ability led him to the staircase. A dense cloud of energy hovered over the floor tiles indicating he did not need to track the *scent* any further. There was his mark. He had to get closer, but there was so much blocking his path, he wasn't sure how to get there other than by digging.

Palan curled his finger tips and stared at his chipped nails. He still wore rings stacked on every other finger, though the added weight was certainly not helpful to him now. "Well. Say goodbye to these uncalloused hands. It's time to work," he said, cringing a little at the thought of destroying his fingernails any further. It had to be done. The circumstances called for him to make sacrifices.

Digging proved to be a laborious task. Though Palan had the upper body strength, honed from years of weapons training, he still felt his muscles burn as he worked to uncover his mark.

Eventually, he reached it. Palan looked down at his palms, so sweaty and caked with ash and blood he had begun to lose sensation. "What a waste," he growled with displeasure.

Palan looked around but couldn't see anything of interest. He closed his eyes, feeling the *scent* as deeply as possible to pinpoint a location. There was something below the cracked marble.

"He went to great lengths to hide you, didn't he," Palan said softly to the object he was searching for. "Wanted you for himself."

He searched for something nearby to help lift what was left of the chipped floor tiles. His gaze fell upon an out-of-place object. It was black and shimmered in the light let in by holes in the walls. Palan frowned as he half-crawled toward it, pushing aside splintered darkwood to reveal a sharp obsidian blade.

"Sweet stars," Palan breathed as he gripped the carved hilt. Turning it over in his palms he saw runes and symbols adorning its surface. It looked like the weapon Nova discovered near Nayeli's body.

The blade intrigued Palan. He wondered why it lay abandoned on the floor of Fenwick's ruined home. A prickling feeling of suspicion covered Palan from head to toe. The discovery of the blade made him think Fen knew more information about their attackers than he had revealed to the rest of them. *What do you have to hide, I wonder?*

He wished he could translate the symbols himself, curious to know whether they would match the carvings on Nova's blade, but he couldn't decipher them on his own. At least not yet. Not until he found it. He was so close.

"You can come with me. And perhaps Fenwick can explain how you got here," Palan whispered, returning his attention to his target.

Palan jammed the black blade under the edge of tile and upended it in one smooth motion. In a hollowed-out space beneath the stone slab lay a small, locked jewelery box. Its polished wooden surface had a red rose carved on top with the elegantly scripted words "I love you" along the side. It wouldn't be difficult to break it open. Something about the design caused Palan to hesitate before destroying it.

"I love you…" Palan repeated the scripted words out loud. The words themselves were not unusual, of course. He imagined everyone had said, "I love you," to someone at some point or another. But seeing them written on the box left him feeling unsettled for reasons he could not pinpoint. Recalling Fenwick's translation of Nova's blade, Palan wondered whether there was a connection or only a coincidence.

He grabbed the freed-up tile and smashed the box. Mysteries could be solved another time. He needed his locket back. It had only been missing for a few days, but Palan hated that he could not pinpoint the moment Fenwick had stolen it from him. How often did Fen follow him?

It was puzzling to Palan that Fen would not have used the locket himself. It was a waste of its power not to use it. But why did Fen go through such great efforts to hide it?

Satisfied he had at last found his treasure, Palan gently pulled the locket up by its thick, gold chain. A cage of golden thorns twisted around an earth-colored stone in the center of the pendant. His heart hammered as he clasped the chain safely around his neck, tucking the stone inside his shirt to conceal it.

With the precious item recovered, Palan rose and walked swiftly back the same way he had come. He was stunned to see how low the sun had sunk in the sky since he first set out. He had been there longer than he realized.

Still, he had found the stone. This was something Palan needed close to his heart. He felt significantly more at ease with its weight resting once more against his chest.

As he made his way back toward the street, Palan allowed himself to relax just a fraction. He could not let his guard slip entirely. He was always on alert.

"Oh. Imagine finding you here," a sharp voice said, cutting through Palan's thoughts.

Startled, he whirled to see Fen, leaning against a sooty, stone fence. Palan swore. How had he missed noticing his presence?

His signature *scent* normally alerted Palan long before he had a chance to bump into him.

"Good to see you too," Palan said, a sarcastic smile twisting on his lips.

"Yeah? I can't say the same," Fen replied, looking Palan up and down. "What are you doing over here? On my property?"

Palan waved flippantly at the air. "Your property?" He snarled. "Do any of us own anything anymore?"

Fen lowered his head. "Well. You may be right there," he said quietly.

"And where have you been?" Palan asked. "Never helping, are you? Always just showing up when it's past time to work."

"I've been working as much as you, Palan," Fen replied. "But... I still wonder why you're here." He stared pointedly at his fallen property.

Palan shrugged. "I'm returning to the library," he said, deflecting. He wondered, once again, how long Fen had been nearby and how much he had seen, if anything.

"Well then," Fen said, brightening. "That's perfect timing. I heard Sonny and Nova recovered several books today."

"Good," Palan said, at least halfway meaning it.

Chapter Eleven

PRECIOUS TRINKETS

Fenwick held a lantern high above him, illuminating his path as he moved through the darkness. The structure of his former home lay in ruins like all the rest of the city. His chest burned with every breath. He spent all his resources trying to appear at ease after discovering Palan on his property. It was agonizing waiting for the safety of night to return to his estate.

He leaned against the remaining stump of a pillar as a wave of anxiety-induced nausea washed over him. Years of intelligence gathering trained Fen to keep a cool head in the midst of high conflict situations, but he could not seem to master his emotions now.

As he passed by familiar treasures, most of which were shattered beyond recognition or repair, grief sank like a heavy stone within him. Fenwick knew each and every item in his home.

He gathered everything with care, enchanting collectibles with melodies that sang out when activated.

Fen built intricate puzzles throughout his estate, designed to play tunes once solved. His love of mystery and music combined to create a home filled with personal comforts. He missed it all.

Distorted harmonies and dissonant notes were all that remained now, playing at random moments without any predictable frequency. Only fragments of his illusions survived after furniture and trinkets were destroyed.

Fen walked across what remained of his home to the place he had seen Palan. He had gone to a lot of trouble to obtain the amulet in the first place and he regretted not hiding it any better. He should've known Palan would track it down easily.

He knelt to clear the tiles where he hid the box. A small smile played at his lips as he recalled watching Palan struggle to pry them up earlier. Uncovering the hollowed-out floor tile was a simple matter of decoding a riddle—an easy riddle at that. But Palan overlooked the details.

The box lay discarded on the floor and Fen's hard work engineering the puzzle was destroyed.

A tear drop splashed onto the surface of the broken box; Fen sniffed as he scrubbed it away with the edge of his cloak.

Memories of Nayeli handing him the hand-crafted gift sprang to his mind.

"I miss you so much," Fen whispered to the darkness. Although Nova had discovered the soul-stars, Fen could not bring himself to search for her light above. He couldn't explain why it brought him further pain. She had always been kind to him. More than kind. Fen loved her fiercely and missed her dearly, though he could never confess his grief to Nova. He was Nayeli's chosen partner and Fen understood Nova's grief over the loss of his partner would be heavy. Fen discounted his own grief in light of Nova's.

Fen hummed a tune to himself. He recalled singing it to her the evening she gave him the cologne she'd crafted specifically for him. It was the perfect blend of rich rose with hints of cardamom and ginger layered beneath. It was meant to call in the one he loved. He still wore it as often as he could, though he used it sparingly. It would eventually run out.

He gently brushed the lid of the box and held his breath, steadying his nerves before he opened it. As he removed the lid, he bit down on his lip. A single, heaving cry escaped his throat as he pushed aside the tangled, dried vines and rose petals at the bottom of the box. There he found the small, glass bottle safe and sound. Palan had not discovered it.

"Thank the gods. Thank EVERY god he never noticed you," Fen said aloud. He knew Palan would not be looking for the cologne, but he feared with his gifted *scent*, he would surely have found it anyway. Deep relief washed over Fenwick. This one precious item had escaped Palan's notice. The cologne didn't matter anymore, but memories of Nayeli's nurturing love were entangled with it, and he couldn't let it go.

Fen wasn't like the rest of his colleagues. While he could move easily through social environments, turning on his charm to entertain people, he felt alone underneath it all. He didn't have a family or even close friends to miss. He had his home, his music, and his puzzles. That was all gone.

Nayeli was one of the few people Fen ever felt truly saw him. She didn't fawn over him the way others so often did. She communicated with him on a different level.

He placed the wooden box back within its niche and tucked the vial into a cloak pocket. Slowly, he climbed over fallen beams and smashed stones until he found what had once been his bedroom. Fen laid down on what was left of his plush mattress. Carefully, he dabbed the smallest drop of fragrance onto his skin and breathed in its rich scent. "For you, my love," Fen whispered to the night. The crafted *scent* never seemed to work, but he still held onto a distant hope that it might. At minimum, it brought him a comforting reminder of Nayeli. He stared up at the constellations until he fell asleep.

In the morning, refreshed and with his mask of cheerfulness restored, Fenwick traveled back to Observation Point. He resolved himself to make more of an effort to be involved in the construction. Nayeli would have wanted it.

As he crested the hill, he found the crew already bustling with work. He stood back, examining the flurry of activity. The progress they'd made was incredible. From his vantage point, the spaceship seemed to glisten in the sunlight. Its shell looked complete. Fen knew the engine was nearly ready to go as well.

"Look who's shown up again," a snide voice said.

Fen pasted a smile onto his face, allowing charm to ooze through almost without thinking. "Good day, Palan," he responded in greeting.

Their eyes locked, each regarding the other with deep suspicion. Palan was openly distrustful of Fen, but Fen took great care to hide his own apprehension in return. He knew better than to reveal his cards to anyone, especially Palan. He dropped his gaze only when he noted the braided gold chain barely visible under Palan's shirt collar.

Now that Palan was once again armed with extra *senses*, Fen knew he would need to be cautious around him. He worried the extra gifts would be used to manipulate those who were unaware of its existence.

Nova interrupted their standoff with a delighted shout. "Fen!" he called out, waving with excitement for Fen to join him. "Come see this!"

Fen met Palan's gaze once more, making sure to appear as unbothered as possible before crossing the worksite to Nova.

He greeted his friend with a friendly pat on the back. "It looks like she's nearly ready," he said as he regarded the ship.

Nova grinned. "Yeah. Almost. I still need your help with some of the calibration. But come and see this!" Nova beckoned and ran ahead up the gangplank into the ship's interior.

In the entrance, he opened his arms wide and announced, "This is it!"

Fen admired the intricate details of the ship's enhancements. A long tube-shaped tank bubbled and swirled along the wall of the ship. It was a system designed to maintain a fresh water supply for the space travelers indefinitely, provided the technology did not fail.

"It's incredible," Fen said, his voice soft. "She would have been so proud of you."

Nova's excitement dropped noticeably, replaced with reflective sorrow. "She IS proud," he said, altering Fen's choice of words.

"Of course," Fen replied. He hoped that were true.

Fen changed the subject, hoping to draw Nova's enthusiasm back in. He charmed his words with faint musicality as he said, "You said you needed help calibrating? Where do you need me?"

Nova smiled, immediately appearing more at ease. "Yes, of course. There are calculations in the observatory. You can look those over."

"I'd be happy to," Fen replied, satisfied his persuasive *voice* still held some power. Together they walked to the observatory to continue their work.

Chapter Twelve

CHICKADEE RIVER

Back at the Chickadee River encampment, Nova examined the dagger as he often did before drifting off to sleep. It had become a ritual. He couldn't glean any further information from the weapon alone. He knew every facet of its surface by then. The revolting words, *"I love you,"* still infuriated Nova. Love was never meant to destroy, yet the blade had ravaged his heart's deepest treasure. He seethed at the paradox of word and weapon.

Exhausted, Nova leaned back against a tree trunk. His fatigue extended far beyond his physical body, right down to his soul. After months of tireless efforts, Nova's vision had taken shape in reality.

He loved standing near the ship's engine core, visualizing himself tapping display panels while drifting through the silence of space. He pictured the darkness through the windows and how different the specks of starlight would look; even the details he would be able to see on the surface of Kelmundy's three moons.

The process still felt like a dream, in some ways. Nova never considered how all their prototypes would function at full scale. All the tales of ancient star travelers which fascinated Nova since childhood were suddenly far more realistic than he'd dared to hope before.

It was remarkable to see the tangible embodiment of his dreams. The ship had jumped from the pages of story books and technical drawings and turned into a new home.

Nova always had an insatiable thirst for knowledge. As he poured over ancient texts during the ship's development, novel ideas flew into his mind. There seemed to be no end to his curiosity, every idea gave birth to ten more. Nova knew he would never be able to investigate them all within his lifetime—that thought satisfied him.

His heart filled with gratitude as he reclined, reflecting on the power of a collective vision. So many people, in the aftermath of a tragedy, had set aside their time and devoted their skills to Nova's idea. It was almost an intimidating thought to be responsible for such a large-scale endeavor.

At last, Nova set the dagger down beside him. Peaceful thoughts of traveling among the stars, bringing him to a soul reunion with Nayeli, eventually comforted Nova enough to fall asleep.

Nayeli visited him often in the dream realms, though Nova never mentioned it to anyone while he was awake. Her appearance was almost a nightly occurrence. Sometimes his dreams brought him more pain than peace. Her love had been so beautiful and precious. Irreplaceable. Every time he opened his eyes, reality forced him to confront his grief. Although Nova did not wish to lose the memory of her, he longed for a dreamless sleep.

In spite of his wishes, dreams overtook Nova as he drifted deeper into rest. Nayeli appeared across Chickadee River. Nova's dream-form sat up as he saw her standing on the far bank, waving and smiling at him.

He walked to the river. Nova searched up and down the water's edge. The current was too strong for him to cross. He wandered, barefoot, along the riverbank.

Nayeli called out to him repeatedly in her clear, soprano voice. Nova shook his head, frowning. "No, I can't! I'll drown!" he called back. His voice wouldn't carry to her, no matter how loud he shouted. She continued calling to him, unmoving from her position on the shoreline.

Nova's frustration grew with a mounting tension in his throat. He looked at Nayeli again, desperate to communicate with his love, but when he saw her, her expression had transformed from a gentle smile to one of horror. Nayeli pointed to the trees, then held her finger up to her lips for silence. Nova focused his sight into the woods where he saw dark shapes—hundreds, if not thousands of them—weaving through the trees.

Even with his sense in tune, he could not make out details on any of the moving figures. They were cloaked, just as Fenwick had been when he snuck up on Nova and Palan at Observation Point.

Nayeli's voice changed, becoming darker, deeper. The image of her flickered as if it were a holographic projection. Her words thundered in Nova's ears as the wind amassed speed, roaring around him.

"You must wake up now," Nayeli's voice said, echoing in every direction. Her dark hair swirled wildly around her head, thick strands swiping across her face as her image faded from Nova's view.

"Wake up! Wake up, Nova! They're here! Wake up!" Nayeli's disembodied voice urged.

As Nova opened his eyes, he jolted forward, heart hammering, trying to catch his breath. He half expected to see Nayeli standing along the shore, but the riverbank was empty now. The only sound was the steady flowing of the Chickadee. He dropped his shoulders in relief.

Before his heart rate could return to its normal rhythm, a shadowy movement among the trees caught his attention. He grabbed the black dagger and leapt to his feet. Peering deeper into the trees, Nova confirmed his fears. There were hundreds of cloaked figures moving quietly throughout the forest headed straight for the encampment.

Nova stood frozen in panic, indecisive of his next move. He opened and closed his eyes multiple times, pinching himself to ensure he was really awake. The shadows in the forest seemed to multiply. His lips turned dry as sand in an instant as he realized it was far too late to warn anyone. An attack was imminent.

Hardly knowing what to do first, Nova dropped to the ground. Palan and Melly sprang to mind. There was no way to save the camp, but there might be time to help the child get to safety. He crawled on his belly until he reached their sleeping tent.

He fumbled as he untied the tent flap, fingers trembling uncontrollably.

"Wake up," Nova hissed as he shook his friend's arm and patted Melly's back at the same time. "Wake up, wake up, wake up," he repeated in a hoarse whisper, unwilling to raise his voice. It was best not to send the camp into chaos no matter how much of a stubborn sleeper his friend was.

Palan lifted his head and elbowed Nova squarely in the chest. "Piss off." He rubbed his palm vigorously over his face and turned to glare at Nova as he sat the rest of the way up. "What the fu—"

Nova slapped his hand over Palan's mouth, ignoring the anger that blazed in Palan's eyes.

"Attack! They're here. Get Melly. We have to go!" Nova said, tension straining his voice.

Palan appeared to absorb the information more quickly than Nova had. "How many?"

Nova shook his head. "Hundreds…maybe thousands. It's too many."

Palan immediately pulled his half-sleeping daughter into his arms.

He reached under his pillow, pulling out a tangle of scarves and deftly wrapped them around himself and Melly, securing her to his person.

The little girl whimpered as she became more alert.

"Shh!" Palan said as he rushed to the corner of the tent and threw a blanket off a small heap, revealing a lock box full of energy weapons.

"Grab what you need," Palan growled to Nova as Melly's cries intensified.

"Daphne!" Melly screeched.

"Be QUIET, child!" Palan rasped. "Gods-cursed stupid doll… where is it?" Palan continued to mutter curses too unintelligible for Nova to work out as they both sifted anxiously through the mess of blankets for Melly's doll.

"Nova!!" Palan hissed as their hands collided.

Nova looked at him in shock.

"Forget the doll. I've got this. Get the others."

Nova nodded his comprehension at the directions. He pulled two energy weapons from the chest, securing them to his person before crawling his way back out of the tent. He held his breath as he glanced toward the trees. They were getting closer.

He tried to focus his *sight* like a shield around himself, hoping an illusion would at least dampen his movements. It wouldn't be as good as their cloaks that seemed to swallow light altogether, but he hoped it would be enough.

He slid forward, thankful now more than ever for his quiet footsteps. Nova threw open the next tent with less caution than he had Palan and Melly's. He called softly to Sonny.

Sonny sat up quickly. She stared into Nova's eyes and rose without a word, seeming to understand their danger instinctively.

Nova tossed a pistol toward her. Swiftly, she swiped it out of the air and tucked it under her belt.

They exited the tent, searching the small, growing settlement for their next move. Palan gestured toward the trees behind their campsite. Nova nodded acknowledgement and the four of them hurried in the opposite direction into the woods. Melly appeared to have found her doll and she stayed blessedly quiet on her father's back.

Palan knelt on the ground, placing one hand on a tree trunk. "We need to go. Now," he said.

"How many did you say you saw, Nova?"

"Too many." Nova replied.

"We need to warn the others!" Sonny insisted.

"What are we going to do? Fight them? I've got *two* pistols and a kid on my back!" Palan snapped.

"We can't just leave them. They could still escape," Sonny answered.

Palan grunted. "Fine. Someone get Fenwick." He spat the name with obvious disdain.

Nova crept along the treeline towards Fen and Isara's tents. The bell tower near the supply center was too close to the water, and Nova did not believe he could reach it without being spotted. Instead, he looked for a safe route farther from the water channel.

A booming crack of thunder rang out across the Chickadee River followed by shouting. There was no more time for warnings. Nova's mouth opened in horror as he watched the throng of cloaked attackers rush across the river. All the physical and *sensory* barriers dissolved in an instant. The attackers shouted and whooped as they kicked up water, dust, and rocks in their charge.

The sleeping survivors awakened, emerging from their tents. Sparks flew as charged energy weapons blasted, swords clashed, and glaives swung.

Nova stared as he watched Isara Blackstone emerge from her tent, a heavy axe in each hand. Her black, curly hair frizzed around her in all directions. She was a formidable sight. Nova only hoped her raw strength would be enough against the energy charges shooting all around them.

He raced to the bell tower and pulled the rope hard, sending its warning gong out into the night. If there was anyone left unaware, they would be alerted by its haunting knell.

A chain of lampposts sprang to light, illuminating the entire campground.

Nova whirled around to see Palan, Melly, and Sonny running away from the camp, to the concealed path they used to travel to-and-from Observation Point.

A bright, yellow bolt shattered on the metal bell behind Nova, narrowly missing his ear. He ducked, grabbing the arm of an assailant who had scaled the bell tower. Nova plunged his dagger through black fabric into human flesh without a moment's hesitation. He swiftly pulled the hood off his attacker who dropped to the ground as blood bubbled from his mouth.

Nova jammed the hood over his own face and detached the attacker's cloak, securing it around himself. His lips tingled as he tucked the dagger back into his belt and absconded the dead attacker's energy weapon to add to his growing arsenal.

Before he had a chance to catch his breath his arm rose to block an incoming blow. His knees buckled and, as he fell, he grabbed the new attacker by the knees to pull him down with him. They struggled on the ground, Nova doing his best to gain the upper hand.

A sudden bolt of lightning struck his assailant who went still. Nova looked into Fen's eyes. He scrambled to his feet, breathless, thankful to see Fenwick's face alive with fury.

"Run. I'll meet you at the hill," Fen said, voice calm.

Nova hesitated as he saw the surge of fighters pouring through the camp.

"Go. To the spaceship. I'll be right behind you," Fen repeated.

"It's not ready!" Nova shouted.

"Ready or not," Fen said with a grin. He turned and continued shooting, leaving Nova to escape.

Hesitating only a split second longer, Nova's feet flew toward the hills. He hoped the cloak and mask would be enough to dampen his appearance so he wouldn't be noticed or followed.

The climb to Observation Point was a blur of brambles and scrapes as he tripped innumerable times. It hardly slowed him down.

He ran through calculations in his mind, silently taking inventory of every bit of the spaceship. It was not ready, but it was close. He hoped it would be close enough to get them safely away from the isle of Asayouga. Perhaps he would be visiting Nayeli's star sooner than he'd anticipated.

As Nova reached the hill, he saw that Palan and Sonny had already fired up the engine. All the lights blazed, turning Observation Point into a beacon bright enough to see from any of Kelmundy's three moons.

As he ran, Nova looked up at the glittering night sky. A chill ran through every inch of his body as he realized the date—the moons had reached their triple alignment. Ancient astral wisdom about the lunar event foretold chaos and calamity.

Nova ran towards the ramp. Bolts of electricity shot past him as Palan shot more attackers whom he had not noticed in his haste.

He bent his head forward and picked up speed as he ran up the metal ramp. Immediately, he and Sonny grabbed drills to detach the platform which Nova shoved from the side of the ship with his boot. He and Sonny reached up in tandem to pull the heavy door down, sealing the hull of the spacecraft.

Nova looked over at Palan who stood near the engine panel.

"I don't have a damn clue how we fly this thing," Palan said, as he proceeded to slam on all of the buttons.

"Fen!" Nova shouted. He turned back to the panel they had just fought to close, ready to grab the tools and release it again. But Sonny squeezed Nova's arm. When he looked at her, she merely shook her head.

"He's as good as dead," Palan stated in a matter-of-fact voice before continuing. "And so will we be if you don't tell me how to fly this gods-cursed SHIP!" he said, his voice escalating back to a shout.

Nova swallowed a lump in his throat. He pictured the brightness in Fenwick's face as he'd saved him on the embankment. He hoped Palan was wrong. But he knew they could not wait.

He screamed directions to both Palan and Sonny. The three of them raced around the ship, flipping switches. Nova watched wide-eyed as bright yellow energy hummed and flowed through the center engine. He gripped a side panel as the ship rocked violently back and forth.

Sonny ducked below the panels for shelter as sparks flew through the interior. They were not ready to fly. The final checks were not in place. But they had no choice.

The launch was fully activated. Nova ran to the windows in time to see Observation Point already surrounded by cloaked attackers. His stomach twisted as he witnessed the swarm around the observatory where all their research lay open and vulnerable to attack. It would be lost now. Some documents remained on board the ship, and that was Nova's only comfort.

The vessel lurched. Nova flew backwards, slamming painfully into a wall. On his hands and knees, he saw Melly holding onto a cupboard door in wide-eyed terror.

Nova dragged himself across the floor to wrap his arms around her in protection.

The ship lifted off the ground, spiraling into the air. Nova fought the urge to vomit. Melly couldn't. She threw up violently. It was the last thing Nova saw before blacking out.

When he came to, they seemed to have gained momentum but instead of rocketing towards the stars, this time they hurtled back down through the atmosphere. Sonny and Melly were both knocked out while Palan appeared weak and sallow as he clung to the engine panel.

"How…" he gasped, eyes connecting with Nova's. "How do we land?"

The ship would land somewhere, regardless of what they did.

"Escape pods," Nova wheezed in response. The two of them hauled the limp bodies of Sonny and Melly across the bridge.

They struggled against the force of the spaceship plummeting through the air.

They stumbled into the pods. Nova propped Sonny against the wall. She slumped forward. Palan held his daughter in his lap. Nova closed the hatch. He swallowed a lump in his throat, knowing he was about to lose all hope of returning to Nayeli.

He hit the button, shooting the pod far away from the main ship. Bracing for impact, he hugged his knees to his chest.

"Hope you can swim," Nova said.

Palan said nothing. They crashed into the ocean.

Chapter Thirteen

BEACH

Nova sat in the sand, exhausted and disoriented. He wasn't aware of how long he settled there, unmoving. He only knew he had vomited seven times since landing. The escape pod somehow survived the crash with minimal damage, but the ship was gone. There was no telling where it landed.

Sonny stood in the water, staring at the sky, still as a statue while Palan held Melly inside the escape pod. The door wouldn't close again, but beyond that, the hull and interior structures remained intact.

Nova didn't know enough about the world beyond Asayouga to figure out where they were. He guessed they were still somewhere among the Ersette isles, perhaps near the mainland.

When night fell, he would be able to use the stars as a reference point. He hoped he could re-orientate himself quickly.

The sun blazed hot against Nova's neck, even though it was only mid-morning. Uncertain what to do next, no one made a move or attempted to speak.

The heat grew increasingly oppressive as the day stretched on, leaving Nova's muscles feeling weak. The four of them moved further from the beach into the rich jungle to escape the direct sunlight. Under the canopy of trees, it was only slightly easier to withstand the scorching heat.

Nova was thankful they already stocked the escape pods before their unexpected launch. Their canteens—charmed to purify any water they were filled with—meant they didn't have to worry about finding a fresh drinking source nearby.

Palan broke the silence first with sobering words. "This isn't the mainland," he said, voice sounding thick and scratchy. He still held Melly close to him. She had gone silent again. Her doll was missing.

"How do you know?" Nova asked. He still couldn't tell. Although he had read plenty about the Isles in his years of study, he could not seem to recall anything of importance just then.

Palan huffed before gesturing off into the distance. The heat was getting to all of them. "The volcano," he stated simply.

Nova shielded his eyes with his hand, squinting at the shapes in the distance. The smoke rising from some of the mountains suggested Palan was correct. But the whole island was covered in steam too, rising from the hot, humid ground all around them.

"Great," Nova responded. Volcanos confirmed they were somewhere west of the mainland. He didn't know why, but the distance they'd flown surprised him. He searched his mind for any details he could remember about the city of Oleress but came up with very little. Though Nova knew a great deal about space travel, it wasn't going to help them navigate the remote jungle isles.

"We shouldn't explore too far without a plan. We will need somewhere to shelter, and the escape pod is more cramped than our tents on the Chickadee." Sonny pointed out.

Nova nodded. The tiny escape pod would provide some shelter, but it wouldn't be sustainable for long.

"Our best bet is to find the main ship," Nova said.

"Or a city," Sonny added.

Palan continued to scan their environment. Finally, he kicked a tree trunk and swore.

"What's wrong?" Nova asked.

"You mean besides everything?" Palan said, rolling his eyes.

"I mean why are you abusing a tree?" Nova shot back.

Palan shook his head. "I simply have a bad feeling," he said as he raised his hand to wipe sweat from his forehead.

Nova eyed Palan carefully. Palan wasn't a man who relied on gut feelings. He usually focused on practical details, facts and data. While Nova's mind wandered off in all directions, including into the stars, Palan didn't take the same view. He focused on the present. It unsettled Nova to hear his colleague talking of instinct.

However, he couldn't disagree. He had chalked his own uneasy feelings up to disorientation from the crash and their unfamiliar surroundings, but something about the steaming, sticky air of the jungle brought further confusion.

"That doesn't seem like you," Nova said at last.

"It doesn't seem like me to allow myself to be launched into space in an oversized bucket fueled by magic either," Palan replied.

"We are still ourselves, even if the place is new," Sonny said calmly.

Nova nodded. "But we do need to make a plan. We can't just sit here."

"We should search the island for any inhabitants," Sonny began, "Perhaps early in the morning, to avoid the heat. We won't get far traveling at this time of day."

"There's a bloody volcano on this island," Palan said. "If anyone lives here, they are not of sound mind."

"It isn't fair to judge people we've never even met simply because they live differently to how we do," Sonny said.

"You should know: I am too hot to make judgments," Palan quipped.

Nova listened to Sonny and Palan argue back and forth a while longer until the hairs on the back of his neck prickled. Nova instinctively closed his fingers around the pistol at his belt.

"SHH!" he whisper-yelled.

Sonny and Palan didn't seem to hear him. Nova thrust his elbow into Palan's side.

"OWW—" Palan started. Nova slapped a hand over his friend's mouth to put a stop to any further protest. Palan bit his palm and Nova cringed hard, managing to stop himself from screaming out in pain himself.

"We're being watched," Nova hissed through his teeth barred tightly together in pain.

As soon as Nova lowered his hand Palan leaned forward, looked Nova directly in the eye and whispered, "If we survive this, you'll pay for that later."

"I think I already did," Nova said quietly as he tightened his fingers over his painfully stinging palm.

The three of them crouched, returning to the beach as noiselessly as they could. Wrapped in carrying scarves on Palan's back, Melly gripped onto her father's shirt as if to provide extra security.

Crack! A loud snap made Nova freeze in his tracks. He clutched Palan's arm, fingernails digging into his friend's bicep.

Palan swore in a whisper. "We've got company."

At least a dozen warriors, dressed in patchy-colored fabric that blended seamlessly with the jungle stepped from the trees, surrounding them on all sides.

Sonny, Palan and Nova stood back-to-back, shielding Melly in the middle of their circle. Nova found himself gaping in wonderment as he observed the way the warriors' clothing shimmered and shifted, blending with the surrounding foliage. Their armor was cleverly designed. Powerful illusions graced the fabrics, keeping them perfectly camouflaged in the jungle environment.

Nova felt frozen in place as the warriors drew their weapons in unison. He closed his eyes, expecting to be shot instantly. There was no one there to help them negotiate. He wished once more that Fen had made it on board. His *voice* was needed.

One of the warriors stepped forward from the circle. He was more elaborately decorated than the others, perhaps denoting his higher status. He spoke in a language Nova did not recognize. To Nova's ears, it sounded like the jungle itself—heated, thick, and hissing with life.

The string of words that met their ears was unintelligible to Nova.

"He's asking how we got here from space," Palan muttered, adding a few choice expletives.

"You have the *voice* now?" Nova asked.

"I have a brain. They saw us land here from the bloody sky, Nova," Palan answered. His voice sounded calm despite everything.

"By the gods," Sonny whispered.

After another string of harshly-uttered words, one of the fighters gestured to the others. He stepped closer to the four of them who stood back-to-back as enemies surrounded them.

"I hope my soul becomes a star next to Nayeli's," Nova said, considering himself already dead.

"I don't rightly care what I turn into anymore," Palan said.

"Can we take them?" Sonny asked.

No one answered. Nova held his energy pistol at his side in a death grip, but he made no move to use it. There were too many to know where and how to start shooting, especially with so many weapons pointing straight toward them.

Mouth dry, he whispered an idea to his companions. "If we all draw on three, we could distract them and you could take Melly. Make a run for the pod," Nova said, keeping his voice quiet in case one skilled with the *voice* could translate his words.

Before anyone could reply, fire rained from the sky. The dozen colorfully-clad fighters surrounding them shouted to each other in surprise.

The grass at their feet lit ablaze. Next, a tree. Nova spun to take Melly from Palan. Palan had already drawn his weapons and aimed into the smoke. None of his shots landed.

More bolts of fire pierced the air around them. There was too much commotion. Nova couldn't tell who or where the shooters were.

He held Melly and ducked his head, running straight toward the beach. If he could make it back to the pod, the hull would provide some protection against the blaze of energy bullets. He hoped Sonny and Palan would find them quickly.

Once Nova reached the escape pod, he crouched with his back against the now blazing-hot metal of the outer hull. Cautious, in case the islanders had already discovered the machine, he inched along the sand until he could peek through the open escape hatch. Seeing nothing, he deemed it safe enough to crawl inside.

He settled Melly against the wall, away from the opening and held a finger to her lips to remind her to stay quiet. Peering back through the open doorway, he searched for any signs of Palan or Sonny, while keeping himself in front of Melly like a living shield.

There was no trace of either of his companions emerging from the trees, though Nova could still hear yelling and shooting. He heard more blasts from energy weapons—most likely Palan's—but he couldn't be certain. Even with his *sight* he couldn't *see* the warriors well because of their illusioned armour.

At last, Palan and Sonny emerged from the trees, running toward the pod. To Nova's surprise, no one pursued his friends as the two sped across the beach.

They climbed inside but the damaged hatch refused to activate, leaving them exposed.

The three of them crouched in silence with nothing but the sound of their heavy breathing and the smoke crackling from the distant trees.

"Well, we aren't alone here," Palan said after a breath.

Nova shook his head in confirmation. Exploring the island wasn't going to be easy. Wherever the warriors came from, the news of their mission would soon reach more ears—Nova had no doubt. Their crash from space had been noticed. He suspected it wouldn't be long before more came to investigate.

Nova and the others kept watch through the open doorway, waiting to see if anyone would emerge from the jungle.

"Nova," Palan said sharply.

Nova glanced at his friend questioningly.

"Look," he said, pointing.

A woman stood in front of them, gripping a bow in one hand with other weapons crossed at her back. She wore knives strapped against her chest and arrows around her waist.

Nova stared in shock as he pointed his pistol at her. He had not noticed her approach, which was remarkable considering she was so overladen with weapons. She was also tiny. She did not have the expected physique of a fighter.

A strange sensation passed over Nova from the top of his head to the bottom of his foot. The entirety of the right side of his body prickled with heat as his gaze locked with hers. A force like lightning ignited between them, passing quickly. They stared at each other without moving. Nova didn't know how much time passed before the woman spoke, her voice heavily accented but somehow still intelligible to Nova's ears.

"Aren't you going to thank me for saving your lives?" she asked, a slight smile crossing her features.

Nova didn't think she was using the *voice* to communicate. Instead, she seemed to be speaking in a common tongue. It did not match their language exactly, but he could understand it. Some of the syllables were unclear, using unfamiliar vowels or different word shapes, but it was enough for them to communicate.

"The fire arrows..." Palan said. "That was you?"

"Yes," she replied with a bow.

"Why?" Nova asked, simultaneously perplexed and dazzled.

"Fire is fun. Unexpected," she said.

Nova paused a moment, surprised by her answer. That wasn't what he'd meant. "But... why did you help us?"

"Oh," she said, stepping back to make a show of her admiration for the small spacecraft. "It's not every day you encounter space aliens," she laughed.

"Who are you?" Palan demanded.

"My name is Edeyn," she replied. "Welcome to Scoria Island."

Chapter Fourteen
RESCUER

"Scoria Island?" Nova parroted the words in a question. He wasn't sure he heard them correctly. Images of maps floated into Nova's mind's eye as he struggled to recall reading or seeing the name in any of his books or studies before. He couldn't connect it to anything.

"That's right," Edeyn replied in her sing-song accent. She appeared to be studying all of them with deep curiosity, her eyes dancing brightly as she surveyed Palan, Sonny, Nova and Melly all in turn.

Nova and Palan exchanged glances and Palan shook his head slightly, wordlessly conveying to Nova he did not recognize the name either.

"I'm not sure that helps us," Nova said eventually.

Edeyn had crouched down to meet Melly at eye level. She smiled at the little girl as she answered Nova, "I can be your guide."

Nova blinked. The intense heat made it difficult to think clearly. "Our guide for...?" he asked.

Edeyn laughed. "For the island, of course! You look like you could use some help."

He chewed the inside of his cheek as he considered her offer. Exploring the island would be dangerous, and they were already suffering from the extreme heat. A local's guidance would be invaluable.

"Why should we trust you?" Nova asked, even though he already did, despite not understanding why. His chest and stomach bubbled with warmth as he looked at Edeyn. There was a familiarity about her, even though he knew without a doubt he could never have met her before.

"Why *wouldn't* you trust me?" Edeyn replied. Her answer flowed easily, as if she had no fear in the world.

Nova stood back, observing as Palan pulled Melly close to him. The child's eyes were wide, as Edeyn opened her palm to present her with a piece of glowing sea glass.

"We've never met you," Nova said, although something in the back of his mind insisted that didn't matter.

Edeyn locked eyes with Nova. Goosebumps covered his arms as their dazzling, bright, emerald color captivated him. He couldn't look away.

Shrugging her shoulders, Edeyn replied, "Trust is not absolutely necessary. We can help each other. There is no need to trust anything beyond that."

Palan broke his silence. "What if we don't want to help you?"

Edeyn laughed and shrugged her shoulders again. "Then you won't, and I won't," she said.

Her answer rendered Nova perplexed. Most people held hidden motivations for offering help, at least in his experience. The ease with which she accepted his answer caught him off guard. Nova knew they were indebted to Edeyn for saving their lives. She must want something.

"This is a trap," Palan said with a growl.

"And what if it isn't?" Sonny said after a deep breath. "We need a guide around this island. She knows how to avoid the inhabitants."

"We can help ourselves," Palan snapped in return.

"Maybe..." Nova began. He shielded his eyes against the blazing hot sun as he looked toward the sky. They had never been in an environment as harsh as Scoria's. They'd already narrowly escaped an ambush. Nova doubted they would be able to navigate the whole landscape safely on their own. The terrain was treacherous and strange. Finding their ship would be nearly impossible without navigation support.

"We might find it on our own," Sonny said, "but we might just as easily die." She turned to look up at Palan, their height difference strikingly apparent as they stood next to each other. "You should think about Melly."

Palan snarled. "How dare you suggest I wouldn't!"

"That's not what I meant," Sonny said with an exasperated sigh. "Why are you always sniping at everyone? We don't know our way around this island or where we might end up. Melly won't be able to manage everything we could come across, and she adds danger to the journey."

While the group argued, Edeyn traced symbols in the sand. She remained unperturbed, at least as far as Nova could tell.

"Wait. How can we help you?" Nova asked, turning to address Edeyn recalling her proposition to help each other, not just her guidance through Scoria.

Edeyn looked at Nova with a dazzling grin. Something about her sudden flash of brightness landed like a gut punch to Nova's soul. He was immediately flooded with memories of Nayeli and her hopeful spirit.

"Maybe I get to join you on your ship," she said.

Nova eyed her with a mixture of curiosity and suspicion. "How do you know about the ship?" he asked.

"Nova!" Palan snapped, combing both hands through his hair in a gesture of exasperation.

Edeyn shrugged. "It's a valid question," she said. "I saw your ship fall from the sky. It was impressive!"

"We don't even know if it's survived the crash," Nova said, alarmed. "It might not even be on this island!"

"Your little ship survived, didn't it? Perhaps the bigger one did as well. And I think I know where it is," Edeyn said, undeterred.

"Don't tell her anything else, Nova," Palan said.

Nova looked at both Palan and Sonny. Only Palan seemed certain they couldn't trust the woman who swooped in to save their lives. He felt a strange calm as he looked at Edeyn. His soul told him she was safe, even if it wasn't logical. He didn't know what to say to the others to convince them. Edeyn appeared unbothered. She watched Nova's face expectantly.

"What did you see?" Nova asked, after a pause. He heard Palan let out a strangled yelp of frustration before stomping down the beach, leaving Melly behind without a word.

None of them pursued Palan. It was difficult to convince him of anything under the best of circumstances.

Edeyn made a humming sound in her throat and tilted her head as she continued to stare at Nova. "I saw this little ship explode from the bigger ship. There was a burst of light and I saw the larger ship crash somewhere on the mainland," she explained. "I don't know its exact location, but I could take you to the mainland."

"How did you know to save us?" Nova asked as he pondered Edeyn's report.

"Oh, I didn't," Edeyn said. "The Agatians saw the crash and I followed. They were not expecting me."

Edeyn pressed her palm to the escape pod, examining it. "I have seen this metal before, I think."

"I doubt that's possible," Nova said. They had invented the material themselves.

"I think I have," she insisted.

Nova ignored her insistence. He knew it couldn't be true, or if it were, it would be a remarkable coincidence.

"Where did you say you saw the ship?" Nova asked, still perplexed.

"Southeast. I'm certain it's near Oleress," Edeyn replied simply. "We would need to go to the opposite end of the island.

And you won't want to bump into Agatia on the way there. There are more of them. A lot more." Her mouth pressed into a thin line as she relayed the information.

Nova registered her expression and realized it was the first time she'd shown anything resembling displeasure or worry in her face. He watched her intently as she chewed the inside of her lip, her brow creased in concentration.

After a moment, her features brightened once more. "I was born here. I've lived on this island my whole life. I can keep you out of harm's way while you look for your ship," she said.

Nova felt his heart hammering faster in his chest. He wondered why Edeyn recognized the metal. Whether she had seen their ship crash or not, she didn't seem to know much more than they did about where it landed.

He eyed her again, wondering what Edeyn's *sense* was. It might have been the *sight*, though she didn't seem to know enough detail about where the ship landed for that to be true. And it wasn't her *voice*, as she had intentionally spoken in a common language that they could at least understand most of; despite how the sounds differed from their own dialect. He supposed she might have the *touch*, using it to enhance her arrows with flame. But a glimpse of a flint box attached to her belt eliminated that as a likely choice, too.

"And you want to go to space," Nova stated.

"Sure!" Edeyn answered without hesitation.

"Why?" Nova asked. "You'd be trapped with a bunch of strangers. Why would you want to leave your home behind?"

Edeyn laughed. "Why would you?"

Nova answered quietly, "We have no home. Not anymore."

Edeyn nodded, her expression merely softening. She smiled, but there was a sadness hidden behind her eyes as she answered. "Neither do I. We are the same, you and I."

Nova's own heartbreak sat heavy in his chest, his grief a constant companion from every moment since Nayeli's death.

"You said this island was your home," he said.

"I never said these words," Edeyn replied.

"You did, you said—" Nova started.

"That may be what you heard," Edeyn interrupted, "but it is not what I said. You have lost much. I can see that." She paused, finally looking away from Nova. "I understand."

The continued heat from the sun, even as it dipped lower into the evening sky, the impact of their crash, and the events of the day all seemed to catch up with Nova at once, leaving him drained and weak. He blinked at the vivid colors stretching out along the water's edge. The sunset was beautiful.

Finally, Nova nodded. He knew they wouldn't get far without help, and this particular help was practically begging them to be included. He wondered about her story, what was behind her desire to lead them. But something within Nova trusted Edeyn at a level he had never felt before. He wondered what Nayeli would think of him for this.

"Ok," Nova said. "Get us safely to our ship. After that, we can talk. We might not even recover it. I can't promise you an escape, if that's what you're looking for."

Edeyn smiled again and replied, "This suits me well. What may I call you, as I guide you, sky-bound one?"

"Nova Nightfall," he answered. He noticed she had not addressed the end of his statement. The nagging fear of her inevitable disappointment in him settled in the back of his mind.

Edeyn smiled and ducked her head.

"Is there something wrong with my name?" he asked, unable to explain why he suddenly felt foolish and awkward in Edeyn's presence.

"Nothing at all, Nova Nightfall. It is a beautiful name. Simply unheard among my people," she replied with the hint of a quiet laugh in her voice.

"Oh," Nova said. "Thank you, then."

Edeyn turned her attention to the beach. "Your grumpy friend is not going to like this." She giggled as she said it, as if the idea of upsetting Palan delighted her. "Also, we must travel in the evening. Not in full daylight. It is too difficult in the heat."

Nova felt the sweat clinging to every part of his body and nodded agreement.

Edeyn opened her pack and set wrapped parcels down on the ground. "Something to eat from the island? You may enjoy these! Especially the little one," she offered.

Sonny knelt down with Melly and allowed the child to unwrap one of the parcels. Nova picked one up as well. The paper was cool to the touch, apparently designed to protect the contents from the scorching elements.

"You have the *touch*, then?" Nova asked as he unwrapped the package. He stared at the contents, fascinated. There were tiny, colorful pieces of dried fruit, berries, and meat. He couldn't identify what they were from *sight* alone.

Edeyn shook her head. "I do not." She didn't offer any further explanation.

Nova was too embarrassed to ask any more questions. He sampled the food, chewing it slowly. It was surprisingly flavorful.

They ate in silence while they waited for Palan's inevitable return.

Chapter Fifteen
EDEYN'S SORROW

Edeyn worked together with Nova, Sonny and Palan to hide the escape pod. After scouting ahead, she guided them down to the rocky part of the beach where it would be easier to disguise the small ship among the dark, grey rocks.

Even though the pod was small, the four of them labored heavily to move it along the sand. At last, they pushed the pod into place nestled between several large boulders. Edeyn stepped back to admire their work, satisfied to see it was well hidden even before they added *sensory* illusions.

Edeyn nearly collided with Nova who was standing much closer to her than she'd expected. She looked up at him in surprise and blushed when their eyes met. The electricity between them was difficult for her to explain. Edeyn didn't usually feel attracted to strangers, but since the moment they first said hello, she felt something awaken deep within her soul.

She allowed a nervous laugh to escape as she recovered her composure. She spoke using the common tongue she had poured years of study into learning, despite never having use for it—until now.

"Sorry, I didn't mean to walk into you," she said.

Nova smiled, never taking his eyes off her face. He seemed to be drinking her in. "It's all right," he replied, without adding anything further.

"Make sure you put a strong enough illusion on it," Palan interrupted.

Nova's gaze lingered a fraction of a second longer on Edeyn's face before he answered Palan. "Yeah. I'll try!"

Edeyn watched him work, enthralled. She found visual illusions fascinating, especially because she could not create them herself. Nova knelt close to the escape pod, his fingers resting against the hull as he perfected the protective illusion.

She forced herself to stop staring and instead redirected her attention to Palan. The tall man carried his daughter on his back, secured there with thick scarves designed to carry her weight.

Edeyn never wanted a child of her own, but children seemed drawn to her anyway. They seemed to trust her quiet nature.

It was a stark contrast to most adults who distrusted her implicitly.

There was a time in the past when loneliness seemed to crush Edeyn. She craved love so deeply that she gave too much of herself in an effort to be seen. Eventually, Edeyn felt comfortable on her own and she stopped communicating with people. Keeping to herself seemed the safest option. Where others might eventually turn on her, she knew she would never betray herself.

When Nova was finished, he stepped back and turned to Edeyn first. Her heart leapt as he smiled at her again. The flutters in her chest made her wonder if she were losing her mind. She forced herself to look calm on the outside, hoping he wouldn't think she was insane.

"I think it'll do," he announced.

"Of course," Edeyn replied, scanning the rocks before shrugging. "I can't see it, and I know exactly where it is. Well done."

Palan grunted. "I can *smell* it," he said.

Nova sighed as he answered, "I can't do anything about that, Palan. You're welcome to add your own illusions, though."

"I will," Palan replied. He set to work, still carrying his daughter on his back, seemingly unaffected by her added weight.

Once everyone was satisfied the miniature ship was adequately hidden, Edeyn nodded in approval, ready to take charge. She was not used to looking after anyone but herself, though she was confident in her knowledge of the island.

"Follow me. We'll need to be cautious near Agatia. Once we've passed that city, we should come to the City of Thorns. From there we can gain passage to Oleress."

Nova nodded in agreement, gesturing to Edeyn to lead the way. Their fingers brushed against each other for an instant, igniting sparks in Edeyn's chest. She smiled again, hoping her expression would conceal how nervous she felt. Marching confidently, she led the way into the jungle where she would bring them safely past Agatia.

It was hard to believe when she left the city that morning it would be the last time she would ever see it. Not that she would miss it. If she never returned to Agatia again it would be too soon. Through all her years living there, she had never once felt like she belonged.

Edeyn had longed for the day she would journey beyond the city's walls and never return. She'd always known the day would arrive eventually. Even though she couldn't explain it logically, she knew the day was finally here. Encountering Nova was a point of fate. She would never go back to the streets that persecuted her since childhood. She had a new purpose to fulfil.

Edeyn recalled a *vision* she had before Nova's arrival. The strength of the images woke her from her sleep. It was something stronger than a dream, signaling to her the events she *foresaw* would come to pass in the waking world eventually. Some of her dream *visions* were coded in metaphors and symbols, but this one was plain as day.

A man stood on a hill, looking at the stars through a telescope. A feeling of longing surrounded him, similar to the way she felt when she observed the moons and stars. The vastness of the night sky reminded Edeyn she was only a small piece of the larger fabric of the universe. She had a home somewhere beyond Kelmundy's plane. Somewhere indefinable.

The *vision* shifted quickly. *Panels of blinking lights, the feeling of hurtling through the atmosphere. There was a flash of burning buildings, thick smoke, and a river. She saw another man fall to his knees by the shores, noticing an object bolting through space above him before he collapsed, his arm around a fallen warrior.*

The unusual *vision* left her puzzled at first, but it was not long afterward she saw the streak of light as a spaceship blasted through the atmosphere. Edeyn knew the moment she saw it that she would soon meet its inhabitants.

Further *visions* swarmed her mind now. *She felt the solid impact of shining, black metal against the forest floor. She saw the sheer rock face rising in a sharp backdrop behind the machine.* Blinking slowly, she thought about what she *saw*. She knew where the ship was, but she would need to be careful about how she revealed her *knowing* to the others. After experiencing a lifetime of distrust toward her *visions,* Edeyn learned to reveal her premonitions without enlightening people as to the source of her knowledge.

She had an idea of how the others might react to sharing a *vision*. Palan was obviously distrustful of her. This was energy Edeyn was used to. But Nova seemed different. Still, she was afraid to test his trustworthiness too closely. She promised herself one day she would tell him how she knew where his spaceship was.

"Nova," Edeyn said, turning back to face the others.

"Yes?" he said, instantly locking his gaze with hers once more.

"If you're able to camouflage our appearance at all, this would be a good time," Edeyn said. "The Agatians patrol this area."

Nova ducked his head, looking sheepish. "I'll try. But I've never been very good at illusions," he admitted.

"Something is better than nothing," Sonny said from behind Nova.

"You did a fine job hiding the escape pod earlier," Edeyn added with cheerful encouragement.

Palan stood silent, looking irritated.

Nova nodded. He closed his eyes, taking in a deep breath. A few moments later, he sighed and opened his eyes. "I did what I could," he said.

Edeyn reached forward to pat Nova's arm in reassurance. She regretted it when she felt lightning fly between them like an ancient power. She hoped no one noticed, but one glance at Nova's face told her he felt it too. She prayed he would not suspect her of doing *sensory* magic on him.

"I'm sure it will be fine," Edeyn said, keeping her voice cheerful. "I know their patrol patterns. Follow me," she said before marching forward once more.

Chapter Sixteen

TREK

Day after day, Palan and the others trekked, single file, through the trees across Scoria Island. After traveling safely past Agatia, Edeyn assured everyone they were nearing the city of Tskela—referred to locally as the City of Thorns. From there they would be able to cross to the mainland.

The jungle was too dense for them to walk side by side. Palan followed at the back of the line while Edeyn led the way at the front, and Sonny and Nova took turns carrying Melly on their backs, swapping shifts every few hours. Palan wouldn't allow Edeyn to transport his daughter. He could see Melly was drawn to the woman, but he couldn't trust her. Trust left people vulnerable to betrayal. That was not something Palan was willing to risk.

Recalling the friendship he once had with Fen and how deeply betrayal hit in the end, Palan was cautious about who he allowed to get close. Nova's patterns were consistent and that kind of predictability was safe. At least he wouldn't have to worry about watching his back around Fenwick again.

Edeyn was an unknown entity. Was she friend or foe? Unable to decipher her motivations, he remained suspicious of her. She had dropped out of nowhere and saving a bunch of strangers selflessly didn't make sense. Palan didn't believe anyone could be as cheerful as she was all the time. It had to be fake. The only other person he could think of who acted like that was Nova. He reflected on the uncanny set of similarities between the two of them. They seemed to match each other on every level. Palan had never seen anything like it before.

Sweat dripped down the back of Palan's neck, soaking his shirt. The island heat was nearly unbearable, despite mostly traveling after sundown and in the early mornings. They trekked in silence, the thick foliage keeping their progress slow.

Further into the jungle, darkness grew deeper. The only sound was their footsteps, gently rustling the brush with every step. Bobbing orbs of light from their lanterns illuminated small areas enough to guide them forward. It was difficult to see much of anything else.

Palan continued to puzzle over Edeyn. Although her demeanor was easy going, he knew she had to be hiding something. Her *sense* remained a mystery. She used enchanted gear for everything, from her weapons to her clothing to the lights they all carried, but whenever anyone asked her about them, she denied having created them herself with any *sense*. She avoided answering direct questions about any of the *senses* either, changing the subject when the topic was brought up.

Left to imagine the possibilities for why anyone would hide their *sense*, Palan's distrust of their travel guide intensified. In any case, Edeyn seemed to be a very good actor. Palan was wary of anyone who wore a mask to such an extent.

Palan growled in irritation, slapping at his ear as a fly buzzed against his skin. In front of him, the train of bobbing lights halted and he could feel all eyes on him despite not being able to see their stares clearly.

"Palan?" Nova called.

"It's fine," he grumbled in reply.

Nova stepped closer into Palan's view and Sonny joined a moment later with Melly and Edeyn.

"We should probably stop soon anyway," Edeyn said, holding her lantern up towards Palan's face, causing him to squint.

Palan marveled at Edeyn's natural power. Not only was their guide shorter than even Sonny, she had a small frame as well. Yet, she carried herself as if she were larger than Palan. Though he would never admit it to anyone, her easy confidence intimidated him as he could not find such certainty within himself. He hated being afraid of someone whom he could so easily overpower, but still, he acknowledged with reluctance that he was, indeed, afraid.

"Why?" Palan questioned. There was still plenty of night left.

Sonny glanced over her shoulder at Melly who was fast asleep.

"The brush is getting thicker. It is too hard to navigate until we have more light," Edeyn answered. She paused a moment, a sound catching in her throat as if she were hesitating about what to say next. "Besides, I feel a presence nearby. I don't think we should continue until we determine who or what that may be."

Palan glanced at Sonny for confirmation, if anyone could *sense* something nearby it would be Sonny.

Sonny shrugged. "I haven't felt anything."

Palan felt the enchanted jewelery against his chest, tucked as always beneath the collar of his shirt. He focused his mind on its energy. Even with its power adding *touch*, he could not *sense* anything nearby aside from small animals, trees, and grass. No one needed to know of his awareness, so he kept the information to himself as always. He enjoyed the strategy of asking questions he already knew the answers to. It was enormously helpful in identifying one's secret enemies.

Edeyn's expression was unreadable. "I know these jungles. There are things you have not encountered," she said.

"You do not have the *touch* nor are you *sighted*. I can't smell anything with my *scent*. What *sense* is alerting you to this...presence?" Palan asked, keeping his tone of voice pleasant.

Edeyn tilted her head at Palan. "Why does it matter to you what *sense* I have?"

Palan felt his spine stiffen, taken aback by her response. "Everyone has a *sense*!" Palan snapped, his vocal folds seemingly recovered.

"Not everyone," Nova interjected.

Palan looked at his friend knowing he was about to info dump.

Edeyn turned to watch Nova as well.

"There is another *sense*," Nova explained. "It is possible to have a *sense* beyond the physical. It is not connected with anything on the body but in the mind. I've only ever read about it in tales, never witnessed it. But I have never seen this island

and I suppose there are many mysteries in the world we haven't observed."

An awkward silence fell between them after Nova's impromptu lesson.

Edeyn broke the silence first. "Thank you, Nova. I've never heard of these tales," she said, her voice still calm and bright. "And I *don't* owe you an explanation, Palan. I know what I know. I have lived here since the day of my birth. You may choose to use my advice or not. That is your choice. But *I* will be stopping here until daybreak."

With her words spoken firmly and calmly, she marched off into the trees, looking for a place to set up camp. Palan watched as she paused, touching tree trunks or crouching to examine the ground until she landed on a suitable spot. She tossed her bag and rummaged through it, laying her gear out on a clear, flat space between two solid-looking trees.

Nova looked at Palan and shrugged.

"Who is she?" Palan said, lowering his voice, not wanting Edeyn to overhear them. "She could be keeping us here to trap us!" "Maybe. Do you have a better idea? I can't get a clear view of the stars here. I can *see* but I don't know what dangers to look out for," Nova said.

Palan didn't realize he was growling until he glanced down at Sonny's hand on his arm. He jerked his arm away quickly. "Don't *touch* me."

"I was only trying to help," Sonny said, dejected.

"I don't need your help," Palan said. "No one here is properly suspicious. You trust everyone except who you should!"

"Are you suggesting we do not trust you?" Nova asked, reading between the lines of Palan's statement.

"You don't! I've never once steered you wrong and yet here you are listening to a stranger with NO *senses* guiding us through the jungle," Palan replied. He felt the unbearable, fiery tension ready to rip its way out of his chest.

Melly stirred on Sonny's back as the noise of the conversation rose. "No one here said you steered us wrong, Palan," Sonny hissed, taking care not to waken the child fully.

"So, we're sitting here for the night," Palan said, throwing his hands up in a gesture of exasperation.

"I am," Nova said. He glanced over his shoulder at Edeyn, then back at Palan. He pressed his lips together in a thin line before silently joining their guide under the trees.

Palan watched as Sonny followed Nova. It didn't seem he had any choice but to join them. As much as Edeyn bothered him, he knew there was no point traversing the jungle on his own.

The group set up camp in silence. There was no use in arguing. Palan settled down to eat a ration, his responsibility to protect his daughter remaining his top priority. He knew protecting her also meant not taking foolish risks, no matter how much he worried about betrayal.

It was a haunting from his past, a reality he could not forget if he wanted to keep himself and his child safe. Betrayal had a way of sneaking up on people who were too open. The twist of its knife left festering wounds more deeply painful than any physical ones Palan had ever experienced.

He sat back, chewing in silence, reasoning with himself. He wasn't really giving any part of himself away, so he couldn't really be betrayed. Eventually, Edeyn's motivations would be revealed and Palan wouldn't need to do anything to force the others to see. It would be Nova and Sonny who would feel the shock of that awful surprise. Not Palan. When she acted against their best interests, he'd be ready. Until then, he would never stop watching for signs of treachery.

Yet, the thought of Nova or Sonny or Melly losing their lives because of their misplaced acceptance refused to leave him alone. He didn't want to think that far ahead. There wasn't any point. They had no home to return to and only the foolish hope of some adventure among the stars to look forward to.

He reasoned himself into comfort and allowed himself to fall asleep. Whatever awaited them at the hands of Edeyn, the island, or anything else, would require his full strength. He knew he needed to rest while he still could.

Chapter Seventeen

SOMETHING HISSING THIS WAY COMES

Nova tossed and turned throughout the night, his dreams fragmented and strange. For the first time since Asayouga's destruction, Nayeli did not visit him in his dreams. Instead, Edeyn's face floated in and out of his slumber, staring at him with deep, soulful eyes. He heard her name echoing in his mind over and over throughout the night.

Nova woke before sunrise. He found it nearly impossible to stay asleep anymore, between the heat of Scoria Island, the strange dreams, and the discomfort of not knowing minute-to-minute where his life might be headed next.

He watched the stars fade slowly from his *sight* as the dawn broke. Glancing at Edeyn, he was surprised to see her already awake, crouched on her sleeping roll, watching him while she chewed a pre-packaged square from her pack of supplies. He'd been so absorbed in his thoughts he hadn't noticed her waking up.

He struggled to stay anchored to reality. There was nothing constant to hold onto, leaving his mind adrift. His home was destroyed. His love was lost forever. All he had left was the dream of launching his spaceship again, and that seemed unlikely.

Thrown into chaotic circumstances, survival was his highest priority. Yet, Nova's mind wandered to dreaming more than ever before. Reality was too much to deal with on its own without anything to look forward to.

The stars pulled his thoughts to the comfort of something he knew would stay the same. Any new discovery in the sky added to his existing framework of information. He never grew tired of learning about the outer realms. Somehow, focusing on the potential dangers of space travel seemed less daunting than the tropical jungle on an unfamiliar island did.

He smiled at Edeyn, hesitating as he tried to think of something interesting to say. Nova couldn't explain the tug in his soul every time he looked at her. The familiarity seemed to stretch deep beyond time as if they had once been together in another universe. He knew it didn't make sense, but he already felt he would break apart if he were parted from her.

Nova's love for Nayeli had been intense, too. He and Nayeli were happy together, and his love for her would never die, but meeting Edeyn ignited an entirely different fire within him. As he sat near her, his heart stirred like butterfly wings. It was as if his heartbeat were one with hers.

He told himself the strength of his affection was merely because Edeyn saved their lives. It was only natural he would feel connected to their hero. Yet another part of him whispered of a love that existed before they'd met as if a seed laid dormant in his heart, waiting for the fire that would burst it open and fuel its growth.

He sounded crazy even to himself. His thoughts shifted to Palan. Nova couldn't blame Palan for fearing the worst. They had encountered a well-armed stranger, about whom they knew nothing at all. Nova knew better than to trust his feelings alone, but that didn't seem to make any difference where Edeyn was concerned. Though, he hoped Palan would not be proven right.

Nova looked at Edeyn again. She was still watching him, a peaceful expression on her face. Dusting himself off, Nova quietly rose from his sleeping roll and sat down next to Edeyn so they could talk without waking anyone else prematurely. They would need to be on the move again soon, regardless.

"Good morning," Nova said with a smile.

"Have you slept?" Edeyn asked.

"Yes and no," Nova answered, unable to resist glancing up at the sky once more.

"Who is up there?" Edeyn asked.

Nova glanced at her in surprise, studying her face, wondering how she knew to ask the question. Of course, he didn't know the customs of the Scorians, but he supposed they may be similar to Asayougans.

Nova opened his mouth to answer but found his voice caught in his throat. Willing himself not to cry, he drew in a long, deep breath before replying. "Everything," he whispered, though he wished he could find better words to explain it all to Edeyn.

He glanced down at the small, gentle touch he felt against his arm before meeting Edeyn's gaze. Her large, green eyes sparkled with tears. Though Nova had said little, he felt in his heart Edeyn understood his answer, and all that he had not said out loud.

"I'm sorry," Edeyn said quietly.

"Thank you," Nova replied. He let out a husky laugh as he finally fought past the swell of grief. He allowed the moment of unspoken understanding and companionship bring a measure of healing to his heartbreak.

"The presence you felt last night"—he paused only because he was uncertain of exactly what he was asking.

Before he could finish formulating his question, Edeyn responded.

"Yes. It was something of spirit more than earth."

Nova frowned. The mystery of Edeyn created a spark of intrigue inside him. He couldn't differentiate the feeling between excitement or fear. Perhaps it was a combination of both. He didn't understand her but she seemed to understand him.

"What do you mean by that?" he asked, unable to dull his innate sense of curiosity.

"It may be difficult for you to understand if you are not open to things that cannot be explained with your logical mind," Edeyn said. Her voice remained calm as if she were used to being misunderstood.

Nova realized perhaps their rescuer and guide was still working out whether she could trust her new companions just as much as they were uncertain of her. "I am interested to hear what you have to say. Not everything makes sense the first time we learn about it. That doesn't mean it isn't real."

Edeyn smiled. She appeared to enjoy Nova's answer. "We are here in human form. Everything around us from the skies above to the seas below is made of energy. We are also made of energy. Some energy exists in a way that can't be observed by humans. We don't match, but I can *sense* what is there, even if it's not completely... human."

"Animals?" Nova asked, absorbing Edeyn's words as she spoke.

Edeyn shook her head. "No. Animals are different still. They're part of the physical world around us. Some energies exist beyond our physical reality."

"Oh," Nova said simply. It dawned on him that he already believed this as well. To believe Nayeli existed in a different form as a star in the sky was to believe in energy beyond their physical reality.

"So what you felt last night was—"

"Not of this world," Edeyn said, finishing Nova's thought. "It's something I don't think your friend is willing to believe."

Nova shook his head in agreement. "No. It isn't. Palan believes only what is in front of him."

"He believes more than that," Edeyn said, "but he is afraid."

Uncertain what she meant, Nova hesitated before responding in Palan's defence. "Well. He's afraid with good reason." He didn't mean to imply there was reason to be wary of Edeyn, but as soon as the words left his mouth, he worried she might interpret them as such.

"No," she said. "It is not 'good reason' that prevents him from accepting new beliefs. It is memory."

"Isn't that kind of the same thing?" Nova asked.

Edeyn shrugged. "Not to me," she said.

Nova fell into silence, wondering if she would elaborate.

She did, eventually. "It's not the same. When we reason, it's based on evidence. Sometimes we use past experiences to guide that, but memory is different. Our bodies remember how we felt in moments of deep pain and that can drive our responses more than logic. We act from the memory of the hurt unless we learn to see it and respond another way."

Nova considered the wisdom of Edeyn's words. He knew Palan felt the stabbing of betrayal in love before, and that had a way of shaping a person forever. He thought of his own loss, the gut-wrenching pain of losing his beloved and his home. The grief sparked an idea leading him to the present moment, camping on a volcanic island, sitting next to Edeyn. Without the circumstances of loss, he would likely never have landed on

Scoria Island or met her at all. His sorrow changed the entire trajectory of his life.

"I think I understand," he said at last.

"You do," Edeyn agreed. "I think we should keep moving along. The presence I felt in the night has passed. It either only exists in darkness or it has chosen to carry itself elsewhere. We were not a threat to it after all."

Nodding in agreement with Edeyn's words despite not fully understanding, Nova answered jokingly as he stood. "I'll wake Palan. I wouldn't want him to murder you on sight."

Edeyn laughed before returning to her gear. She packed her things remarkably quickly.

Palan was already half awake and easy to rouse.

"Edeyn says it's safe to continue," Nova told him.

"I'm sure," Palan growled. Everything was always a growl. Despite his obvious disdain for following Edeyn's plans, Palan gathered his things. He spoke softly to his daughter to wake her without startling her. It was still a shock to wake up in their strange new surroundings. Heavy humidity, the scent of flowers, and fruit thick in the atmosphere were unlike anything on Asayouga.

Sonny woke easily as well and packed her things without a word. She was the first ready to leave after Edeyn. Nova was last, having committed himself to everyone else's needs before his own.

They returned to their single-file trekking, mostly in silence. The heat changed as they made their way across the island. Though it was still hot and humid, the further inland they went, the less oppressive the humidity became. The ominous sounds of the volcano, however, alerted him to another problem. Nova wondered how difficult it would be to cross the streams of lava he imagined they would soon encounter. But, once more, he felt his trust in Edeyn had not been misplaced. He may not understand their connection, but he felt a sense of peace in her presence. She would know how to lead them through the difficult terrain.

After carrying on for some time, Sonny halted in her tracks, holding up a hand for the rest of them to follow suit. "Um...Edeyn?" Sonny started.

Edeyn turned, waiting for Sonny to continue.

"Are there snakes on this island?"

"Yes," Edeyn answered without concern in her voice. "There are many snakes on this island."

Sonny looked not at all reassured.

Nova squinted; curious what had alerted Sonny. Using his *sight*, he could make out the shapes of hundreds, if not thousands of small, black, wriggling bodies in the tree branches, on the ground, everywhere.

"Do any of these snakes travel in...gangs?" Nova asked in alarm as he felt his heartbeat increasing.

Edeyn immediately unstrapped daggers from her waist belt, one in each hand.

Nova looked at her. Though grateful for her willingness to fight for them, he wondered how she had so easily pickled up the presence of inhuman energies the night before, but missed an entire army of snakes.

"Violet adders," Edeyn said. "I hope you have good aim."

"Not all of us," Sonny said. She rubbed her hands together.

With his *sight*, Nova could *see* a ball of heat growing and glowing. He drew his energy pistol, ready to shoot oncoming snakes.

"Wait. On my count. They will all attack once startled. We should be ready," Edeyn said urgently.

Nova looked at her, ready and waiting for her order.

"3...2...1... Fire." She leapt forward with her daggers and Nova shot at the writhing shapes nearest to him in the grass. A bolt of heat swooshed past Nova's ear, setting fire to the thick brush before them. He heard the squeals of pain as snake bodies burned in the flames.

The snakes seemed to multiply in number, advancing swiftly just as Edeyn had predicted. Nova continued shooting, but as many as he hit, more seemed to swoop in to take their place.

"Nova!" Palan shouted.

Nova snapped his attention in Palan's direction, firing almost before he saw the snakes. There were hundreds converging rapidly across the jungle floor.

"Thank you!" Palan shouted as he ran, aiming upwards and blasting the trees. Dead snakes fell around him like rain but they didn't slow him down.

When Nova looked down, he was horrified to see snakes sliding across the tops of his boots. He stomped on their heads without thinking.

A scream pierced through the air. It was Melly, terrified, taking shelter behind a rock, actively swarmed. Nova shot across the grass quickly, grabbing the "I love you" dagger from his waist belt and stabbing it into as many snake heads as he could along the way.

Swiftly, Nova scooped Melly into his arms and took off. She was no safer hidden on the ground than carried on his back. "Let's get you out of here," he yelled over his shoulder.

He ran without stopping, crashing through the underbrush and rocks. The rocks became thicker, sharper, and blacker as he raced away. There was no time to stop to register their surroundings. He carried Melly as far as he could before he slowed down.

The air became less thick and stifling. Nova paused to gain his bearings. They had gone further than he'd thought. He blinked up at the clear blue sky before turning to take in their surroundings. The jungle trees were nowhere near them now. Instead, their environment had shifted to outcroppings of igneous rock, the ground a dusty, desolate grey as far as he could *see*. Nova shifted Melly from his back to his chest and held her close. They were alone.

Chapter Eighteen
SCORIA ISLAND

Nova sat against an outcropping of blackrock, holding Melly gently against his chest. They were both quiet, though the child let out an occasional whimper. He stroked her hair comfortingly, shushing her with his voice as he took stock of their surroundings.

He could not *see* their companions even with his *sight*. He had run much further than he realized. Nova now regretted his actions, though he held on to hope Palan would be able to use his *scent* to track them down. The rocky terrain seemed to dampen Nova's *sense*. He worried the environment would also make it more difficult for Palan to catch the *whiff* he needed to locate his daughter. They needed to find their way out of the volcanic zone quickly if Palan were to have any chance tracking them.

The shiny black surfaces and sharp edges protruding from the ground around them felt strangely familiar to Nova. He puzzled over it, searching his mind for the missing connection. His hand moved to the dagger at his belt as the solution dawned on him. He didn't need to look at it to recall its unusual shining black surface.

"I guess we know where you come from now," he whispered to the killing blade as he patted it without drawing the weapon.

Startled by Nova's voice, Melly looked up at him, her face still dirt stained and streaked with tears.

Nova smiled down at her. Their emergency escape meant he had brought nothing with him, their supplies abandoned somewhere in the jungle. All he had were his holstered weapons and a water gourd tied to his belt.

"Don't worry, little one. Your dad will be with us soon," he told her, though he had no idea whether or not that were true. He hoped it was for both their sakes.

"Snakes kill him," she said.

Nova shook his head in reassurance and replied, "Nah. He's a fighter. Your dad won't fall to a bunch of snakes."

Melly heaved a shuddering sigh and snuggled against Nova's chest again, accepting his answer as truth.

Nova wished he could reassure himself as easily. He chewed his lip, holding the girl in silence. He needed a plan. It wouldn't be long before Melly grew hungry, and there was no hope of foraging food from the barren terrain.

Nova did his best to strategize a route out of the area. The jungle would provide cover, but there were many hidden dangers there. He would be able to re-orientate himself when darkness arrived. He knew the star positions like the back of his hand. Even without knowledge of the island, he hoped he could use the constellation points to navigate them to a city.

He would have to distract the little girl until nightfall. Edeyn had described cities to the southeast beyond Scoria's volcano. Even without knowing their exact location, Nova considered finding a civilized area was their best chance at survival. It would be easier to make a plan to reunite with Palan and the others from there.

As daylight stretched on, the heat intensified. Nova wiped his brow, but he could not stop perspiration from trickling into his eyes, or down his face and neck. Although exposed to the direct sunlight in the rocky landscape, the air was not as oppressive as it had been within the jungle. Even with reduced humidity, the sunlight was only marginally more bearable.

Nova closed his eyes, feeling drowsy in the hot sun. He knew they would not survive for long if they remained exposed to all the elements. A distant, thunderous rumble roused him, causing his eyes to flutter open.

He frowned, hearing the unusual thunder roll again. As he stood, he shielded his eyes with his palm and searched the sky. It was dazzlingly bright and cloudless without any sign of an approaching storm. He couldn't perceive any logical reason for the sound. It left him uneasy.

He set Melly down on the ground. "Wait here a moment," he told her as he wandered, scouting for clues. The ominous rhythm echoed across the open sky again. Nova struggled to make sense of the noise.

"No!" Melly screeched.

Startled, Nova returned to the child's side and patted her head. "I'm not leaving you, ok?" he said, interpreting her fear.

Melly was unwilling to be left behind in any capacity. She hugged Nova's leg, refusing to let him move without dragging her along the ground with him.

The thundering sounded again. Deciding he had little choice, Nova picked up the little girl. He held her against his hip as he walked cautiously, gripping the deadly blade in his free hand. It would be completely impossible to fight with her attached to his side but leaving her to sit alone in terror seemed needlessly cruel.

Smoke, ash, and steam clouded the air, blocking his view. Nova focused his *sight*, concentrating hard to *see* through the thick pall that hung over the rocky area. He took slow, cautious steps as the landscape revealed itself. The area's dampening effect made it much more difficult to process what he *saw*. As the sound continued at intervals, Nova realized the noise had not been thunder after all, but the steady beating of drums.

He stood still to listen, shushing Melly's soft cries. Nova cursed silently to himself.

"Shh," he said both as urgently and gently as he could, pressing a finger to her lips.

She quieted somewhat but her body convulsed with hiccups.

He closed his eyes to concentrate on the sound. The thrumming steadily increased in volume, though he still couldn't *see* anything. He licked his lips as he looked around for somewhere—anywhere—to take cover. In this environment, there was nothing that would conceal them for long.

He scanned the area until he found a larger outcropping of rocks and hurried to crouch behind them. Nova doubted the rocks would provide enough cover. Exhausted, both from their escape and the heat, he couldn't muster up the energy it would take to create a *sensory* illusion. They remained exposed from nearly every angle.

The drums grew louder and louder. Nova closed his eyes to concentrate on his breathing, forcing his racing mind to calm. There was nothing he could do to protect them further, and he knew it. He only hoped the people they met would be kind to Melly. With no hope of rescue this time, Nova held Melly as they waited like prey to be discovered.

Nova glanced uncomfortably over his shoulder at intervals as his heart hammered in his ears. The looming drum beats grew to a roar until a voice shouted and the sound came to an abrupt halt.

Pressing his back firmly against the rocks, Nova squeezed his eyes shut and held Melly's head against his chest protectively. The sound of hundreds of footsteps all stomping at once met his ears. When he dared to look, he saw hundreds of weapons pointed at them. Warriors, dressed in black with weapons and unfamiliar-looking gadgets strapped to their armored suits, surrounded them.

Nova took note of the differences between the Agatian fighters who surrounded them on the beach, and the squad that stood in front of them now.

The original warriors had camouflaged, soft, flowing cloth armor, while these were covered in dark, shining plate mail that matched the deadly rocks surrounding them.

One of the soldiers stepped forward, his voice low as it reverberated from behind his suit of armor. Even though Nova recognized their language was not his own, he understood every word. He wondered if the commander had the *voice*, or if one of his gadgets had been enchanted to interpret his language in real time.

Nova observed all kinds of unfamiliar technology attached to their suits and weaponry. He had never seen anything like it. Strange gears and flashing lights adorned belt buckles, gauntlets and helms. A grated piece at the front of their helms was the only visible opening on their armor. He assumed they *saw* using an enchantment.

"Where do you come from?" boomed the question.

Nova had no way of answering. The truth would sound absurd, and he didn't know enough about the island to make up a convincing lie.

"I'm not from this island," Nova said, feeling defeated.

"What is your name?" asked the armored fighter.

"Nova Nightfall," he said, seeing no point in giving a false identity. His only hope now was to protect the little girl.

"And the child?"

"The child is mine. Melly," Nova lied. "Please," he added, "do not harm her."

"We would never harm an innocent," the voice replied. "You will, however, come with us."

At the commander's nod, a pair of soldiers stepped forward, in one smooth synchronous motion and lifted Nova by the elbows. Melly still clung to Nova's chest with no sign of letting go.

Their captors took them without resistance. Nova feared if he stepped out of line, they would be killed instantly. With no other choice, they marched, following the soldiers' lead.

Chapter Nineteen
TRACKING

A growl bubbled deep within Palan's chest. He was furious. "Where *is* she?!" he said for the umpteenth time.

Palan, Sonny and Edeyn stood surrounded by the bodies of dead snakes, breathing heavily after the exertion. Palan didn't notice Nova or Melly's disappearance during the chaos, but discovering their absence now left him in a blind rage.

He white knuckled the grip of his pistol as fear set in his soul. The snakes had activated his adrenaline already. The terror knowing his daughter was missing went far deeper than that.

Palan glanced at Sonny, fury snapping into his eyes. "Where?! You *feel* nothing?!"

Sonny squeezed her eyes shut and took in a slow, deep breath. "I'm sorry, Palan. I don't know where they are."

"You *felt* nothing at all this entire time?" Palan belted, wild with fear and panic.

"I was a bit focused on the vipers threatening to poison me to death," Sonny said, slightly defensive.

While the two bickered, Edeyn remained quiet, observing their interaction, shifting back and forth from foot to foot with a glaive in each hand.

"And you? Do you have no *sense* at all?!" Palan had turned his attention to Edeyn.

She narrowed her eyes. "Excuse me?"

"You have nothing to offer to this expedition! Why are you even here?" Palan snapped. In the back of his mind, he knew he should go easier on his companions, but losing his child overwhelmed him.

His thoughts blurred as he struggled to think clearly. Melly's absence stole all his attention. Any other objectives disappeared and his anguish burst out without his consent like the swarm of venomous snakes they killed.

"Are you quite finished?" she replied, her voice testy.

Palan kicked a rock and stomped in a circle. It was only then he recalled his amulet, still tucked safely inside his tunic. He didn't want to reveal its existence to the other two, but he needed its powers more than ever. Although the extra *senses* remained active as long as he wore it, Palan connected much more strongly with it when he held the stone piece in his palms.

Time was of the essence and he needed to sneak away to use it, but how?

Until his opportunity to use the amulet came, he was left with his own gift, his *scent*. Though he had no idea of the last time he saw Melly or Nova, he would be able to find their trail if he honed in with his *sense*.

Palan discovered his ability to detect *whiffs* had grown confused and scattered as they trekked their way through the jungle. As he focused, his *scent* was flooded with information but most of it was not what he was searching for.

A mix of tropical fruits, humid air, the trace of metallic rocks, the trees, even the dead snakes all swarmed Palan's mind. He forced himself to continue searching for the right *scents*.

First, Palan searched for Melly's signature *smells*, hoping their familial connection would make it easier to pick up her *scent*. Her essence was natural fabric, sugared candies, and the old doll she always carried with her, straw, her hair, and steam. He came up with nothing. At one point he believed he caught the faintest *whiff* of straw, but it faded before his *scent* could grasp it properly.

Next, he hunted for Nova's familiar blend of aromas—a mix of cold spring air from the outdoors after re-entering the warmth of a home with a fire burning in the hearth, an earthy, rich plum, and a soft note of vanilla. But with his abilities still dampened, he came up blank.

"Why are they not showing up?" Palan said. He growled again, enraged. He knelt by the rock where he'd seen Nova run to Melly. They must at least be together.

Edeyn eyed Palan calmly. "Sometimes I think all of you with the *senses* rely on them far too much. You know there is life beyond just your *scent*, right?"

Palan clenched his fists, resisting the urge to launch himself at Edeyn. She was so tiny next to him. He thought of how easy it would be to strangle her, allowing himself to entertain the idea in his mind, if only for a fleeting moment. Though, despite her stature, part of him was intimidated by her inner power.

"Now is not the time to lecture me on how I rely too much on my abilities!" Palan said, raising his voice by several degrees. "I need to find Melly. She is *all* I have left. She could be hurt. Alone. Stranded--" Palan's voice broke and suddenly it felt like silence engulfed the land. Though he often appeared as a wolf ready to attack, Palan clearly had a soft spot, and her name was Melly.

"It's not a lecture, whatever that is," Edeyn replied calmly. "It is simply a fact. You could use your mind to find her, but instead you wail about how you cannot *sense* her." Edeyn shook her head as she re-sheathed her weapons and equipment. Without missing a beat, she rose and walked into the trees.

"Where the blazes are you going?" Palan screamed. He looked to Sonny who shrugged and followed after Edeyn.

"Come along, angry daddy," Edeyn called out in a sing-song voice without so much as a glance over her shoulder. "Time to find your light."

"Don't ever call me that again," Palan growled. The two women continued on without responding. Reluctantly, Palan re-holstered his pistol and followed through the trees. Edeyn seemed to have a direction in mind.

"Where are we going?" he asked, impatient and anxious.

"To find your daughter," Edeyn replied, striding purposefully forward.

"How do you know where she is?"

"I don't," Edeyn said, voice flat, "but I have an idea of where Nova went. And that's more than we can say for you."

"What if she's not with him?" Palan protested.

"She is," Edeyn replied.

Palan resigned himself to following Edeyn's lead as the resolute way she spoke reassured him that Nova and Melly were together. He still didn't trust her, but he felt there was no choice. As he followed behind, silently, he pulled the amulet from his tunic and held it in his hand. As the *senses* within it activated more strongly, Palan felt like he could breathe again. Holding it tightly, Palan scanned their surroundings.

It was a risk to gather information using the amulet. He didn't want to alert the others to the fact that he had it. But finding Melly was more important than his secret. He had to try. Palan looked with enhanced *sight* through the underbrush, absorbing all he could in his vision of the ground. He looked for anything that may give away their tracks—depressions in the dirt, footprints, broken twigs, anything.

He *saw* very little of use. He had forgotten Nova's ability to tread lightly and now resisted voicing the bubbles of frustration that caught in his throat.

Sonny looked at him with a questioning glance. Clearly, he was not entirely successful at suppressing his displeasure.

"You good?" she asked.

Palan laughed bitterly. "I've never been better. My child is missing in the middle of a jungle. I'm ecstatic."

Sonny nodded, compassion gentling her expression. "I see. I thought you were saying something, that's all."

"No," Palan said. He hoped Sonny wouldn't notice the tightness of his fists as he gripped the gemstone in his palm. To him, it was so obvious, but he knew they weren't looking for anything unusual. So long as he kept his wits about him, they wouldn't notice anything amiss.

As the three trekked forward in relative silence, Palan returned his attention to the amulet, now activating its *sound* abilities. He still couldn't understand why his *scent* picked up nothing. He almost thought he was imagining it, but maybe the island itself was dampening his *senses*. It suddenly occurred to him perhaps that was why the island's inhabitants seemed to rely more on technology than innate *senses*.

Regardless, he fought desperately to *hear* anything that might lead him to his daughter. *Sound* seemed the least likely to assist Palan, but he clung to the hope of anything. Even heavy breathing from Nova or a soft cry from Melly would do.

Nothing came. Palan shoved his hand into his pocket to deposit the amulet there, but just as he was releasing his grip, the sound of drum beats thundered through his ears. He felt it radiate through his whole body and froze in his tracks.

"Wait," he said in a husky command.

The women halted, turning to the frazzled man in curiosity.

"Do you hear that?" Palan asked. The thundering rippled again through his ears as he held tightly to the stone hidden within his pocket.

The roaring beat grew louder, its rhythm pulsing throughout Palan's body. "There it is again. There's no way you don't hear it," he said. He licked his lips, surprised to find they felt mostly numb. He had forgotten he was holding the stone, the *sound* was so mesmerizing, so consuming.

"I do hear... something," Edeyn said after a slight pause.

Sonny shook her head and added, "I truly do not."

"It's loud. It's everywhere," Palan said again with horror. He hadn't picked up any other *sounds* but this one held his attention.

"My *touch* seems to be useless here," Sonny admitted. "I *sense* nothing. If I'm honest, I hardly even *sense* you two and you're right in front of me. I'm sorry."

Edeyn stared down at her boots and shifted uncomfortably from one foot to the other, losing the slightest air of confidence which she had previously carried.

Already primed not to trust Edeyn, Palan took her change in countenance as an opportunity to pounce. "You're doing something to suppress us, aren't you!" he accused.

Edeyn snapped her eyes up to Palan. "No," she said.

"Sonny can't *feel*, I can't *scent*. Nova couldn't *see* clearly. You're the only one who seems to have any *sense* of direction. You're doing something!" He yelled, unable to control his rage.

Edeyn's expression went cold. "You may wish to lower your voice."

"Or what? You'll kill me?" Palan spat.

"No. But *they* might," Edeyn replied.

Palan spun around, expecting to see more soldiers. Still, all he heard was the drumming. "WHO?! The trees?" He took a menacing step toward Edeyn, ready to clamp his hands around her throat. He was certain he could overpower her without much effort.

She stood her ground and drew both her glaives in one smooth motion without breaking her gaze away from Palan's.

Enraged, Palan roared and leapt at Edeyn. Attempting to break through what he thought was an opening, Edeyn raised her weapons without hesitation. He grabbed the polearms and pulled Edeyn hard toward himself. He did not succeed in moving her. It was like she was rooted to the ground.

Edeyn and Palan's eyes locked, glaring at each other, both frozen in time, each waiting for the other to crack.

Palan dropped his grip first, throwing force into Edeyn as he let go. She did not move a muscle.

"We don't have to trust each other," Edeyn said, voice unwavering. "But I do hear the drums, and I know this island. If Nova went that way and the patrols found them out in the open, we might already be too late."

Palan roared and balled his hands into fists. Fire coursed through him. He knew, despite his distrust of Edeyn, he would get further by following her than not.

He closed his eyes and breathed slowly, focusing on the *sound* again, allowing himself to match the rhythm of the beats to his own inhaling and exhaling. He hated the fear that bubbled through his voice as he spoke. "Too late?"

"Not dead, I don't think," Edeyn said, quickly reassuring him. "But the Tskelans will capture them, and there isn't much shelter if they've made it to the firelands."

Too afraid to ask any more questions Palan stammered. He was living his worst nightmare and he was being led by someone unproven. But he had to trust her, it was the only way he'd find Melly and Nova. "The firelands?"

Edeyn re-sheathed her weapons and turned away from Palan. "This is Scoria Island," she said, as she walked. "We might be in a jungle now, but most of this island is rock and lava. The firelands are all around the volcano. It's mostly bare darkrock, surrounded by magma and smoke. There's nowhere to hide and… the darkrock mutes your *senses*." Edeyn paused, tossing a glare over her shoulder at Palan before she continued. "An effect you already observed on your own."

Palan scowled but did not reply. He thought Edeyn might be telling the truth about the island, and he didn't want to admit he had jumped to conclusions about her character.

"Well," Sonny said, "now perhaps you can stop wasting time attacking our guide and focus instead on finding your daughter."

"I didn't ask for your opinion," Palan said as hot shame twisted through him.

They moved quickly and the drumming grew steadily louder. The sound, though ominous, helped solidify their direction. Palan hated not being able to access his own *sense*. He never realized how much he'd taken his abilities for granted.

The buzz of *scents* from the world around him was always there like comforting background noise. It reminded him where he was in the world, where he had been already, and where he still needed to go. Now that part of his mind felt like an empty void. He was surprised how much he missed even unpleasant smells. Without his gift, it was as if a part of himself had died.

Edeyn led the way to the edge of the jungle. She paused and crouched. The land sloped upward in front of them, and the drumbeats rolled loudly enough no one needed gifted *senses* to hear them any longer. Their sound was undeniable. She beckoned Palan and Sonny to her side. No longer resisting her orders—primarily Palan—the two followed her direction, crouching next to her.

Edeyn leaned in and whispered, "We're too late."

Palan shook his head as his stomach clenched in fear. "We *cannot* be too late."

Sonny touched Palan's wrist, a gentle warmth flowing into his body.

He guessed she was trying to relax him. Palan wondered if she'd realized she was transferring her energy to him.

"We are." Edeyn gave him a sympathetic look before continuing, "Unfortunately. But that's only for plan A."

Palan never had a plan. His only thought was getting Melly back, holding her in his arms. He hadn't thought about the steps to find her or anything before the end point. Now, the end goal eluded him. He fought the feeling of panic rising within. He was ready to run for the drums without looking back.

"We can enter Tskela on our own," Edeyn said. "But we must wait."

Palan nodded.

She looked into Palan's eyes with a soft, forgiving smile. "We *will* find them," she said, her voice warm with promise.

Palan needed to believe Edeyn. No other outcome would be acceptable to him. She was right. She had to be.

Chapter Twenty

CAPTIVES

Bewildered and tired, Nova held Melly on his hip as their captors led them through a busy, colorful marketplace. As the drumming continued, people scattered to the side, creating a pathway for the soldiers and their captives to march.

Nova felt the overwhelming pressure of all eyes watching him. He tried not to look directly at anyone. There was already so much around him to absorb, details to memorize that might help them later.

Unable to gather the level of detail he was used to with his gifted *sense*, his head felt cloudy. He had no idea if they would be able to escape, but he remained on high alert, ready to give himself and Melly their best chance if an opportunity did arise.

The muscles in his neck ached where Melly continued to cling to him for what seemed an interminable journey. Her little hands doing their best to remain clasped.

Their captors led them through a maze of streets. It was as if they were parading Nova and Melly as prizes.

Finally, they came to a halt in front of a decorated platform on which sat a throne. Its occupant slouched, leaning their cheek against their fist. They appeared bored with their role as they tapped their foot slowly, seemingly uninterested in Nova and Melly.

The drumming ceased at last and Nova's ears rang in the sudden silence, though the busy marketplace still buzzed behind them. He could still hear the drum beats thrumming in his head even though the physical sound stopped.

The captain stepped out, leading a group of soldiers to approach the dais, but the monarch did not adjust their position to greet them. They exchanged words in a language Nova could not understand. To him, it sounded different compared to the warriors they first encountered on the beach.

It didn't take long before their fates were decided. Nova was shoved forward and ushered into a looming, stone fortress. The halls were so narrow the group had to usher through single file, a line of soldiers in front of the captives and a line in the back.

Melly reached out to touch the walls as they trudged their way forward.

"Careful," Nova whispered in the child's ear.

Melly continued without heeding his warning. She looked around with keen curiosity and interest. Nova hoped she would remain unafraid as it freed his mind to pay attention to every twist and turn they took through the corridors.

Before long, they were taken into a sparsely decorated room with a solid wooden door. The furnishings, though limited, seemed much more comfortable than any prison cell Nova had ever seen.

The soldiers ushered them inside, said something Nova could not understand, then left. The door clanged shut behind them and the clunk of the lock echoed through the room. No matter how comfortable their room looked, it was still a prison cell.

Nova set Melly down. He dreaded the unknown hours ahead of him if he were to remain imprisoned with a small child. The silence of the small, stone chamber was a stark contrast to the drum beats and the noise of the city. Panic exploded inside his chest as reality sank in.

He replayed the memory of the snakes in his mind over and over, imagining all the possibilities of what he could have done differently. He had run to protect Melly. His choice of actions was born of love. But now he wondered whether he made the right decision. He had no way of knowing whether they would ever be able to find the little girl's father again.

Nova slumped against a wall, sinking to the ground in despair. He didn't want Melly to notice his panic, so he forced himself to breathe deeply, remaining calm on the surface. Though, nothing could stop his thoughts from spiraling in all directions. He questioned his every decision, wishing he could create a different outcome.

Nova couldn't shake the feeling he'd led them into a fate perhaps worse than what they would have faced if they'd stayed and fought the adders.

The noise of Melly's laughter brought Nova back to reality. Confused, he snapped his attention to where he left her. She hadn't moved, but she now stared in front of her, smiling and giggling with amusement. She seemed mesmerized by a presence invisible to Nova, pawing at the empty space as if trying to catch something. Nova's spiraling thoughts halted, temporarily distracted by the child's antics.

He tilted his head, observing her. He hadn't seen her play even once since they'd left Asayouga, especially since they'd lost her doll.

Now she sang and chattered to an imaginary playmate. He moved closer to the child to examine the space more carefully.

He saw nothing except the crumbling, dirty stone walls of their newfound prison cell. Suddenly, a stream of light glittered in front of his eyes but when he blinked it disappeared. He fluttered his eyes thinking the light would make its return but it didn't, so he dismissed it as his imagination.

The child shook her head, still giggling. "No, no!" She laughed, grasping her invisible friend, jumping up and dancing in a circle.

Although afraid to interrupt, Nova was unable to stop himself from asking, "Who are you dancing with, Melly?"

She continued laughing. "You can dance too, Nova!"

"I'm good," Nova said, his voice trailing off as he watched her in curiosity. A warm, glow flooded through him, making him feel as if he were floating. He found himself observing his own emotions as if they did not belong to his body. Complete peace didn't match their present uncertain circumstances and surroundings. It was puzzling, though not unwelcome.

He leaned in and watched Melly as she continued dancing and smiling. The glitter of light appeared once more, but this time, Nova perceived a flash of dark, curly hair, and eyes that held the depths of the stars. He gasped aloud as recognition flooded him.

Nova sat down hard, managing to choke out one word from his dry throat. "Captured," he whispered.

"I'll find you," the light seemed to breathe back before disappearing suddenly. Melly ceased her cheerful playing.

Had the light spoken back? Did that voice belong to Edeyn? "*I'll find you.*" Her words echoed even after the light disappeared, comforting him like a blanket.

When Melly looked at Nova she fell back into her silence.

Though filled with disappointment, Nova smiled and pulled the child against his chest. He stroked her hair in reassurance as he stared at the place where the light glimmered moments before. He couldn't imagine how it was possible. Had the heat somehow corrupted his mind? Even so, a small part of Nova knew, deep down, he had just spoken with Edeyn.

~~~

Edeyn let her eyelids flutter closed in a brief, nearly imperceptible blink, allowing the *vision* to fill her mind's eye completely. Palan's obvious distrust of her required taking greater care than usual when activating her gifts. Although she had a lifetime of practice guarding herself from the suspicions of friends and family, Edeyn's unease around Palan was particularly strong. It was as if he knew about her hidden *sense*, despite all her best protections.

Edeyn made peace with her differences long ago. She could not recall a moment where *visions* like hers had ever been wanted. *Knowing* things when she shouldn't have known them tended to make people, at best, uncomfortable, and at worst, dangerous. A deeply innate sense of self-preservation encouraged Edeyn to practice precautions every time she received a vision or message. It was second nature for her to steal away secret fractions of moments to absorb the information she needed without anyone else's awareness. Yet, despite a lifetime of self-discipline and inescapable solitude, Palan's animosity toward her presented a particularly difficult challenge.

The man never seemed to lower his suspicion. He watched her continuously. Edeyn could see their energy connect in the air like the crushing of tectonic plates in an earthquake. It was a strong enough connection even Nova and Sonny could perceive it. She knew she perceived energies different from most people. While she believed everyone experienced shifts, most people only experienced them on a subconscious level.

A quick snap of the child's laughter reached Edeyn's ears. With another flash of light, she could see Nova, an expression of shock clear on his face. She couldn't *see* any details in their surroundings. There wasn't enough to tell where exactly they were, but she promised herself she would try to connect with them again soon. She prayed she would receive a clearer picture before reaching the city where she would have to mute her *senses* or risk becoming overwhelmed.

"I feel like my shoes are melting off my feet," Sonny commented.

Edeyn immediately lost her *visions* and smiled at Sonny. "Don't worry. It is hot, but not melt-your-feet hot."

Palan huffed.

Edeyn did her best to ignore the sharp prickles she felt digging into her skin as tension leaked into the air like a noxious cloud. As pressure built in her chest, she forced herself to slow her breathing and release Palan's emotions from their entanglement with her own.

"We're nearly there," Edeyn said.

"If you're leading us into a trap, you will regret it for eternity. I can promise you that," Palan threatened.

"By all three moons, I wish you would drop your vendetta, Palan," Sonny exclaimed.

Edeyn raised an eyebrow as she glanced at Sonny. Sonny struck her as powerful yet timid. She couldn't recall hearing her speak so directly before.

Palan snarled in response. "You're naive."

"That may be," Sonny said, "but what choice do we have? We need to find your daughter. You being endlessly perturbed has not made this walk in the heat any more bearable!"

"Talk to me when it's *your* daughter," Palan said, his anger sounding more muted than before.

Edeyn felt the sudden shift in tone as a pulse through her body like steam releasing from a bubbling kettle. Once more pushing Palan's energy to the side, she allowed her eyelids to flutter closed.

This time she clearly envisioned Nova's face staring at something in the space between them. For a split second, their eyes connected and Edeyn jumped. She had always been able to view auras from a distance, but she had never encountered anyone noticing her back before. The look of recognition on Nova's face startled her. Instinctively, she glanced behind her to verify Palan hadn't noticed anything amiss, even though she quickly realized how absurd that thought was.

Puzzled over what just occurred, Edeyn frowned. She knew it was impossible for Nova to make eye contact with her through her *vision*, yet she was completely certain he had. She couldn't deny the way Nova's expression brightened in sudden awareness. Electric currents sparked as their gaze connected, the same as it always seemed to when they were standing face-to-face. He definitely saw her, somehow.

Edeyn stopped in her tracks and gripped the hilt of her glaives as if to draw them.

Sonny responded to Edeyn's sudden change in demeanor, unholstering her weapon without hesitation. "I don't see anyone," she said, though her stance suggested she was more than ready to shoot.

"No," Edeyn said, dropping her grip. She hadn't intended to give away her discomfort so obviously. "I'm sorry. I just need a moment, please," she added, waving at Sonny to lower her weapons. Behind her, she heard Palan hum low in his throat again. She fought to ignore it, though her stomach twisted in an anxious response against her wishes.

Edeyn held her breath before returning to her vision, bracing herself to see Nova again. This time they connected more quickly.

Fire shot through her as their eyes connected.

"Captured," Nova said in Edeyn's mind. His voice was as clear to her as if he stood beside her.

She stared into the *vision*, simultaneously perplexed and fascinated. She wondered if he could hear her thinking back to him. "We're nearly in the city. I'll find you," she thought.

To her amazement, Nova appeared to receive the message. His expression looked just as shocked as her own. The *vision* vanished.

Intrigued at this new manifestation of her abilities, Edeyn felt a fresh wave of confident resolve. "Just a little further," Edeyn announced aloud. She led the way to Tskela again.

Chapter Twenty-One
Rose Garden

From the moment they entered the city of Tskela, Palan felt increasingly uneasy. The bustling city streets triggered memories of Asayouga before it was decimated. It seemed both familiar and completely unfamiliar which was an unsettling and overwhelming combination to experience.

He kept his eye on Edeyn, as always. Despite his continued apprehension, uncertain of how much she knew or how much he could rely on her, Palan had to admit a degree of gratitude for her continued guidance.

The panic of losing Melly had not dissipated, and Palan's search for clues of her whereabouts continued. There were many unfamiliar aromas to adjust to which confused his ability to identity specific *scents*. Even without the island's *sense* dampening environment there were challenges to picking up the *scent* he needed.

Begrudgingly, Palan admitted Edeyn wasn't responsible for their dulled *senses* after all. Although he remained uncertain whether it was merely the island itself or intentionally diluted even further by the island's inhabitants, Palan noticed how it became even more challenging to access his enhanced *sense* as soon as they'd reached the city's outskirts.

He'd stopped reaching for the amulet as its powers diminished beyond usefulness the deeper into Scoria Island they traveled.

Edeyn walked ahead of them, Sonny in the center and Palan a slight distance behind, taking his time to observe the sights and sounds. Without relying on his *scent*, he was forced to concentrate using his mundane senses instead, actively observing the details around him.

The group came to a halt when Edeyn paused at a market stall to converse with one of the sellers.

"These are so beautiful!" she exclaimed, as she picked up a hand-crafted mug from the table of wares. She switched to a language Palan couldn't understand.

Though he could feel his impatience threatening to boil over, Palan stayed silent. He forced himself to wait instead of reacting, but it took all his energy to appear calm.

The two women chattered back and forth. He watched as Edeyn responded, gesturing with her hands as she spoke. She leaned to the side, lowering her palm to indicate a person of smaller stature. It dawned on Palan that Edeyn was asking the shopkeeper if she'd seen Melly.

The merchant shook her head but pointed. Palan turned his attention in the direction she showed them. A short distance away, he noticed a large archway where guards stood on either side. A flutter of hope rippled through his chest, though it was quickly replaced with fear and frustration at the necessity of rescuing his daughter from a guarded fortress.

Edeyn and Sonny explored the items on the merchant's table and Palan took the opportunity to observe more of their surroundings. There was a central path but the streets were crowded with maze-like offshoots and alleyways.

The *scent* of the sea, humidity, and the stony smells of the nearby volcano were still the most prominent aromas Palan could detect. A sudden thud against his side confused him.

When he looked down, his eyes widened as the sight of a small child hugging his leg. Palan stared at a mop of curly, black hair so similar to Melly's. He ducked to swoop the child up into his arms but stopped short when their eyes met. It wasn't her. His heart sank as he and the strange child locked eyes in mutual confusion.

As soon as the child noticed her mistake, she burst into tears. Palan instinctively crouched in front of her, pulling a small stone from his pocket. He held it out in his open palm without speaking. He'd been collecting unusual stones and shells ever since they landed on the island. Sometimes he gave them to Melly to occupy her. Some he kept for himself, uncertain why they fascinated him.

The child's sniffling subsided as she marveled, first at the stone with curiosity, then at Palan, then back at the stone. He waited, unable to communicate in the child's language, not wishing to frighten her with his unrecognizable speech.

Eventually, the little one picked up the stone to examine it. Lost in amazement at the small treasure, she appeared startled when a feminine voice spoke, drawing her attention away from the object. The little girl held out the rock to her caregiver with obvious excitement, babbling something in their own language. Her guardian responded as she picked up the child. The woman smiled gratefully at Palan before wandering away.

Palan smiled and held up his hand as they went, without either of them exchanging a single word. His stomach twisted into knots at the thought of his missing daughter. He couldn't act impulsively. He knew he could not allow his desperation to take over. But in that moment, he felt he might fall to his knees under the weight of his fear.

A soft touch against his arm brought Palan out of his despair. He was surprised to see it was Edeyn. It struck him as comical how much fear he felt every time he interacted with her, despite how tiny she was in comparison to his tall, wiry body.

"There's some good news," Edeyn said softy as she gently drew Palan further from the stall and back toward the busy street.

"You know where she is?" he asked all too hopefully, betraying his internal anguish.

"Not exactly," Edeyn said. "But people have seen them."

"What do you mean?" Palan asked. His lips had gone inexplicably dry. It felt effortful to speak.

"A few days ago, there was a military parade," Edeyn explained. "The woman said there were prisoners...a man carrying a little girl. She didn't know what happened to them, but she definitely saw them."

Palan felt his heartbeat in his throat. "So, they're prisoners."

"Possibly," Edeyn said. "They may have been let go for all we know. A little girl would pose no threat to them."

"But where would they have gone?" Palan asked.

Sonny spoke up, then. "I think it's best we find somewhere to regroup and decide where we go from here."

Palan glanced down the street at the guarded archway. He could *sense* nothing of Melly but he felt a pull within him he couldn't ignore. "They're still there," he said.

"Most likely," Edeyn agreed, her voice quiet but still distinct above the innumerable voices around them.

Palan fell silent, thinking about what to do next. He stared at the archway as if it would display an answer for him if he waited long enough.

"Let's go," he said eventually, striding purposefully down the sidewalk.

Both Sonny and Edeyn sped up to match his pace.

"Palan," Edeyn said gently as she grabbed his arm.

Anger shot through his body and he shoved Edeyn aside, turning to glare at her, eyes flashing. "Stay off of me," he hissed with vehemence.

Edeyn's expression remained stoic as always. She met Palan's gaze with her perpetual calm and Palan hated her even more than usual.

"We need to re-group. Find somewhere to make a plan and figure out how we're going to get inside," Edeyn said.

"And we don't even know where they are," Sonny added, though she was out of breath from having to catch up to Palan and Edeyn.

Palan gestured vaguely ahead of himself. "We know they're there."

"Yes, but we need more than that," Edeyn replied. "Sonny is right."

Although Palan knew the women were correct, it infuriated him to slow down. He wanted to charge through the gates, weapons drawn and ready, to rescue Melly immediately. He would fight a thousand guards bare-handed if he had to. Slowing down to calculate their next move was wise, it was necessary, and he absolutely did not want to do it.

"Where? We have no money," Palan said.

Edeyn smirked as she corrected him. "Correction. You have no local currency. I, however, have enough. We will find an inn and do our planning there." She glanced over her shoulder, scanning the street with a frown before continuing. "I don't know the city well. We may have to explore a while before we find somewhere suitable."

Palan gave a nod of resignation. "Fine. Lead the way, then," he said.

The three of them wandered along the walkways. Although his *sense* was severely reduced inside the city, Palan still caught the strong *scent* of salt in the breeze, along with the steam and stone from the nearby volcano.

They passed the busy market again and rounded a corner to a street lined on one side with shop fronts. Across from the shops was an open, well-kept garden. There with manicured pathways and shrubbery dotted with flowers as well as a smooth stone gazebo that peeked out from deep within the maze of hedges.

"That's beautiful," Sonny remarked as she paused to gaze across the street.

"It is," Edeyn agreed.

A powerful *whiff* of roses reached Palan's awareness. He scanned the flowerbeds, and although he couldn't spot them, he assumed there must be rose bushes inside the garden.

"Yeah. Flowers are pretty. Can we find an inn now?" Palan asked in annoyance.

"Wouldn't you like to walk through there?" Sonny asked.

"No," Palan said. He had no desire to stop and look at flowers. That was something Sapphira would have done. But there were more pressing matters to attend to. Palan's priority was his daughter, and those worries consumed all of his thoughts. He could think of nothing else.

"I would," Edeyn said, "But perhaps we will have time for such things later on. We must focus," she said. They slowly continued, all three of them wary in the unfamiliar city.

Palan nearly collided with Edeyn when she halted suddenly in front of a dark wooden door. A worn-out sign hung on it; written in a language he couldn't read.

"We might as well check in here," Edeyn said.

Palan grabbed the door handle and ushered them all inside the dimly-lit inn. They stepped inside to a room filled with patrons conversing at various tables. Palan's inability to understand their language left him disoriented and disconnected. They would be completely reliant on Edeyn for communication.

He gripped the amulet inside his pocket, squeezing it more tightly than usual as if to force the magic to work. It provided little to no clarity. He picked up short phrases and single words, but it wasn't enough to let him know what anyone was really saying, at least not without giving himself a headache from deliberate concentration.

Palan resigned himself to following Edeyn's lead as she confidently strode to the counter. He released the amulet from his grip with a sigh. As Edeyn struck up a conversation with the woman behind the desk, Palan scanned the room again.

It was still sunny outside but somehow the light barely filtered through the windows and the only thing it seemed to illuminate was dust. Volcanic ash and the salt of the sea clouded the atmosphere of the small interior. It didn't seem to matter where they traveled on Scoria Island, the volcano, along with the surrounding ocean, seemed to influence the entire landscape whether they were indoors or outdoors.

The *scent* of roses wafted through the room to Palan's awareness once more and he frowned. He made a mental note to walk through the garden on his own later on. A thought nagged at the corners of his mind and he knew he wouldn't be able to rest until he followed the thread to its conclusion. He just needed to confirm he wasn't imagining the *scent*.

Palan's mind returned to the present as Edeyn concluded her conversation with the innkeeper. She smiled as she held up a key. "Upstairs," she commented as she led the way through the lower tavern tables and around to a side staircase.

Despite open windows at the top and bottom, the narrow stairwell was even darker than the main room. Palan followed behind Edeyn and Sonny to the top of the steps. They made their way through a long hallway until Edeyn unlocked the door to their room, marked with numbers in an unrecognizable script. Palan knew he couldn't memorize the foreign numbers so he took note of items throughout the hall for something to help him recall the room's location. Above the handle of their room was a small emblem resembling a hawthorn bush etched into the wood. Palan suppressed a shudder as they made their way inside the small inner chamber. He would feel more comfortable when they could leave the City of Thorns far behind.

"There's only one bed," Sonny remarked.

Edeyn set the key on a small table next to the bed. "I'll leave this here so any one of us can use it," she said, without responding to Sonny's comment.

Palan glanced at the key from the corner of his eye, an inescapable tension building within his chest. Tskela made him nervous, but he couldn't pinpoint what left him feeling increasingly unsettled, apart from the obvious. The inn walls seemed to be getting smaller, as if they were closing in on him.

He turned his attention to the bed situation and saw an opportunity. "You two can share the bed. I'll stay in the hall," he said. He hoped his suggestion would give him the chance to explore the garden without alerting the other two. It would be much easier to sneak away after they'd fallen asleep if he were not also in the room.

Edeyn eyed him cautiously before nodding her head. "There is enough room on the floor in here," she said.

Palan snorted, disgruntled. "You don't realize how tall I am. The hall is fine," he said, insisting.

"Suit yourself," Edeyn said, "But stay close by. We should stick together as much as we can if we're going to have any success rescuing your daughter."

Palan looked her squarely in the eyes, almost daring her to admit out loud she had somehow read his thoughts. "Why would you say a thing like that?" he asked as his lip curled into a sneer.

Edeyn smiled easily and began removing her weapons and supplies from her person, unburdening herself. "It's just common sense," she said in a cheerful voice. "You don't know the language, after all. Even I don't know the city terribly well."

It bothered Palan that Edeyn knew more than she was letting on. He couldn't allow her to get under his skin, but he didn't like the idea she read his thoughts without his permission. Could she read his mind? He wondered what else she might know, and that brought him serious discomfort.

He pushed aside his feelings, unable and unwilling to dwell on the what-ifs about Edeyn. There was too much weighing on his mind.

Palan pulled a small chair away from the wall and straddled it, leaning his body over the back, resting his chin on his arms. He watched as both Edeyn and Sonny eased their burdens, removing their boots, rubbing their own feet and aching limbs. Palan felt the same aches but could not relax. He would rest, perhaps, after his daughter was safely in his arms or when they could settle somewhere in safety. He knew that wouldn't be any time soon, if it ever happened again. They had no home to return to.

"We need a plan," Sonny said, the first to break the silence.

Edeyn nodded, eyes distant as she chewed her lip. "We do but..." she began, trailing off.

"But we don't know where they are. We don't know how to get in. And we don't know where to escape to," Palan said, stating their grim reality. "In essence, we know nothing. And we're not going to know it after sleeping here for one night."

"No," Edeyn agreed. She sat down on the bed, stretching her body like a cat before settling back against the pillows and closing her eyes.

"So, you're going to sleep? Helpful," Palan sniffed.

"I'm not going to sleep," Edeyn said, still with her eyes closed, "but I haven't laid my head on pillows in an age and they feel very good."

"They do!" Sonny said in enthusiastic agreement as she settled herself in the bed as well.

Palan rolled his eyes. "Are you going to spare one for me or am I supposed to sleep on the hardwood with nothing?"

"I'm not giving you one of my pillows," Edeyn said with a laugh. "But we can ask for more for you when the time comes." She propped herself up into a seated position. "Now, we need to think about this logically."

"As opposed to what we have been doing to this point?" Palan sneered.

Edeyn continued, ignoring Palan's comments. "We already know a little about where they're held."

"We do?" Palan asked, raising an eyebrow.

Edeyn looked at Palan directly and nodded. She seeming to decide something in that moment. "We know because I've been *seeing* them."

Palan sat up straighter in his chair. His mind raced as he wondered if Edeyn had really been reading his thoughts the whole time after all.

"What do you mean?" he said, unable to keep the intense suspicion out of his voice.

Sonny had also sat upright, though she looked far more curious than Palan felt. "I thought you said you were not *sighted*," she said.

"I'm not," Edeyn replied. "At least, not as you'd be familiar with. I don't have a primary *sense* like the rest of you."

Palan felt his stomach sink like a stone. "Then how...?" he said, though he was already beginning to understand, and he didn't like the explanation.

"I have another *sense*, like an inner knowing. It's not as useful as being able to heal or learn any language or see long distances, perhaps. But it has its uses."

Edeyn's shoulders slumped and she sighed. It was the first time Palan had ever seen her confidence waver in the slightest.

She continued. "I can ... see *visions* in my mind. I can feel energy around me—"

"Like my *touch*?" Sonny interrupted.

"Not like that," Edeyn said. "At least, I don't think it's the same. I can *sense* energies that others cannot. Things from beyond the physical plane"—she cautiously bit her lip—"I was able to connect with Nova earlier."

Every bone in Palan's body froze. "What do you mean by...connect?" he asked, forcing himself to speak above a whisper.

Edeyn frowned, chewing on her lip as she seemed to be deciding how to answer the question. "I mean I could see him in my mind, him and Melly, and... he answered me."

Palan's lips went numb. He hadn't just been paranoid after all. Edeyn could actually read thoughts.

"I know what you're thinking," Edeyn said with a smile, "And no, I can't just read your mind without focusing on doing that."

Her distinction was not of any comfort. He scraped his chair back abruptly. "I'm going for a walk. We can discuss our plan more when I return," he announced.

Edeyn and Sonny exchanged glances and Palan did his best to ignore them before stomping out of the room.

Chapter Twenty-Two
Garden Stroll

Without thinking, Palan marched across the street, making his way through the hedges toward the gazebo.

His steps slowed as he reached the white wooden structure covered in thick foliage. His heart raced and he clenched his fist around the amulet again, squeezing his eyes shut. Palan fought to quiet his mind which was still buzzing with constant worry about his daughter's safety and the revelation about Edeyn. He reviewed his every thought since they'd first met her, trying to reassure himself she hadn't read anything he wouldn't want her to know. He'd been right not to trust her.

He wracked his brain, trying to remember if he ever heard of anyone with her powers before. Palan recalled Nova mentioning something about a sixth *sense* that included telepathy, but it was more of a legend than anything anyone had witnessed.

Abilities like Edeyn's were rare enough to be thought of as myths. Palan shuddered.

Now in the foreign garden, Palan smelled roses that, as far as he could tell, did not grow there. He considered the possibility that he had injured his head when the spaceship crashed, or that he had somehow been poisoned by one of the violet adders, despite knowing he was never bitten.

A strong waft of rose petals engulfed Palan and he spun around, scanning the flower beds, shrubs and trees around him. The gazebo was encased in climbing vines with exotic flowers Palan could not identify—clearly native to the island and not something he grew up seeing on Asayouga. What he couldn't find were roses.

The disembodied *scent* dredged a memory to the surface. He recalled the scene clearly.

~~~

Sonny held a palm up to Palan, silently begging him to stop his pacing. Her sleeves rolled up to her elbows, she looked all business. Palan wanted to throttle her.

Screams ripped through the walls of Sapphira's home. Palan bunched his hands into fists, digging his fingernails into his palms as the sounds of Sapphira's labor continued. It had been hours. No one had warned him.

If he hadn't chosen that moment to pay her a visit, he would have missed the birth of his child. The thought enraged him. Even though Sonny had let him into the house, willingly, Palan resented her for not making an effort to reach him sooner.

He knew in his heart that Sapphira did not want him there at all. He shoved the feelings of shame below the surface where they could not bother him. A voice at the back of his mind whispered to him to leave her be, that she was right to be wary of him after everything that had gone wrong between them. But he needed to see his child. He couldn't leave.

Eventually, Sonny convinced Palan to take a seat in the living room. She brewed tea for Sapphira and offered a cup to Palan as he slumped into an armchair. He drifted to sleep, waking hours later to a dark house and silence apart from a few soft, contented grunts coming from a small bundle of blankets.

Sonny smiled as she placed the newborn into Palan's arms.

Awed, he cradled the infant as if she might break if he held on too tightly.

"Congratulations, Palan. You have a daughter," Sonny whispered.

Palan's eyes blurred with tears as he stared down at the little one. She had a head of thick black hair already. Her features were perfect in every way. He looked at Sonny with a grin.

Sonny smiled back. "Her name is Melvene," she said.

Palan nodded as he caressed the top of his daughter's head, tracing her features with his index finger. "Hi, Melly," he said, his voice betraying his emotion.

After several moments of reverence passed taking in the sight of his new daughter, he asked to see Sapphira.

Sonny nodded. Silently, she took Melly from Palan's arms and stepped back. "Yes," she said. "But Palan..."

He hesitated, bracing himself for Sonny's next words.

"She's been through a lot. Please don't press her," she added.

Palan looked at Melly's cherubic features, determined not to let the past interfere with her. "I wouldn't," he said, vowing to put aside his pride.

He climbed the stairs, entering Sapphira's room only after a soft knock to announce his presence.

She gave Palan a worn smile, her appearance weak and pale.

"Hello," he said, voice husky. He sat on the edge of her bed, silent, gazing at her nightstand. It was covered in dishes, empty tea mugs, a plate of snacks that needed to be cleaned up, and a vase filled with roses.

Palan stared at the flowers.

Moments passed before Sapphira covered Palan's hand on the blanket with her own. "Did you see her? Isn't she beautiful?" she asked.

Palan tore his gaze away from the roses, though his heartbeat thundered in his ears at the sight of them. Who had given her flowers, he wondered. It didn't seem like something Sonny would do. She was there for practical purposes. Fenwick's face appeared briefly in his mind's eye but he dismissed it.

"She is the most beautiful person I have ever seen," he replied, without another glance at the nightstand.

~~~

A gust of wind returned him to the present. Palan stormed up the steps of the gazebo. Benches lined the sides of the wooden structure. He smoothed his hands over the railing, finding sets of initials carved by couples all across its surface. Some of the paint peeled back, weathered over time.

He looked up, still able to make out lights shining on the exterior of the inn across the street, though only the upper level and roof were visible from his vantage point. His thoughts returned to his daughter. He had failed to protect her twice. Once was already unforgivable. How could he have allowed it to happen again. He knew Nova would try his best to keep her safe, but he couldn't know that he would even survive to protect her. The thought filled him with dread.

The unmistakable *scent* of roses overwhelmed him once more, reminding Palan he had come to the gazebo for a reason. Their perfume permeated the whole garden. Furious that he could not find the source, Palan grabbed a fistful of vines and tore them from the gazebo pillars. "Where are you?" he gasped.

He staggered, dizzy from the overpowering smell. There were no roses. Not anywhere.

Palan's knees buckled. He stumbled to a bench where he slumped against the arm rest. "I know you're here," he rasped, enraged and fearful. It was impossible. And yet—

Chapter Twenty-Three

Assassin

Fenwick Greensong crouched to look his captive in the eyes, gripping the man's throat with one hand, a dagger in the other. From the corner of his eye he could see Isara's body, still and unmoving.

He had lost his ability to feel at some point. There was too much to absorb already and one more death could not sink into his soul without destroying him. So, Fen wouldn't let it.

"Tell me why," he said, his formerly clear *voice* void of all its usual charm. That was all he wanted to know now.

His captive looked him in the eyes with nothing but coldness. Fen knew he would get no information from this man, and he felt the flames of anger bubbling through his chest as he leaned in closer, eye to eye.

"Tell me, or I kill you right now," Fen hissed.

"You'll kill me either way," the man choked out, his words blocked by the pressure Fen continued to apply against his throat.

"True," Fen said. "Tell me anyway." This time he used the full strength of his *voice*. He knew the man would not be able to thwart it in his weakened state. As added insurance, Fen slowly, methodically tore through his captive's clothing with his dagger, never shifting his focus from his *sense* or breaking eye contact.

A hint of fear covered the man's face but his reply relayed none of it. "I won't betray anyone in my death. So go ahead."

Fen growled dangerously. The memories of loved ones flashed in his mind, fueling his resolve for justice. He thought of all the needless bloodshed that occurred and his anger intensified. Isara. Nayeli. Sapphira. He needed an explanation for their deaths, for such utter catastrophe. Asayouga was betrayed, but why were the attackers back again?

"I'll decide how you end," he said, still pushing the full power of his *ability* through every syllable he uttered. There was nothing left to lose.

"You. Already. Know," the man replied.

Fen winced at a jolt of pain through his wrist. He looked down to find the man's gloved hand—adorned with the emblem of a hawthorn bush—gripped tightly around his forearm. Before he could stop it, his arm was yanked forward and the dagger plunged into his captive's chest.

Blood bubbled from the man's lips even as the trace of a peaceful smile crossed his features. Fen stared, eyes widened in shock. His *voice* had failed him and he had no further answers than moments before. He stood, swearing as he did. The tightness in his chest expanded, nearly overwhelming him as he glanced once more at Isara's body. He hadn't really believed it were possible for her to die. She was too strong, too powerful.

Fen lifted his face to the grey sky and closed his eyes, trying in vain to center his breathing and find thoughts that made sense to his racing heart. Before he consciously realized where he was going, Fenwick started walking the path to Observation Point.

Memories of years of research and effort floated through Fenwick's mind as he walked. Every step he took seemed to tie together more and more connections. He relived an impossible number of memories as if he temporarily existed outside of time itself.

Thorns. The emblem of the Thorn Network confirmed who Asayouga's destroyers were. A sickening knot twisted in Fen's stomach. He had a blind spot.

After being in the Rose Network for so long, guarding precious knowledge from outsiders, he failed to protect Nova's research and all of Asayouga had paid for it. Guilt tore him up inside as Fen's mind imagined all the actions he could have taken to prevent the attacks.

When he reached The Point, the observatory was already gone. Stones lay scattered across the hilltop, crumbled and destroyed. Flames and smoke filled the grim, dark sky. Nova's spaceship was gone and the landscape was empty of human life now.

Fen sat in the grass and buried his face in his hands. Not one attack but two. The reality of the losses sank into his very soul as he squinted again at the blackened sky, obscured heavily with smoke. He couldn't see the new constellation but he knew that even if he could not see it, it was still there.

"How did we miss this?" Fen whispered to the night. He glanced at his forearm, tracing the outline of his rose tattoo as the pain of heartbreak ripped through his chest.

"*I will find my love, always across the dark expanse.*

Your brightness reaches beyond the fires of time

Breaking the smoke, filtering to my ears in my moments of pain

I can feel you in my heartbeat

Carried with me beyond time

I cannot see you sheltered in the stars, but I know that you are still with me,

Reaching me because your love extends beyond even my dying breath,"

Fenwick sang the song softly to the night, the words flowing through him before he even knew what message he was weaving with his *voice*.

When he finished composing the short, gentle melody, the fog cleared from his mind. He began searching bodies around the hillside. Though he didn't find much of use, Fen eventually pulled out a note, neatly folded and tucked into a shirt pocket.

Carefully, he smoothed the paper flat, staring at the unfamiliar words that blurred before his eyes as he struggled to decipher the Tskelan script. The note conveyed an order from someone reported to own a market stall in Tskela. The foreign name stood out to him, ringing a bell in connection to the stolen technology.

He needed to reach Tskela. He didn't know whether Nova and the others were still alive. The spaceship could have launched successfully. Wherever they were was beyond Fenwick's reach.

Pieces of the puzzle came together in Fen's mind. The Tskelans destroyed Asayouga to eliminate their technological rivals. They already had all the information they wanted. This proved they didn't see any further utility for the city. Fen owed it to his fallen loved ones, to his home, to find out more. Asayouga's traitor could still be out there.

He would travel to Tskela and see the situation for himself. Whether it brought any clarity to him or not did not matter anymore. There was nothing left for Fenwick to do but discover. Perhaps he would understand all that transpired before his own death, or perhaps he would not. His success did not matter when all that remained for him on the isle were reminders of death.

~~~

He had never set foot in the city of Tskela before, despite all the years he worked for the Network. He knew they had technology Asayouga did not. Some of it, Fenwick had the privilege of acquiring for himself, such as his enchanted cloak which had proved useful on many occasions.

Where Asayouga had embraced the *senses*, Tskela and Scoria had not done the same. The island around them naturally dampened their abilities and the people of the island adapted their lives to the land itself.

The power of the *senses* was seen as a threat to the forces in power. *Sensory* dampening technology was developed and integrated into every facet of the City of Thorns, right down to the building materials used to create every home or business within the city. While the people of Asayouga worked to enhance the *senses*, Tskela worked to lessen their effects.

Even as he walked carefully along the streets of the city market, Fenwick Greensong wore his *sense* dampening cloak to prevent those with the *sight* from perceiving him as easily as they would unrestricted. He didn't love the feeling of his suppressed *voice*. It felt as if an invisible hand gripped his throat, preventing his powers from escaping, or truth from being spoken.

Ironically, the city itself was a *sensory* marvel. Dampening technology was built into every stone. The walls were built to block *sight* and *sound*, the bricks and shop stalls and fabrics dampening *voice*, *touch*, and *scent*. Yet, the city was so full of activity—from the shipping dockyards to the market stalls to the fortress in the center—it felt just as alive as Asayouga always had.

Fenwick scanned the crowd for signs of his target. His mission now was his alone. He only wanted answers to understand why thousands had died. He knew it wouldn't bring them back. But searching for justice gave him purpose. He would devote his life to answers before leaving the planes of Kelmundy.

Tskela looked a little different to how he imagined it. Most of his work with the Rose Network was in deciphering messages coming to their island home. Venturing into the places he read about was a very different experience.

Now that he was there, he felt strangely at home. Perhaps it was simply the energy of being near other living humans again. His journey from the shattered Asayouga had been long and isolated. The bustle of the city relaxed him, reminding him he was never truly alone while he still drew breath.

At last, he spotted her. Fenwick leaned against the side of a building, allowing his hood to fall back from his face. He did his best to look casual standing there as he peered across the street near the market stalls at his mark.

The way she moved, the way her clothing flowed around her curves momentarily enthralled Fenwick. Her distinctive, red-gold locks of hair cascaded down her back. She was truly beautiful. He hadn't expected that. Fen had no idea if the information he had regarding Lani Gemward was accurate, but he had to start somewhere.

It had already been a long journey. Uncovering the note at Observation Point led him to many locations across the isles as he investigated the information he found. All of that led to the name Lani Gemward. She was the one with the market stall in Tskela. She was the key.

Fen had checked himself into a nearby inn where he merely existed for days and days as he attempted to recover his mental balance. He almost had the energy now to cross the street where Lani stood, preparing to greet her, but what he saw next froze him in place.

A man, clothing tattered and filthy with ash and mud, carrying a little girl, flanked on either side by well-armed guards. Fen's heart hammered in his throat as he recognized Nova and Melly. They were heading toward the fortress gate. He had to hold himself back from calling out to them directly. It was like seeing two ghosts.

Fen still had unfinished business. He watched Nova and Melly a little longer until they disappeared behind the gates of the fortress. He would look for them next. Part of him had already known they were somewhere on the island. In Agatia, he heard the rumors about the crashed "space people." There couldn't be too many space travelers wandering the Isles. He had been too afraid to hope they were really still alive.

Seeing them again now brought a desperate ache into his heart. The urge to abandon his plans to chase after them was a powerful one. They were like family to him. Especially Melly.

Fen squeezed his eyes shut, promising himself he could still find them just as soon as he was done. He had already come so far, and he did not want to give up on the possibility of justice for Asayouga.

He forced the two of them from his mind and crossed the street to Lani Gemward's market stall.

Fen ran his fingers gracefully above the jewelry on display at her table, pretending to be interested while watching her in his peripheral vision. When she turned his direction, Fen remained nonchalant.

Travelers came to the city daily, so the sight of a foreigner would not be a surprise to the shopkeeper. Lani Gemward watched Fen as he continued to browse until their eyes met. A spark of recognition shot through Fen, which he couldn't quite explain. He was certain he had never seen Lani before in his life. He knew what she looked like and where to find her only from the intelligence he had gathered. But this was different. It was like he already knew her from somewhere.

Fen quickly recovered his composure and smiled at Lani. He could feel his natural charm flowing through him even without the ability to use his *voice*.

"Can I help you?" Lani asked in a rich, full tone.

"Perhaps," he said, never taking his eyes off of hers.

"Are you shopping for anyone or anything in particular?" Lani asked.

Fenwick allowed a slow smile to cross his lips. "Is anything here charmed to help with the *voice*?"

"Of course," she answered easily. "We have all kinds of *sensory* jewelry."

Fen nodded as he held up a long necklace with a pink gemstone wrapped in golden wire. "This one," he said as he dropped it into Lani's open palm.

"It will cost you," Lani said, "but it's a beautiful choice. You have great taste."

"Perhaps we can strike a bargain," Fen suggested as he reached into the inner pockets of his cloak and withdrew a handful of gemstones.

"These are lovely but..." Lani paused in hesitation. "How do I even know they're worth anything?"

"Are they worth anything to you?" Fen said gently. Even with his muted powers, he knew how to use his natural voice to change a mood to whatever he desired.

The woman hesitated a moment before nodding her agreement. She knelt to pull sheets of delicate, colored paper from below her table. "I'll wrap the necklace for you," she explained, taking the handful of gems from his palm. She gently set the items on the rustling paper and began wrapping them. Fenwick watched her expertly fold the paper; She carefully snipped and tied waxy twine around the small package.

"I'm sure she'll love it," she said, handing him the gift box.

"No one said it was for a woman," Fen said with a charming smile, leaving the meaning of his words a mystery.

Lani's eyes widened for the briefest moment in surprise. "No... I suppose you didn't. Him?"

Fen chuckled. "Perhaps. There is someone...rather something... I need to find," he said, trailing off as he turned his head to gaze off into the distance, purposely drawing her attention past the marketplace itself.

"I'm not sure what you could mean?" she said with a frown.

"Do you happen to know the way to the tech center? I've heard they're building a ship that can sail amongst the stars," Fen said, *voice* smooth as silk. It was a risk. He couldn't know exactly how she was connected to everything, but he had to take the chance and play the part. At worst, he would make a fool of himself.

Lani shook her head and replied, "We common folk do not have access to such information."

"Common folk, sure," Fen said lightly as he intentionally brushed his fingers against the back of Lani's hand. "But you are not common at all, are you?"

Lani's mouth pressed into a tight line at Fen's words. She took a step backward and reached one hand behind her back.

Before she could draw her weapon, Fenwick leaned forward, his lips inches from hers and whispered, "I'm not here to play games, Lani Gemward. I have nothing and no one left to lose. You can help me find it or die here in the market stall."

Lani's dagger flashed as she drew her blade and brought it to Fen's throat.

He chuckled from deep within his chest, unwavering. "You wouldn't dare."

"You don't at all know what I would dare, Fenwick Greensong," she replied, her voice shifted from its earlier ease into cold, hard steel.

Their recognition of each other rang out in the moments that followed, locked at a standstill together. "True," he said.

The seconds seemed to stretch on as if moving through multiple lifetimes. "But I know what I would dare. And I don't care if I live or die," he said, keeping his voice to a low rumble. The pain in his chest had not left since Asayouga's destruction. Since he lost his heart.

He welcomed death as it would end his torment, but he needed to find out all he could first. It was a matter of justice, really. For all who had died. Now, of course, he knew that Nova and Melly were nearby, yet in that moment with a weapon at his throat, he wasn't sure it mattered anymore. They left him behind, after all. How could he forgive them leaving him for dead?

The starcraft, though. He could still find that. He could still find out whether the rumors were true, whether they had used Asayougan technology to initiate space travel on their own. He might yet unravel the mystery that Asayouga had burned for.

"Well, that makes two of us," Lani seethed. "And I'd sooner die here than betray my home."

"Blonde hair. Deep, soulful eyes. I've seen her," Fen said and saw the fear strike Lani's soul as he described her lover.

"I know exactly where to find her," Fen said. "One soul for another. I could make her the payment." It suddenly came to him why Lani seemed so familiar. He *had* seen her before. The memory of a shifting glance in the gaming house he frequented with Palan came to the forefront of Fen's mind. She enjoyed sitting in a corner near the piano, often with Hazel Pippit, though not always.

"You couldn't know—" Lani started, but she halted her speech, uncertain as she called Fen's bluff.

That was all he really needed. Just her hesitation. It confirmed the information he'd gathered was correct. The fear of losing someone important would be enough to overwhelm her love. Hazel was probably dead, but Lani didn't need to know Fen was bluffing. His *voice* would aid him in his deception.

"Just give me a location," Fen breathed as his grip tightened around Lani's throat. He hoped he would only need to threaten. "Then you will never see me again and you can live your life in peace."

Lani looked into Fen's eyes. "She wasn't supposed to die, you know. We were supposed to let her go."

Fen froze. His heart hammered so hard in his chest, he worried Lani may be able to hear it. Was she talking about Nayeli? He used all his strength and resolve to keep his voice steady in spite of the fear.

"Well, you failed," he said. Nothing could bring her back now. He didn't even know how to absorb what Lani told him.

"Or maybe we weren't your only enemies," Lani said.

Cold, dark hatred filled Fenwick's chest, furious at Lani's implication—that someone on Asayouga was responsible for the death of thousands. That someone among their own intended to kill Nayeli. But as much as it infuriated him, he knew she was telling the truth. It was why he now scoured the Ersette Isles alone.

"Where. Is. The. Star. Ship," he said through his teeth. Rage ripped through Fen and it took everything he had to keep from shaking.

"No where you will ever find," Lani said.

Fen stabbed her with all the force of his strength. Blood bubbled up into Lani's mouth and gushed out. He watched as her eyes grew wide. She was dying and she knew it. Her eyes would haunt him even when his own soul joined the stars in the sky. In her dying breaths, she didn't take her gaze away from Fenwick's.

At last, her body crumpled to the ground. Fenwick stood over her, breathing heavily, hardly believing what he had just done. He could barely see as rage blinded him. Shouting erupted around him causing Fenwick to break out of his frozen trance. The guards—alerted to the incident—rushed toward the scene.

Swiftly, he ducked under the table and patted down Lani's clothing, looking for any clues that might lead him to a Tskelan research facility. He could hear the clamor increasing behind him. If he did not find something—anything—quickly, he would be captured and most likely put to death.

His shaking fingers hovered above Lani's ring finger adorned with a gigantic pink crystal carved into a tangle of thorns. Behind him he could hear the guards shoving past panicked civilians to get to him. It was now or never. Fen released her hand and slid under the table at the rear of the market stall. Luckily, his cloak still provided concealment as he crouch-ran through the streets, dipping under tables, hanging clothing, scarves and booths. He took a last look behind him to see the collective attention of the crowd was drawn to Lani's dead body.

Chapter Twenty-Four

SUPERNOVA

Nova held a sleeping Melly against his chest. The walls felt as if they were closing in on him. He waited, hoping for Edeyn's energy to return to the room but it never did. He had enjoyed the feeling of connection with her even from afar and felt a deep grief within him at the interminable silence now within his thoughts.

Since the moment he first saw Edeyn, he knew she was special. Her unique mystery may have frightened Palan, but Nova felt peace in her presence similar to the way he did with Nayeli.

He needed to stay focused on guiding him and Melly to safety, but his cluttered thoughts kept returning to Edeyn, and he could not seem to stop them. The more he tried to let go, the worse it seemed to get. Memories of Nayeli confounded his feelings for this new person. He couldn't forget his life's greatest love. He wished he could see her star. It would reassure him of his purpose.

Nova despised feeling constricted. He ran from the jungle to protect the child but it landed them in worse danger. Now they were trapped, and he didn't know how they would escape. It didn't seem possible or likely. He forced his thoughts into the present, to focus on Melly's safety. Even as he strategized for freedom, his mind still buzzed with thoughts of both Nayeli and Edeyn.

Nova didn't care to fight. He'd never been much for conflict, physical or otherwise. But he found himself wishing he still had his weapons. He had twisted the black dagger around every night as he pondered Nayeli, the stars, and anything else on his mind. It became a comfort, over time. Now he was without it and it left him feeling empty, amplifying the feeling of dread and panic at being trapped within the small prison cell.

He felt stifled, as if someone were choking the air from his lungs. Every moment barricaded from seeing the stars made him panic more, as if he would physically die if he couldn't see the constellations. It was not enough to know Nayeli was there beyond the cold stone walls. He needed to see her with his own eyes. He was afraid the last link to her essence would disappear if he couldn't confirm it still existed.

Without his weapons, he didn't have the obsidian dagger to soothe him. No matter how cruel the weapon's reminder had been, it still connected him to Nayeli's existence.

Nova knew he would need to master his thoughts if they were to have any hope of escaping. But his *sense* was of no use in their environment, especially under the dampening effects of the city.

After holding Melly for so long, Nova's arms began to throb. Though small, her body's weight took its toll on his muscles. As gently as possible, Nova eased Melly onto the ground beside him, worried the slightest jostling might wake her. As well behaved as the child was, he could not simultaneously manage her needs and his thoughts at that moment.

After successfully placing her on the ground, he gazed down at the sleeping child's face. His heart shattered all over again. Her features bore such innocence and hope despite all she had endured in her short years of life. Nova wished he could reverse time for her, so she could know peace instead of pain. He gently brushed tendrils away from her angelic features and smiled.

Hot tears splashed onto his hand and he quickly stood, clearing his throat in an attempt to deny the pain. There was no one around to witness him falling apart and yet it still embarrassed him. He knew if he let himself feel everything, he would never stop breaking until he crumbled to ash and joined Nayeli in the stars.

The tears continued to flow without his permission. An agonizing shout of pain released from Nova's throat, completely unbidden. He gasped, inhaling tears and mucus, sending him into a fit of coughing. Adrenaline jolted through his body as he checked to see if he had awakened Melly, terrified his blubbering was enough to disrupt her slumber. To his relief, she slept on, not even stirring. He watched her for several minutes before he allowed himself to breathe properly again.

Nova leaned his palm against the stone wall and drew in slow, deep breaths. He squeezed his eyes shut and images of Edeyn immediately flooded his inner vision. He blinked rapidly, as if he could clear the visions from his mind. When that didn't work, Nova pressed the heels of his palms into his eyes in anger.

"Stop!" he whispered fiercely. "Just stop! Leave me alone!" He suddenly resented his inexplicable connection to Edeyn, despite how strongly his heart yearned to be near her. He also hated that he did not seem to have a choice in the matter. Was his love for Nayeli even real? He knew it had been and still was, yet Edeyn seemed to haunt his every waking breath as well as his dreams. There was no escape.

He wasn't sure he wanted to escape her, either. Edeyn hadn't done anything wrong. She offered care and listened to his grief. There was nothing upsetting about that.

Even now, he could feel her energy searching for him. He couldn't explain how that was possible, but he knew it was. Just as he knew the constellations still existed in the daylight when he could not see them, he knew Edeyn was with him, in some capacity, despite her lack of physical presence.

They would be reunited. He wanted that. But first he had to survive the current crisis.

His body tensed again at the noise of shuffling outside the door. Nova froze as he heard the thud of the lock against the door handle and the shriek of a key turning.

Quickly, he rubbed a corner of his shirt across his face, trying to clear up any trace of tears. He hoped his eyes were not puffy, though he didn't know why it mattered what his captors thought of him.

The lock released and the door swung inward, revealing a man standing in light armor with no expression on his face. The man held a black sphere in front of his mouth and spoke, "You may come forward now. The king will see you." The words sounded as if they were being wound through a hand-cranked music box, tinny and choppy. Nova realized the sphere was a *sensory* device, designed to replicate the *voice* and transduce the words from one language into another.

The muddled thoughts of Nayeli and Edeyn ceased battling within him as Nova resolved to focus on every detail in their unfamiliar environment. Survival instinct renewed his spirit. He knelt next to Melly and gently shook her.

"You don't need to bring the child," the soldier said.

Nova looked at the Tskelan guard and shook his head. "No. She stays with me, or we don't come at all." He could not risk separating the child from another caregiver. She had already lost too much for one so young.

The guard displayed no visible emotion but for some reason, Nova could *sense* his annoyance anyway. "Fine. Don't delay any further," he said.

Nova nudged Melly again, a little more urgently.

The child cried out in her sleep, squeezing her eyes tightly and erasing her previously peaceful expression. Nova regretted having to pull her back into conscious suffering. Her dreamland seemed to be the only quiet she ever got.

"Wake up, sweetheart," Nova said, keeping his voice gentle despite the impatience he felt emanating from the guard in the doorway.

"The king cannot be kept waiting. His majesty's time is valuable," the guard said, again holding the sphere in front of his mouth.

Though flutters of urgency raced through him, Nova did his best not to let the words press him into a panic. "Please, Melly... I'm so sorry. We have to go."

Blessedly, the child roused from her sleep, raising her arm to reach for Nova. He swiftly pulled the child into his arms and gently kissed her cheek.

"Let's go," he said as he nodded at the guard.

The guard led them down the long, dimly lit corridor. This time, Melly seemed more alert. Though there was not much to look at down the narrow hall, she cautiously took it all in with curiosity as they passed by.

Nova's thoughts still raced. He wanted to stay anchored in the present, but flashes of Edeyn's energy filled his mind again. As they emerged in the outer courtyard and followed the guard past a stone fountain surrounded by flowers, Nova thought he saw a woman sitting on a bench who looked just like her.

When he looked at the bench again, there was no one there. It felt as if he were being forced by some dark entity to see Edeyn's face everywhere; as if she had been duplicated over and over again, as if she were the only woman alive now or ever.

Nova drove his gaze forward into the back of the guard who continued to lead them through the fortress. They wove through so many courtyards, balconies, staircases and corridors Nova became thoroughly confused as to their direction.

Eventually, the guard led them into a large inner room filled with elaborate décor. The king lounged in a soft, red armchair, his boots propped on a footstool as he looked utterly bored.

Nova surreptitiously examined their surroundings, though he couldn't absorb much detail. He didn't want to arouse more suspicion by looking too long at anything. Only two guards stood by the door on either side of the entrance. Apart from that, the king was alone.

The ruler eyed Nova and Melly with disinterest. He did not move from his reverie to greet them. He barely acknowledged the guard who brought them forward.

"Your majesty," the guard said as he halted in front of the chair.

Nova halted as well, holding tightly onto Melly who was, as usual, remarkably silent.

The king spoke to the guard in a single syllable.

The guard and the king exchanged words back and forth until the king sat forward in his chair. He gestured with his fingers for the guard, who responded by crossing the room to place the speaking stone into the king's hand.

"I'm told you were found wandering about near the volcano," the king said.

Nova nodded, uncertain whether the stone would pick up his own voice if he spoke. He had not witnessed technology like this in action before. There had been little need for it in the isolated city of Asayouga.

"That is inadvisable. Particularly with a child. Not to mention..." The king's voice trailed off, but he gave away no emotion in his silence. "Not to mention, suspicious."

Nova remained silent, though internally his mind was racing. He felt himself breaking into a cold sweat. Had the Tskelans seen their spaceship? Did they know Nova and Melly were connected to the crash? He had no idea what the Tskelans knew or didn't know and he didn't know what to say without giving something away inadvertently. Telling them the truth—that he launched a spaceship from the island of Asayouga after the city was destroyed by an unknown force—seemed unwise. Nova braced himself, hoping the king would say something he could work with.

"We don't typically find anyone in the firelands. Exposed to the elements," the king said.

The king's words brought a beam of clarity to his scattered thoughts. Nova understood a kernel of what the king was looking for. They were foreigners. No native to the island would be wandering near the volcano, especially not with a small child. The environment was entirely inhospitable, the heat unbearable with no shelter in sight. Between the ash and lava, and the glistening darkrock that attracted sunlight like beacons, it was no place to wander.

"Where are you from?" the king asked after allowing space for his words to sink in.

Nova's mind raced, a million thoughts all piling on top of each other as he tried to come up with a believable response. He could lie and say they were from Oleress, but he'd never seen the mainland outside of a book. He wasn't at all sure he could recall details about it if they asked, especially when under as much stress as he was. Telling the truth would lead to further questions and, likely, even greater suspicion. He didn't know what to say but he had to say something quickly.

"Well? This is a simple question, isn't it?" the king asked. This time the slightest cruelty slipped into his voice.

"O-of course," Nova said, though it felt a monumental effort to move his tongue which felt as heavy as wet bags of sand.

"So then answer, please. Where are you from? I will not ask again," the king said.

With difficulty, Nova chose the truth. There was risk no matter what answer he gave, and the easiest path forward was to speak what he knew for certain. He had never been very good at tracking lies.

"I'm from the island called Asayouga. To the west of here," Nova said, in a surreptitious deep breath.

The king stiffened. He narrowed his eyes slightly as he turned to speak to the guard. Lowering the sphere, he fired off a string of questions in a language Nova could no longer decipher. After a brief exchange between them, the king returned his attention to Nova.

"What brings you to Scoria?" the king asked in an overly pleasant tone.

This was a question Nova absolutely could not answer. They crashed there from the sky. There was no logical explanation. Asayougans didn't sail anywhere. "We came on a—"

Nova hesitated before completing his answer "—on a ship." It was only a partial lie, after all.

"Funny. We have never received any sailors from your island in our dockyard."

"We do like to keep to ourselves. But we've begun exploring more," Nova responded without missing a beat.

"Well, what gives you the right to explore this island as if it is your own? This world does not belong to you."

Nova wished he could tell the king how mutual the feeling was. He didn't want to be there anymore than the Tskelans or Agatians wanted him to be. He wanted to be in the sky, in the void with Nayeli. That was all.

As Nova fumbled to find his voice and answer in a way that might remotely convince this king he and Melly were no threat, a clash broke out from beyond the king's chamber. A guard burst through the doorway drawing all the attention to the entrance.

Although Nova could not understand what was being said, he observed the frantic breathing of the guard and heard the noise rising up from the marketplace below.

The king stood abruptly and the speaking stone rolled out of his hand, bumping across the stone floor until it stopped at Nova's boot.

The king barked orders and the guard who escorted Nova responded in a note of protest.

Quietly, keeping his eyes on the commotion around him, Nova crouched slowly and picked up the small stone sphere. He slipped it into his pocket, unnoticed.

After a rapid exchange of words, the escort guard bowed before turning swiftly on his heel and marching back through the door.

With the guards' attention briefly diverted, an impulse came over Nova. He acted quickly, running to the window on the far side of the room, where heavy velvet curtains waved gently in the breeze.

The door guards reacted instantly, rushing across the chamber. There was a drop to a staircase beneath the window ledge and he knew the landing was going to hurt. He had to try.

Guards and merchants scurried frantically on the street below them, but no one was paying attention to the tower windows. *Looking* into the distance with his enhanced *sight,* he *saw* a throng of people converging on the center of the marketplace. This might be the only chance he would get. It was now or never.

"We're going to fall now, sweetheart. It might hurt a little," Nova whispered.

Melly looked at him, eyes trusting as she nodded.

They jumped.

Chapter Twenty-Five
THE BEST LAID PLANS

Palan sat up on the cold, hard floor. The sun shone its early morning rays through the window at the end of the hall, the building already sizzling with heat. The unmistakable *scent* of hot glass drifted to his awareness.

Palan paused to orientate himself to his surroundings. It had been confusing to wake in new environments almost nightly since they'd left Asayouga. Existence felt impermanent as they wandered across the Ersette Isles. Each time he woke, his body and mind stitched themselves back together slowly until he remembered where they were.

He stood and stretched his legs. Everything ached. He felt ancient in that moment and whispered several curse words to himself as he twisted and stretched to remove the twinges from his stiff muscles. Movement helped, but it was difficult sleeping on the ground all the time. Palan seemed to discover a new pain every day.

Edeyn was fully dressed, looking immaculate despite being up at first light. Her beauty appeared effortless while Palan struggled to re-emerge as a full-fledged human each morning. Sonny looked less than enthused at the early hour, which offered him some comfort.

"We have a lot of work to do today," Edeyn said in a cheerful voice.

Her eagerness made Palan want to vomit. "When don't we have a lot of work to do," he grumbled in response. His internal tension after visiting the garden the night before tumbled in his brain. He did not share his thoughts with the women, deciding it would be safer for everyone involved to keep some secrets to himself.

"Do I get to gather my things first?" Palan asked in a sarcastic drawl. Part of him hated that every word he spoke sounded like it had been dipped in poison, but he when he remembered all the burdens he carried, he justified it to himself; soothing his conscience even if momentarily.

"Of course," Edeyn said without missing a beat.

Palan couldn't tell if he bothered her or not, and *that* bothered him. He snatched up the blankets he used as a bed and stomped into their suite throwing everything into his bag. With his weapons secured against his body once more, he briefly patted the pocket containing his amulet, purely out of subconscious habit.

"Let's go," he said, gesturing toward the stairs, prompting Edeyn to take the lead.

They trooped into the common room and Edeyn strode with confidence to the counter, ordering food while Sonny and Palan found seats at a table near the front window.

Palan looked out across the street at the garden, remembering the *scent* of roses in the absence of any such flowers. Understanding clicked into place, causing anxiety to flutter more strongly in his chest. Knowing both Edeyn and Sonny would be able to pick up on his feelings, he did his best to mask his tension on the outside. He hoped the two women would not notice how perturbed he felt.

"The fortress is fairly well guarded," Edeyn said as she sat to join them.

Palan appreciated her for a moment, knowing she meant business. "We know."

"But we *could* get in. The Tskelans have a time for public inquiries and grievances every day around midday. We could seek an audience at that time. With some planning, it may be possible to create a distraction while one of us slips away into the inner fortress. That will probably have to be me because I know where I saw Nova."

Palan clenched his fists. The thought of putting his trust in anyone else to recover Melly was too much. Especially her. Especially Edeyn.

Just as he thought her name, the woman locked eye contact with him. He met her gaze strongly, refusing to waver. He wasn't going to allow her to intimidate him with her powers.

"There's a higher chance of failure if you were the one to go in, Palan," she said.

Her plan was logical, but he didn't want to acknowledge it.

"And I certainly couldn't sneak past anyone," Sonny said with a shrug.

She did have the most lumbering walk that Palan had ever witnessed, but he felt it would be rude to mention it out loud. She couldn't help how she walked.

Palan sighed heavily. He didn't want any of this but he recognized he really didn't have much choice. He didn't know what lay ahead but that didn't matter as much as the safe return of Melly. What came afterward would have to be revealed when the time came. He had lost all faith for a positive outcome, at least not for himself. His heart had fallen so far into darkness he could not see any escape, but he still believed Melly could live a happy life.

"Fine," he said, begrudgingly. "So, Edeyn will find them and release them. But I haven't a clue how to talk to the Tskelans." If he revealed the amulet and its powers, the communication issue would be solved. Palan was determined only to reveal it if he had no other option.

Edeyn paused with a pensive expression. "I hadn't thought about that part," she admitted. Silence fell over the three of them as they considered this complication.

The food came and they ate quickly. Savoring any bite was time wasted. After a sip, Edeyn rested her mug down on the table. "We will have to buy something in the market. It won't be perfect. Some type of amulet, or maybe a bracelet. Something that can be concealed. But this city is full of *sensory* objects that will unlock the *voice*."

Palan felt a twinge of guilt. "That's going to cost us," he said.

"Yes," Edeyn said, "But I think I might have a solution for that."

"As long as it doesn't involve whoring, I'm listening," Sonny said.

Both Palan and Edeyn turned their faces to Sonny, expressions unified in surprise.

"It was a joke?" Sonny said as she looked back and forth between them. Flushed with embarrassment, she quickly buried her face in her mug.

"I was not going to suggest such a thing," Edeyn said once she regained composure.

Sonny nodded with a sheepish smile. "Go on," she said, gesturing for Edeyn to continue.

"We'll offer an exchange. I have some coin left but I don't want to spend all of it. I think if we offered it along with precious stones that would make a difference," Edeyn said, looking at Palan.

"Why are you looking at me?" Palan asked, raising an eyebrow. "Do I look like someone who walks around with precious stones on me...? You know what, don't answer that. Please."

Edeyn touched the bridge of her nose before lowering her arm and responding, "Well, as a matter of fact, yes."

"Excuse me?" Palan said. He felt rage rising once more within his chest—not that it was ever really absent. His thoughts immediately went to the amulet. She must have known about it after all, but he didn't want to bring it up in case he was wrong. Instinctively, he needed to protect that secret.

"When I found you on the beach—" Edeyn began.

"You didn't find us on the beach," Palan snapped, cutting her off midsentence.

Edeyn fell silent, tilting her head, expression peaceful as she held eye contact with Palan.

Did she know? Had she seen the amulet on the beach? Palan silently cautioned himself to be more measured with his answers, not to react so impulsively, but his thoughts and emotions spiraled like a storm rolling in beyond his control.

"When we were on the beach," she continued, "you were often wandering and picking up treasures for your little one. I know you didn't give them all away to her."

Relief flooded Palan as he realized she wasn't referring to the amulet after all; she was referring to his growing collection of baubles. "I didn't, but so what. They have access to these same beaches. These are not precious to them."

Edeyn smiled brightly as she answered, "Actually, that's where you're wrong!"

"Hmm," Palan growled.

"They're always in need of gemstones, sea glass, shells... anything that could hold the *senses*. Some objects are better than others for holding power. Of course, I don't know exactly what you have..." she said, trailing off and glancing at Palan's chest.

He told himself to be still, knowing now that she may not suspect he was hiding anything. "I thought you could read my thoughts," he said with a derisive snarl.

"Sure. But I can't know your every thought every moment of the day. That would be madness. And incredibly draining. I prefer to simply communicate," she said, voice remaining placid.

Palan gave in and reached into his pockets to remove a small satchel he used to collect the items he found interesting on their travels. Most of them he had hoped to give to Melly. Giving them to Edeyn was ultimately for his daughter's benefit as well.

He set the pouch on the table and loosened the drawstring with his fingers. Once the strings were completely unknotted, Palan gently turned the bag over allowing all the tiny treasures to roll onto the tabletop.

All three of them stared at the objects as if they expected them to speak.

"Well. I told you. I don't know that there's anything useful here," Palan said after an awkward silence. He suddenly imagined them all as little children, sharing awe and wonder over their toys.

Edeyn frowned and reached forward hesitantly, picking up a small, sharp ivory object that looked like a fang. "What's this?"

Palan shrugged. "I don't know what any of this is!" he said, absolving himself of any responsibility.

Edeyn looked at him, her face bright with excitement. "You really don't?"

Palan huffed in annoyance. "No, I really don't. Why would I know anything, I could be wrong! I've never been to this bloody island before and I wish I could get away from it."

Edeyn graciously ignored his defensiveness. "This is a tooth. I think it may be from a jaguar."

Palan shook his head again and gestured vaguely.

Edeyn stared at the tooth, holding it up in front of her with her elbows resting on the table. "Yes," she said after a moment of consideration. "This will do."

Sonny reached across the table to examine the tooth for herself, and Edeyn relinquished it, dropping the shiny, sharp object in Sonny's hand.

"Jaguars are revered as extremely protective animals. A fang given willingly to the earth without you hunting this animal down or even defending yourself against an attack—this item is a gift not a trophy. It will be able to hold the most powerful *sensory* magic," Edeyn said.

"Couldn't we enchant an object ourselves?" Sonny asked as she squinted at the sharp fang, holding it so close to her face she couldn't possibly be seeing it clearly.

"We could, but we would need to find someone with the *voice*. And we do not have that. This will do in exchange for an enchanted piece," Edeyn replied.

"Fine," Palan said, relenting. He had no attachment to that particular item. He barely remembered picking it up.

Edeyn leaned back in her chair as she safely stowed the fang inside her money pouch. She touched the straps of all her weapon holsters as if running through a mental checklist of items, making sure they were all in place before nodding. "Let's go."

"That's it? We're not planning beyond this?" Palan questioned.

"We can talk again after we find what we need," Sonny said.

Edeyn nodded in confirmation.

Palan grumbled his reluctant agreement. He wanted to know every detail he could before proceeding. But it seemed he wasn't going to be given that luxury.

The three of them scraped their chairs back from the table and made their way to the marketplace. Though early in the day, it was already full of merchants and buyers alike. Palan followed Edeyn while Sonny wandered off to a stall filled with fresh baked goods.

Edeyn walked with confidence as she always did, knowing her purpose and her aim. Palan didn't fully trust every part of her, but he trusted she would act predictably, and that was enough for him now.

As they wove their way through the stalls, around other shoppers, Palan kept his eye on the fortress with its imposing pillars and high walls. He knew getting Melly and Nova back safely was a long shot. So many variables could not be accounted for ahead of time. Although he desperately wanted to believe it was possible, rescuing his daughter seemed unattainable.

He returned his focus to Edeyn. If he thought too many steps ahead, he would collapse in despair. Edeyn had been right to take the journey one step at a time. They would re-group as soon as they had what they needed.

A sudden *whiff* of roses reached him again, surpassing the mishmash of marketplace smells. Palan spun around to look behind him. It was as if Fenwick were right there, but Palan saw only a sea of strangers. The *scent* vanished as quickly as it had arrived and Palan caught himself growling again.

He couldn't tell whether he was losing his mind or if he was truly *sensing* Fenwick. It wasn't logical for Fen to be there. But the alternative meant he may be losing his grip on reality, and he did not like the idea of that either. The smell of the dusty stone streets, clay wares, baked goods and other assorted objects reclaimed their prominence in Palan's awareness.

They stopped at a stall overlooking the shipping docks on the street below. Citizens could access the lower streets and waterways via stone staircases that curved along the upper levels to the lower. Colorful flags flew from looming turrets along the fortress walls. Palan analyzed his surroundings once more. Despite his dulled *senses*, the *scent* of the sea was powerful. As much as sea salt permeated the air—combined with heady spices, heat, and fish—the *whiff* of roses overcame him again despite his dulled abilities.

He gripped the edge of the market stall where Edeyn conversed with the shopkeeper. Though he was within earshot, Palan could barely make out their conversation. The *scent* was sickening. Overwhelming, even. He squeezed his eyes shut as his head throbbed, as if closing his eyes would dull his *sense*.

Palan fought the urge to vomit as he didn't want to ruin whatever negotiation Edeyn was attempting to work out with the shop owner. He simply could not be responsible for losing their chance to get Melly back. He forced himself to breathe slowly but the nausea caused his skin to prickle as bile rose in his throat.

"Leave me alone," he whispered under his breath. "You're not here. This isn't real."

In spite of Palan's best efforts to hide his sickness, he saw Edeyn eyeing him in confusion before turning back to the shopkeeper with a smile. They seemed to have come to an agreement.

Edeyn thanked the shopkeeper as they completed their deal.

The *scent* of roses wrapped around Palan again causing his vision to blur. The world around him swirled and danced as he fought to stay upright. He had never fainted before in his life and he wasn't about to start now. But it was all he could *smell*. Nothing else existed besides the roses.

Screams erupted across the marketplace and chaos soon followed. Palan staggered as he fell against a stone wall, struggling to regain his balance. Panicked shoppers whizzed past him as he forced his eyes to stay open.

Palan scrunched his face tightly as he tried to concentrate but he couldn't discern any useful details from the confusion surrounding him. People scurried in all directions, the noise level had risen to an unbearable level and his vision continued to blur.

Unable to withstand the pressure any longer, Palan vomited all over the stone street, splashing the top of his boots. Before he could recover, he felt fingers squeeze his bicep in a tight grip before supportive arms wrapped around his chest. He staggered again. Edeyn stood in front of him, staring at the fortress a moment before guiding them through the marketplace to the lower docks.

As he glanced over his shoulder, Palan caught a glimpse of the back of a cloak, embroidered with roses, trailing around a corner before disappearing from view. There was only one person he could think of who wore a cloak like that. The floral *scent* dissipated as Palan stumbled down the steps. He willed himself to keep up with Edeyn and now Sonny who somehow rejoined them amidst the chaos.

Freed at last from the inundation of rose *scent*, Palan felt himself reconnecting with his body. Although he trembled, his vision cleared and his headache lessened. Dread settled into his chest, replacing his nausea from earlier. Fenwick was alive.

Chapter Twenty-Six
DOCKS

Edeyn raced to a covered archway, pulling Palan along by his arm, trusting Sonny would follow without direction. She braced Palan's shoulders in an attempt to steady him, guiding the tall man to sit on the stone pavement. Screams of panic continued to erupt around them.

Palan looked absolutely dazed. When Edeyn looked into his eyes she saw nothing but fear. Had he seen a ghost? She had seen plenty of those, so it was no shock to her, but she knew it could be to those who never experienced a haunting before.

She knelt in front of him, setting the newly-wrapped bundle from the shop down at her feet. Closing her small hands around Palan's wrists she looked into his eyes. As calm as she could she asked, "What happened, Palan?" He did not respond.

Sonny joined Edeyn, kneeling in front of Palan. "Let me try," she offered. Edeyn nodded and sat back to watch, fascinated to observe Sonny using her *touch*.

While Sonny made use of her abilities, Edeyn took the opportunity to see what Palan saw. She closed her eyes to tune in to Palan's mind. The immediate tangled mess of chaotic thoughts nearly threw her off balance. "Whatever he saw has him in complete disarray." She shook off the first try and went in again but this time she was prepared, pulling an energetic shield around herself before entering Palan's mind.

Mostly, she sensed fear there. There was a name Edeyn couldn't quite grasp. Someone Palan was afraid of, though when Edeyn tried to look more deeply into the thought, it disappeared. Even though she knew he wouldn't understand how to block her searches consciously, she had encountered hiding thoughts before. When someone really wanted to keep a secret, it could be difficult to follow the information into the darkness of their mind.

She removed her energy after turning up very little. Sonny appeared to be having more success rousing Palan.

Palan blinked as he slowly emerged from his stupor. Edeyn knelt beside Sonny and stared into Palan's eyes. He looked back at her, expression blank. It was as if he didn't recognize Edeyn.

"Palan?" Edeyn said gently, patient as he regained his awareness.

"What?" he said at last, his voice sounding weak.

Edeyn and Sonny exchanged looks. "What happened?" Edeyn asked.

He shook his head. "I don't know," he responded.

Edeyn didn't doubt that was the truth. He seemed unable to tell them anything further.

"I didn't see what happened in the market," Sonny said. "It feels like madness."

Edeyn nodded. Even though she did not have the *touch* like Sonny did, she could relate to feeling the shifts in energy profoundly. She had the advantage of understanding how to protect herself so it wouldn't overwhelm her, and she was uncertain whether Sonny would have the same ability.

"I think there was a death," Edeyn said. She hadn't seen it with her eyes, but she experienced the event with her *knowing*. She hoped the other two would not ask her to explain how she knew when she didn't have any evidence of her declaration. But she *knew*.

"Oh," Palan said, still in a whisper. It was as if all his usual energy had been drained from him.

Sonny peeked into the street before ducking back into the alcove. "The guards are distracted. We might be able to sneak into the fortress if we hurry," she suggested.

Edeyn nodded. "Listen, we can still use this," she said, returning her attention to their shop purchase. She rustled through the parchment and held up a floor-length dress with pink and cream and blue colors.

"Oh, that's beautiful," Sonny commented.

"Yes," Edeyn agreed.

"A dress," Palan stated.

"Yes!" Edeyn said brightly as she set the garment into Palan's lap. "Put it on quickly. It will help. We may have time to use this distraction to get into the fortress to rescue Nova and Melly.

Palan stood up as if he were on fire, seemingly recovering from his sudden wave of illness. "Why did you buy a dress?" he asked though his tone sounded more accusatory than questioning.

"Because it's enchanted to pick up the *voice* and it won't stand out as using the *senses*," Edeyn explained.

Palan raised his eyebrow. "I am meant to be wearing this."

"Right…" Edeyn said, trailing off in confusion.

"You bought me a dress. You bought ME a dress," Palan said.

"It's much better to be wearing the item," Edeyn said. "If we had chosen a sphere it would be too obvious that you didn't know the language."

Sonny chuckled. "I think Palan may be upset that you assumed he'd wear a dress. Not that you chose a garment to wear instead of an object like a speaking sphere," she said as she gently touched Edeyn's shoulder.

Edeyn frowned, still confused about the upset. "Well, it doesn't matter, does it? It was the best I could find!"

Palan let out a frustrated sigh and picked up the dress. "Did you have to choose something so frilly? A simple gown would have been better. Or a scarf. A shirt. Really, anything other than this?" he asked with a hint of amusement in his voice.

"I wasn't thinking about that, I guess. You're tall and this seemed like it would fit. Also, you were too busy vomiting to help pick something better," she snapped.

Palan shook his head. "I thought you said a bracelet or something," he said, exasperated. Without waiting for an answer, he pulled the dress on over his clothes.

"You can see your shirt through the top! Take it off!" Edeyn demanded.

"You're just being nitpicky now," Palan commented as he removed his tunic. He crumpled it into a ball and threw it at Sonny who responded by shoving it into her pack.

Edeyn took a step backward to survey Palan thoroughly. She tilted her head to the side and reached to re-arrange some of the ruffles.

"You're kind of right," Edeyn said with a sigh.

"What did you say to me?" Palan asked, laughing.

Edeyn couldn't remember him speaking to her without a hint of poison in his tone. "It really doesn't suit you at all. And this was all they really had with *voice* enhancements. I guess it'll do," she replied soberly.

Sonny covered her face with both her hands, stifling a chuckle.

Disgusted, Palan let the dress crumple to the ground in a pile at his feet. "We don't need it anyway, now," Palan said, "But we'd better hurry."

"You don't know, we could still use it if we need to speak to a guard," Edeyn said, but resigned herself to Palan's refusal. She wished they hadn't bothered with shopping at all.

Edeyn leaned out of the alcove and looked up and down the roadway. The screams died down as shoppers cleared the market quickly enough. Some still lingered, perhaps out of morbid curiosity.

"We don't have much time. I think we can make our way to the fortress now. Although I don't know what to expect," she said.

Edeyn froze mid-step, dropping to her knees as the intensity of a *vision* flooded her mind without warning. *She saw Nova, and Melly's deep, dark eyes. The air rushed from her lungs as if she had dropped from a height. A loud clang like thunder filled Edeyn's ears as darkness overtook her.* She blinked a number of times, struggling to see clearly. Some of the shadows dissipated but she felt like she was looking through a shimmering veil.

Edeyn touched her forehead in confusion, unable to conceal the aftermath of her *vision*. She had never experienced one quite as vivid.

Sonny appeared at her elbow. "What's wrong?" the woman asked softly, her arms around Edeyn to stabilize her.

Edeyn looked at Sonny, stunned with the strength of what she had experienced. She lived her whole life *knowing* things without knowing why. She was no stranger to these *visions*. Yet this one was on a level she never thought possible. It felt as if her body had temporarily transported to an entirely different realm, then returned again just as abruptly.

"I…" she began and trailed off as another flood of sensations rushed through her. *She saw the child's wide eyes once more, staring. A hand reached out for Edeyn. Edeyn reached instinctively to grasp the little fingers in return, even though she knew it wasn't really there. She felt the uneven, harsh thudding of footsteps running along stone, then heard a high-pitched scream. Ice cold water surrounded her. Her breath was stolen from her lungs.* She blinked again and staggered, sliding her body down against the stone wall to the ground.

Sonny knelt in front of her and grasped her hands. "What is it?" she asked, her voice thick with concern.

Palan assumed a protective stance guarding the entrance to the alcove as Sonny attempted to soothe Edeyn.

Edeyn's voice caught in her throat. "I don't know but—" she looked at Palan, her eyes wide with fear. "They aren't in the fortress anymore."

Palan spun around. The momentary softness he'd shown her vanished and his hands clenched into tight fists.

"What?" he hissed.

Edeyn burst into tears, overwhelmed with everything she had seen. "I saw them jump and… Oh Palan! I'm so very sorry," she gasped.

"What do you mean?" Palan said, barely above a whisper.

"I felt them drown," Edeyn said weakly.

Silence seemed to crush Edeyn despite the commotion of the streets. The thought was too horrible to process. Her *visions* were not often wrong, yet she wished she could nullify what she'd seen this time.

"The ship," Palan said after a moment.

Edeyn stared in confusion.

"We need to find the ship. Whether he's alive or not. Let's get out of here. Let's go home," Palan said.

Edeyn's lips felt numb. "I have no home," she whispered.

"Neither do we," Sonny said.

Edeyn remained silent. Was this an invitation?

"We'll find the ship," she said as she stood, wiping tears from her eyes with the back of her hand. "Come let us find passage to Oleress."

Chapter Twenty-Seven

LOVE IN LOST PLACES

On his stroll down the gangway to the docks, Fenwick paused and drew in a deep, refreshing breath. After days at sea, he welcomed the feeling of solid land beneath his feet. The memory of the ship's steady rocking still affected his balance as he disembarked.

He closed his eyes as he steadied himself against a wooden post at the end of the shipping dock. The wind tugged playfully at his cloak and he smiled as he enjoyed the warm sea air.

He didn't have a plan, but that was becoming normal for him. From the moment he found himself alone and abandoned on the bank of the Chickadee River, surrounded by many of his fallen friends, he was living one moment at a time.

Seeing Nova and Melly alive in Tskela left Fen bereft. He'd been so close to reuniting with his friends, only to find himself separated from them once more. He never imagined Nova would leave him behind in the first place.

Ever since Nova's spaceship launched from Observation Point, Fen had been on a journey of his own, figuring things out as he went. A vague desire to piece together the remaining mystery surrounding Asayouga's demise—and the loss of his dearest friend, Nayeli—pushed Fen to continue his search. Fighting through feelings of hopelessness, he drifted across the Ersette Isles, embracing the uncertainty of his existence.

A sharp jab shot through Fen as a passerby slammed into him. "Watch where you're going!" he yelled, adjusting his *voice* to the language most of the crew and passengers used.

The man swore at him in return before sauntering off without an apology.

Fen shook his head. He regained his footing enough to carry on to the city of Oleress.

The city's white, shining stonework rose before him—a stark contrast to Tskela's aesthetic. Oleress was surrounded by light. The City of Thorns felt heavy and stifling between the humidity and the thick volcanic fog in the air. Oleress, in comparison, was free from the oppressiveness of Scoria Island.

Taking a moment to marvel at the construction differences, Fenwick noted the cities were a product of their surroundings. The architecture of both cities reflected their environment, with Tskela using Scoria's abundance of darkrock in their building structures, and Oleress using lightrock from the nearby mountain range.

Fen strolled until he reached the outskirts of Oleress. Still haunted by images of Lani's body as it collapsed to the ground in Tskela, he found himself reliving the moment over and over. He marveled in horror at the ease with which he'd killed her.

Killing Lani Gemward wasn't necessary. Although Fen tried to reason away his feelings of guilt, he wished he had spared her life. She was undoubtedly part of the information leak leading to Asayouga's demise. But even though he confirmed his suspicions, Fenwick was a lover not a killer. He didn't quite know how to reconcile the discrepancy between his internal identity and his actions in the Tskelan marketplace.

Fen now knew who and what was responsible for the destruction of his home. Lani wasn't innocent. She was part of the Thorn Network. Asayouga's traitor communicated directly to her. She had been directly involved in the fall of the city. But reassuring himself didn't seem to lessen the guilt of taking a life.

Pain twisted deep within his gut as he remembered his home.

There was plenty of time to ruminate on the attacks during his long, lonely journey. Fen felt responsible for the catastrophe, even though he knew he couldn't be. Not really. If only he'd paid closer attention to the signs, maybe he could have made the connections sooner and Asayouga would still be standing. But love—or desire, at least—blinded him to the truth for too long.

In spite of the painful memories it brought, Fen held on to the rose symbol Nayeli gifted him. The symbol represented love and passion—feelings he wasn't sure he would get to experience again. She'd designed the signature *scent* to draw in his heart's desire. It never seemed to work. He was bitterly grateful for its failure now.

As he recalled Nayeli's beautiful face and gentle spirit, his heart filled with sorrow. Every part of Asayouga's destruction, every soul that watched over them from the night sky, weighed on Fen's shoulders.

His hope dwindled. He had briefly felt re-inspired upon seeing Nova and Melly in Tskela. Because he fled, he doubted he would get a second chance to reunite with them. It felt like he had let them down, even though they were unaware of Fen's presence nearby.

He prayed some miracle of fate would free them even without his help. He wondered what had happened to Palan and Sonny since the ship's emergency launch. The ache in Fen's chest felt like a heavy pile of rocks. He accepted he may never again feel the lightness of hope. He could go on, of course, but too much had occurred for him to ever return to the innocent thought of peace.

Fen wandered into the city, his steps slowing as he took in the unfamiliar surroundings. The gentle notes of strings and melody entered his awareness and he spun to search for their source. A minstrel stood on a small, raised platform in an open square within the street, playing a lute and singing into a voice amplifier to a small crowd of passersby.

Fen approached the platform, drawn in by the song, though he couldn't quite piece together why it called to him. He felt a wave of nostalgia, a familiar heart-pull of energy that reminded him of love and heartbreak and home. He forbade himself to shed a tear. Memories were all he would ever have of home or love.

As Fen came to a halt amidst the gathering of strangers, the singer's lyrics enchanted him.

"*The night that never ends,*
returns love to you in starlight," the melody flowed.

He froze, his eyes widening as he was overcome with soul recognition. It was as if his love were speaking to him through music. It wasn't unusual for Fenwick to make connections through songs—that was common with the *voice*—but this tune captured him in a tight grasp.

"Isn't it a beautiful piece? I heard him sing it once before. I think it was a year ago," said a smooth voice at his side.

Fen cleared his throat and turned to smile at the speaker. He was once again stunned when he gazed upon the man standing next to him. His deep, brown eyes stared into his own. His face was framed by thick, black curls. His features reminded Fenwick of the loved ones he would never see again.

"It is lovely," Fen said as he recovered the ability to speak. It was as if the stars were sending him a message of hope, a reminder of love sent through song. Fen wasn't sure he could find any solace, but he held onto the warmth the music brought him anyway.

He wondered if memories would haunt him for the rest of his days. A passing thought entered his mind unbidden: Perhaps he would not need to live too many more days before his soul went supernova. He, too, would become a new star in the sky upon his death.

Grief swept over him, but he quickly corrected himself. As much as Fen longed for suffering to end, he didn't feel his mission, his purpose, had truly been fulfilled. He needed to hang on a little longer until it was.

"Have you heard Nayven Roseword before?" the woman asked.

The syllables resounded like echoes of the name "Nayeli." Another stab of memory cut through him like a dagger. He cleared his throat, unable to push back the flow of emotions any longer. "Ah, no," he said. "Forgive me. I must go."

He pushed past the man as he fought back a wave of intense emotion. He forced himself to walk down the road until he knew he wouldn't be perceived by anyone, then stopped, pressing his palms against the corner of a building. Fen's chest heaved as the full onslaught of sorrow flowed from him, untethered. He allowed his tears to spill onto the stone pavement under his feet before pulling in another deep breath. "It's only a memory, Fenwick. I will always have reminders of home," he whispered in reassurance to himself.

He looked up at the sky, filled with sunshine, and waited for the heavy pull of longing to subside. Although his loved ones were gone in physical form, he felt a sense of peace knowing a part of them would always be there, above. Their stars were still floating somewhere in the cosmos, and although he could not see them in the brightness of day, he knew they still existed. The knowing was enough.

His thoughts returned to their regular pace, no longer knocked out of alignment by unbidden memories. Now refocused, Fen looked for signals that would lead him to the research station. He knew very little about the layout of the city but he hoped he could rely on his *voice* to decipher signs leading to the university. The research station wouldn't be known to the citizens, but Fen knew from his work within the Rose Network it was concealed somewhere on Oleress Campus.

It was easy to spot the university grounds; its impressive structures stood out along the Oleress skyline.

Fen passed a large, multi-storeyed building on his way to the stone structures. A sign read, "Library of Records." He paused in front of the wide, stone steps, tempted to explore the library first. The scent of books would surely comfort him. But he forced his mind to remain focused on his mission instead.

After weaving his way along the campus paths, Fen eventually found a small, crumbling stone building a little way off the pavement. Whatever path once led to the structure had long ago overgrown, clearly abandoned after the original necessity of the facility ceased.

The heavy door swung open as he pushed against it. A quiet, ancient energy filled the room around him. It felt as if the door was a portal to another world entirely as Fen stepped into the dim, dusty room. It was mostly empty. Sunlight filtered through the windows along the far side of the room but somehow the light didn't provide much illumination at all.

Along the wall opposite him were walls of shelves filled with old books. There were a few tables with chairs haphazardly pulled up to them and lanterns placed in the centers of each table.

Fen wandered along the shelves, scanning titles as he trailed his fingers against the book spines. He wasn't at all certain what he was looking for but he thought it might occur to him as he browsed.

After a moment, he stepped backwards, scanning the entirety of the room. He knew he was in the right place but felt strangely out of sync, uncertain what his next action should be. As he closed his eyes, he was once again filled with bright flashes of memory. His chest filled with immediate anxiety, wishing he could, for a few moments, forget the past.

"Please," he whispered to the silent room, "show me where to look." Fen didn't know exactly how the universe worked and he didn't strictly believe in any deities the way so many others did, but sometimes he felt as if he were communicating with something else when he spoke aloud. He knew he was only talking to himself, but it made him feel as if he were not alone.

Fen stared blankly at the bookshelves, not thinking anything in particular, uncertain if he were waiting for someone to answer him out loud. That's when he noticed a book with a small symbol carved into its spine—a dove holding a flower in its beak.

Fen couldn't explain why the faded symbol stood out to him. Instinctively, he pulled the book from the shelf and opened it, finding a key within its hollowed-out pages. He stared for a while before placing the book onto the shelf.

"Thank you?" he said out loud as he grasped tightly onto the key. Somehow, finding an answer re-connected his mind and his body. Fen searched the room in earnest, peering under the tables, tugging on the bookcases, pulling at the other book spines.

He reasoned that a hidden entrance must be somewhere close by. After inspecting every part of the room and finding nothing, Fen let out a sigh of frustration and returned to the door, ready to search the outside perimeter next. A distant thrum of energy reverberated from below his feet, confirming he had found the lab, even if he could not see the way in.

Fen squinted as he exited the darkened building, the return to direct sunlight causing an immediate headache. After his eyes adjusted to the shift in lighting, he paced around the building, crouching to dig through dense, thorny bushes along the back of the stone façade. He glanced over his shoulders more than once to ensure no one was watching.

"I look like a creep," he muttered to himself as he continued to dig. He knew his cloak concealed him somewhat from immediate notice, but he felt self-conscious regardless.

At last, he found what he was searching for: A wooden storm door locked down and covered beneath stones and dirt behind the unkempt flower bushes. He inserted the key into the lock, struggling with it for a moment before it gave way. He swung open the door and peered down the steep ladder. It was dark but he could see a glowing light in the distance beyond view of the top of the staircase.

Fen carefully positioned himself on the ladder and gently eased the door shut above him, trying his best to remain quiet as he did so. He moved his feet, one by one, down the ladder to the lower vestibule. Pressing himself against the wall behind him, he peered around the corner where he saw a glowing light.

Across the dark, empty stone room, there was a corridor. Fen narrowed his eyes, noticing a strange gimmer hovering over the surface of the pavement. Goosebumps covered his arms, alerting him to potential danger. He pulled a small stone out of his pocket and tossed it across the floor, like skipping a rock on a river. He heard a click and fire shot out from the walls.

"Ah. Lovely touch," Fen muttered, thankful for his own foresight but uncertain how to proceed. He examined the pavement closely and noted the way some stones were slightly raised while others sunk down further. He threw another pebble at the depressed tiles until he was satisfied with his route and tiptoed his way to the far corridor.

He made his way toward the expanding light. When he finally reached the far entrance, he lingered in the shadows, staring in awe at the sight below. The research facility was deep in the ground with a spiral of levels curved around the central opening of a long, vertical tunnel. When he peered over the edge, there it was in all its glory—a spaceship. This one was much larger than Nova's and looked far more sophisticated.

Nova had done well with so few materials available, but this structure was a true marvel.

Fen kept to the shadows along the wall where the lights wouldn't shine directly on him. There were not many spaces to hide. If anyone spotted him, he would not be able to evade capture.

He hadn't expected a fully-constructed ship. Asayouga had dealings with Oleress, providing an exchange of knowledge, but he still hadn't expected them to have such advanced magical technology. Clearly, Oleress didn't share everything with their allies. Fen wondered if the Tskelans had tried gathering secrets from Oleress, too.

As two workers ascended the steps nearby, Fen searched frantically for an exit strategy. He ducked down a side corridor, willing himself to remain invisible as he waited for the workers to pass.

He crouched, leaning his head just past the corner to make sure the coast was clear before sneaking down the metal staircase to the lower floor. He made his way to a room at the head of the spiral, where a wide screen-like window covered the front. Carefully, Fen snuck in the side door, keeping low as he wove between the rows of desks lit with equipment.

A screen, lit with orange number strings and lines of text, grabbed Fen's attention. He peered closely, concentrating his *voice*, mouthing the words as they appeared. It seemed to be live data recordings from what Fen could tell. Everything about the condition of the spaceship.

He marveled at the sheer volume of information. Fen cautiously attempted to navigate the system as he looked through folders of data. Most of them remained locked, but the title of one caught his eye: *Asayouga I.V.* He attempted to select it but a small panel popped up, prompting Fen for a passcode.

He placed his hands against the screen, barely allowing his palms to touch its surface. After a quick glance around him to make sure he remained unseen, Fenwick closed his eyes, slowing his breathing down as he focused the power of his gifted *sense* on the strange device.

Fen had broken codes before, but he'd never encountered a system this advanced. Navigating the labyrinth of code with his mind proved challenging as he crossed roadblocks and barriers specifically designed to keep out intruders who might be gifted with the *voice*.

Determined, Fen focused as clearly as he could, willing himself to succeed. A series of strange letters and numbers appeared in his mind's eye and he hurried to replicate them on the keyboard before losing them from his memory. Fen heard the machine click as the file unlocked.

There were years' worth of records from Oleress' contact with the Rose Network. He scanned the data quickly. Fen grabbed his notebook to jot down names, dates, places, and anything else he could. One name stood out and his chest knotted tightly in recognition.

As he read the Oleressan reports, understanding clicked at last in his mind. He was right about who betrayed their information, but it wasn't the full picture. Fen saw multiple names. All of them were dead now, except for one.

Oleress also seemed to have data on Nova's unsuccessful launch. He smiled as he noted they had never found the crash site. All the work they'd done to cloak Nova's ship worked, as far as Fen could tell. There were several speculative crash site areas listed, but nothing was found.

Clicking through folders, Fen found another on Tskela. His eyes skimmed the information within. Tskela had never successfully found the research station in Oleress, by the look of it. Whatever information Oleress and Asayouga exchanged remained unknown to Tskela.

The sound of footsteps alerted Fen that he was no longer alone. He closed the file and swished behind another row of desks, keeping his cloak closed around him with the hood pulled far down over his face. He waited, holding his breath to keep silent, until he could see his way safely through the door and back into the hall. The only thing he needed to do next was get out of the research lab.

Fen crept up the stairways, making his way at an agonizing pace to the exit. He could see it in view when the most incredible snapping of stone reverberated throughout the underground tower. The ground began to shake and alarms sounded all across the facility as every worker raced from their positions, filing quickly down the staircases.

Fen took his chance amidst the commotion to flee the facility.

Chapter Twenty-Eight

THE VIGIL

Edeyn led the way off the ship onto the dockyards, Sonny and Palan not far behind. She struggled to make firm plans while her thoughts and feelings were entirely pre-occupied with *visions* of Nova. Her thoughts were heavily colored by both sorrow and worry, making it difficult to think clearly.

To add further challenge, Palan seemed to have given up all his previous snarls and raging for complete silence. The tension punctuated every step of their journey together.

Edeyn guided them through the city with its impressive stone walls towering high into the sky. The architecture was delicate—beautiful in a more ethereal sense than the city of Tskela, which had a more ornate aesthetic.

Although Edeyn was not certain they would find answers in Oleress, even the remote possibility seemed better than nothing. Despite the *vision* of the drowning, hope lingered. She couldn't ignore the intuitive pull toward the lightstone city. Ignoring her abilities in the past had been detrimental. Now there was much more riding on her *knowing* than her own wellbeing. She didn't want to give false hope to Palan, so she held onto the glimmers she received as to Nova's whereabouts, hoping perhaps she could change his fate or that her *vision* had been wrong somehow. She didn't speak her thoughts out loud, certain Palan would later murder her if she made anymore missteps.

She faced the others as she paused to get her bearings.

Sonny shielded her eyes against the late afternoon sunlight and turned slowly in a backward circle, taking in the sights. "I'm guessing that's where we're headed?" she asked, pointing at a complex of large, impressive stone buildings and structures.

The Oleress campus stood out. Edeyn looked ahead for a moment before nodding in agreement. "I guess we couldn't miss that, could we?"

"I can only imagine the libraries in that place," Sonny said, her voice filled with wonder.

Edeyn glanced at the other woman. Her inner *vision* flooded with an image of Sonny standing behind a tall desk, stamping book covers and shelving books.

"Is that what you did at your home?" she asked. "You worked in a library?"

Sonny sighed heavily. "Yes. I was a record keeper. I helped Nova with his research many times. It broke my heart to see it all burned."

Edeyn gave a solemn nod to acknowledge Sonny's grief. She wondered if the woman had any family in Asayouga. She realized Sonny never once mentioned any human attachments. Only books.

"Was it as big as this place?" Edeyn asked.

"Well..." Sonny began and trailed off. "I don't know. I haven't seen the library here. But it was impressive. To me, it was home."

Edeyn could not relate to having a home, even an unconventional one like Sonny and her library. She had lost most of her early memories and the few snatches she could conjure up were steeped in misery. She always held onto an inner longing for "something" indescribable and non-specific that would bring her to a brighter place, not plagued with challenges. Glimmers of the longing pulled at her heart here and there throughout her life, but the moments were fleeting.

She didn't like to focus on it too much, but when she first saw Nova, his energy matched her soul's searching. It was as if his soul was the home she had always wanted. She had no way of knowing if he felt anything similar for her. Sorrow cut through Edeyn as she recalled the visions of drowning. If he were gone, her longing would never have resolution.

If Edeyn's *visions* were true, her "home" in Nova was already lost. The fleeting moments of desire settled as she thought of Nova, but it was covered in pain as she realized she would never know if he felt it too. Had she merely imagined their bond? Flights of fantasy helped her escape challenging emotions before. As a result, Edeyn didn't always know with absolute certainty what was real and what wasn't.

Her gifts were unusual. Since she didn't have a physical *sense* like everyone else, the only *sense* she did have was commonly maligned. She had locked it away even from herself throughout most of her childhood. Even though she was safe to use her gifts now and she knew she could take care of herself, the habits of her old life lingered.

They headed to the large campus, keeping their silence. Though Palan followed Edeyn, she could feel his silence like a looming shadow with every footstep. She tried to shield herself from his darkness, but the tightness in her chest remained. How much of it was simply the anxiety of worrying over Nova or how much was Palan's energy? Edeyn couldn't seem to sort it out entirely, and ultimately it didn't matter because it felt the same either way.

They trekked through the campus paths, observing the way the grounds were so beautifully kept with neatly manicured lawns, colorful groves of fruit trees, and lush foliage and floral arrangements. In addition to its stunning visual appearance, it also smelled heavenly.

At last, they approached a large stone building, a little better decorated than the others around it. Although Edeyn had never visited it before, she assumed—based on the symbols decorating its exterior—it was the temple. Accommodations there would be free so long as they held vigil for a few hours at the temple's altar. She hadn't told her travel companions about that part of the deal yet, though she planned to take on the entire burden herself so as not to inconvenience them. She supposed Sonny would at least be able to wander off to access the library while she fulfilled the requirements. She only needed to decide what to do about Palan. When she glanced over her shoulder at him, she re-confirmed how shocked and distant he was. She only hoped he wouldn't do anything impulsive once he snapped out of his stupor.

Edeyn ran up the steps ahead of the other two and turned to face them both. She drew in a deep breath as if she were about to deliver a speech. "Look. We can stay here for free. I can ask about news of the crash. Someone here has to have seen it, so there must be information out there. The only thing is, the temple adepts will require us to hold vigil to account for our time in their accommodations."

Palan didn't so much as blink in response.

Sonny glanced up at the tall man and then smiled at Edeyn. "I'm not entirely sure what that entails, love, but we don't have much other choice do we."

Edeyn nodded. "Well, we could find a way to earn some coin, but I think this is the quickest. We'll be able to carry on with our travels much sooner this way. I don't mind holding the vigil for all three of us."

Sonny shook her head as she gestured at Palan. "No. You and I can split the time. I don't know what this walking tree stump is going to do, but I don't think we can expect much out of him at the moment."

Palan didn't respond.

Edeyn eyed him and then nodded. She decided to avoid addressing him directly. "You could try to find the library. If anyone knows what's going on, that would be the place to look."

Sonny scanned her surroundings. "You know, if you don't mind, I think I will do that. I think I know exactly where to find it. Are you certain you can do all this alone?"

Edeyn laughed, though she didn't intend to. "Of course I can. I've been alone my whole life. I don't mind at all." She couldn't comprehend the look Sonny gave her in response. She tried to tune into the other woman's energy but was unable to make sense of what she *perceived*. Pity? Admiration? She couldn't tell.

Sonny shifted uncomfortably before nodding. "Ok. I'll join you again soon," she said before lumbering down the steps and down the path leading to the library.

The doors swung open easily despite their weight, and Edeyn stepped into the sanctuary. She could feel Palan's presence following behind her but she did not turn to check. Instead, she made her way through the rows of benches adjacent to the back hallways, well-lit with soft, yellow light.

A figure, dressed in a white robe with a beautifully embroidered hood, stood outside an archway leading into an open courtyard decorated with carved stones and water fountains.

Edeyn led the way into the courtyard until she found the presiding sanctuary attendant. She approached and knelt before them, unloading her burdens at their feet as was the respected custom. She bowed her head, awaiting their response.

A musical, genderless voice greeted her. "Welcome, traveler. Should you wish to stay the night, you must tend to the courtyard lanterns for a period of seven hours. Our rooms are open to you and your companion so long as you remain at rest."

Edeyn nodded her agreement. "Thank you. I will take the vigil myself. My companion is unable to do so. We have a third traveling with us who may enter later this evening."

"She will show you to your chambers where you may retire after your vigil." The attendant nodded, indicating the woman standing next to her. "Your companions may rest there freely."

Edeyn stood, gathering her belongings once more and followed the cloaked woman down the corridor. When they reached the rooms, she allowed Palan to enter first. He settled onto a cot without a word. She shook her head, knowing he would likely stay parked on the bed until she returned.

She set her weapons and pack down under a small table that had been pushed beneath an arched window before patting Palan's leg. "I'll be in the garden... Sonny will be back later."

He didn't answer nor did she expect him to. Edeyn left the small chamber to begin her vigil. The return to the silence of her own thoughts would be strange after all this time leading others.

Back in the garden, she washed her hands and face and donned the designated white robe, lighting her candles before beginning her slow, even pace around the fountain. She only wished it were evening so she could gaze up at the stars. Seeing the constellations always brought in Nova's energy. A small wave of grief washed through her at the memory of him.

Instead of pushing her feelings aside, Edeyn allowed silent tears to flow as she carried out the observance. Without intending, a *vision* filled her mind, almost as clear as if the events were unfolding right before her eyes.

She saw a long, dark column, staircases spiraling all around it with a large machine in the middle towering up through all the floor levels from the ground to the ceiling which could open up to the stars. A man in a dark cloak skulked along the walls and a strong scent of roses met Edeyn's nostrils.

The *vision* faded as quickly as it appeared. She frowned as she caught herself standing still. Her heart hammered in her chest as she returned to her pacing of the courtyard. It was difficult to carry out actions in the present at the same time as *visions* overwhelmed her. She recalled her earlier *vision* of Nova's ship: A flash of a mountain of darkrock and the spaceship smashed at the foot of the cliff, somewhere beyond Oleress. This new *vision* showed a research facility, somewhere deep underground.

The scent of roses was undeniable. She wondered what it meant. Finding Nova's ship suddenly seemed more complicated than ever before. Edeyn carried out the rest of her vigil deep in contemplation.

Chapter Twenty-Nine
It Isn't What It Looks Like

All of Palan's thoughts were distorted. Sounds echoed strangely to his ears, his eyes saw blurry, surreal images. It was as if the whole world were underwater.

He vaguely recalled sailing to and reaching the city of Oleress, but the details were indistinct.

Palan blinked slowly as the *scent* of roses once again filtered into his awareness. It jolted his thoughts away from his despair and back to the present. His heart raced in his chest as he spun around, taking in the view of the furniture, the bed, the breeze gently drifting through the open window.

He had no memory of getting there, but the place seemed peaceful. Except for the *scent* continuing to haunt him. Instantly, Palan gripped the windowsill and looked outside, searching desperately for the sight of the flowers which would put his mind at ease. Of course, he couldn't find the source of the phantom smell.

Hurriedly, Palan grabbed his pistols off the mattress and buckled them to his belt. He didn't recall divesting himself of the weapons in the first place. He wondered whether he had done it himself or someone else helped him do so. Either way, the mystery unsettled him as he struggled to recall anything he had done in the past several days.

Poking his head out the doorway, he looked up and down a long corridor decorated with lamplight and smooth stone sculptures. He proceeded down the hall, noticing the stillness of the quiet night air.

Eventually, he emerged in a courtyard with an elaborate fountain in the center. Spotting Edeyn, dressed in flowing white robes and holding a candle in front of her as she paced evenly around the room, Palan went out of his way to walk in the opposite direction.

Annoyingly, she seemed to be alerted to his presence as soon as he entered the courtyard. They made unwelcomed eye contact and stared at each other for a moment. Saying nothing, Palan walked more quickly across the courtyard and emerged in a sanctuary where the moonlight filtered in, gracing the stone tiles. There he slowed his steps.

"Where the hell am I..." he whispered to himself.

A cough alerted him that he was not alone in the sanctuary. He nodded in wary embarrassment as another robed figure standing near a small altar glared at him. Religious surroundings always made Palan uncomfortable. He hoped he hadn't disturbed any vengeful deities.

After another moment's hesitation, Palan exited the sanctuary. He had questions, but he chose not to ask them. The only person he could ask would be Edeyn, and he didn't want to engage with her mind reading if he could avoid it.

He knew they were in Oleress, but it looked nothing like what he anticipated. Closing his eyes, Palan noticed his *scent* flowed freely, unlike in Tskela. A smile tugged at his lips as he enjoyed the return of his abilities. His *sense* guided him down a path in the direction of the floral aroma he now dreaded.

Palan steeled himself to track down the origin of the disembodied *scent*. He already knew who he would find at the end of the trail. But he needed to know he wasn't going mad. Pushing aside the fear threatening to engulf him, Palan followed the *scent* until he reached a small dirt path leading up to an abandoned building. Was Fenwick really alive and in Oleress? He had to find out.

A *whiff* of dust greeted his nostrils even before he yanked open the heavy, worn door. When he stepped inside, he discovered thick particles hanging onto every exposed surface.

He erupted in a fit of coughing as the *scent* overwhelmed him. After having their *senses* muted in Tskela and across Scoria Island, the intensity of his full ability was jarring. He wondered if everything always smelled this strong.

The rose *whiff* seemed to tangle itself within the dust particles, making it heavier than before, threatening to choke him. It was not unusual for a *scent* to dominate all of Palan's thoughts while he tracked it but the roses seemed particularly potent. Nausea threatened to overtake him again but he fought through it. He convinced himself it was only fear amplifying the effects.

Still puzzled, he looked around the dark room. It looked abandoned and he wondered if it was a dead end. Confused, Palan paced the room. It was mostly barren aside from the bookcases which looked to be untouched.

He clenched his fists tightly, trying to focus even more firmly on the *scent*, silently begging it to reveal a trail. The air around him seemed to take on a pinkish hue as he stared, as if the smell had taken on physical shape.

Palan glared at the wall where most of the *scent* concentrated. He turned, marching outside and back down the crumbling steps, stomping around the building to the other side. He crouched, digging carelessly through spindly, bare branches covered in sharp thistles until he found the doorway. Although it surprised him to find the door unlocked, Palan descended into the darkness below him without stopping to question the reasons as to why.

The *scent* completely enveloped him. He could see it everywhere as he looked across a large, seemingly empty chamber toward a light flickering in a distant corridor. Palan pressed himself up against the stone walls, moving as quietly as he could around the perimeter of the room in the direction of the light.

The sound of stone scraping against stone made Palan freeze in mid step as bolts of fire shot out from the walls. He stumbled back to avoid the flames, but as he did, he heard another loud snap. The ground rumbled beneath his feet. Palan realized his careless mistake too late: He had set off a trap. Dust and broken rock rained down around him.

"Oh, hells," Palan said aloud as he struggled to keep his footing. Frantically, he looked for an exit, but no escape was evident. The entrance he came in was inaccessible to him now, already buried in rubble. He would have to find a different way out of the chamber. Darkness surrounded him as the quake knocked out the lighting. Palan strained to make out details in the soot-filled chamber. He crossed his fingers as he ran for the corridor he had seen before, praying to all the gods he did not believe in that it hadn't completely collapsed.

Tremendous force shook the ground under his feet. The walls seemed to vibrate as the sound of collapsing stone increased to an unbearable roar.

He pushed forward. Even in the midst of the earthquake, the *scent* of roses continued to swirl around him, plaguing his last steps as he ran for his life.

Palan thanked the stars as he found the corridor. He scrabbled over a heap of stone, finding the rest of the hallway intact. Using his hand along the wall to guide him, Palan walked until he emerged in a strange, multi-leveled chamber. Every floor flashed with bright emergency lights while workers clad in white and black uniforms rushed down the staircases toward the bottom level. Palan gripped the railing and looked down what seemed to be an intricate spiral. At the bottom sat an impressive, shining black spaceship. Palan's jaw slackened in awe. Light pulsed along the hull of the ship as it whirred and hummed with a soulless heartbeat. The ship was similar to Nova's but much more sophisticated in appearance.

Alarms sounded and lights flashed up and down the spiral interior. Staircases cleared as workers sped to the lower level. Palan followed suit, hoping to blend in. He raced down step after step, boots clanging against metal floors as he ran. The staircases seemed to go on forever, and he found himself thankful for the weeks of trekking through jungle with its uneven terrain, uncertain he would have made it with any less stamina.

At last, Palan emerged on the ground level, out of breath. He pressed against the wall again, trying his best to keep to the shadows, but the sight of the spacecraft enthralled him. He stared up at it, its height seeming more impressive from below.

Looking around for an escape, Palan prayed to every god he could think of, begging for a way out of the facility that didn't involve launching himself into space as a stowaway amongst a crowd of likely hostile strangers.

To his relief, while many of the crew boarded the rocket, others filed through a set of double doors at the far side of the lower chamber. Ceiling panels swirled open above him, making room to launch the ship.

Palan ran for the double doors. He hoped his strange presence would go unnoticed amidst the chaos, allowing him time to slip away when they emerged above ground. Palan fell into line behind another uniformed worker. More staircases. He kept his head down, trembling almost as much as the earth around him.

At last, he could see the night sky with the constellations shining clear above him. Palan wasted no time ducking out of the line, darting his way across the campus as fast as he could. Everything shook. Buildings crumbled, their walls collapsing. People ran, screaming, through the open courtyards as they tried to locate safety.

He staggered in the direction of the temple. He couldn't lose track of Edeyn. As much as he despised her, he felt his last hope of finding Melly slipping away from him as his heart seemed to hammer in his throat.

Palan arrived in time to see the roof cave in. He backed up several paces, coughing as debris shattered through the atmosphere around him. Falling to his knees, Palan found his own body shaking with tears. "Mel," he croaked, his voice weak with agony. "No."

All Palan's breath fled from his lungs as an arm wrapped around his throat, pressing into his windpipe. *Roses*. Palan's vision swam before him as he gripped, digging his fingernails into the exposed flesh of the assailant's wrist.

His head stung as the barrel of an energy pistol slammed against his temple and Palan slumped, unable to find the will to fight.

Rolling onto his back, Palan knew before he looked who he would see. He stared up into familiar green eyes. "I've been looking for you," he said softly.

With a voice smooth as silk, Fenwick replied, "I don't know why. You left me for dead."

Chapter Thirty
SHIFTING

Edeyn ran from the building, her cloak pulled around her mouth. Her premonition had saved her—barely.

She clung to her pack, one hand tightly gripped on her glaive. She didn't have time to grab all her gear and was left with whatever she could carry in each hand. Her eyes widened in shock as she turned in time to watch the top of the temple collapse entirely. Debris spewed everywhere as the earth's rumbling gradually slowed.

Edeyn's hands trembled as she fastened her weapon safely to her back where it belonged. It felt strangely imbalanced having only one. The only other piece she retained was a small dagger strapped to the inner lining of her boot. She had chosen not to divest everything before changing into the vigil robes. She silently thanked her past self for breaking the rules and keeping the blade as she stood staring in horror at the chaos around her.

Flames streaked through the night sky and Edeyn gazed at the sight of the rocket ship launching into the darkness of space. She tried her best to reorient herself, but nothing looked as it had when they arrived. The campus was swarming with terrified residents as buildings collapsed.

The people of Oleress hustled, lost and confused, flooding the streets as structures near campus continued to fall. Some flocked to the city center while countless others stood frozen, watching the destruction.

Edeyn's gaze landed on the crumpled form of a man near a patch of bushes. A sudden lurch of recognition sickened Edeyn as she rushed across the lawn to Palan's body. She crouched and placed a hand on his shoulder, frantically scanning his body for wounds. Although muddy and disheveled, he did not appear to be bleeding. Nevertheless, he lay unconscious.

Edeyn turned her ear close to Palan's face and—to her relief—felt warm breath brush against her skin. She shook him gently, preparing herself for his sudden return to consciousness.

She scrambled backward when Palan roused. He stared into Edeyn's eyes, his own expression marked by confusion. As soon as Edeyn confirmed Palan was not about to jump at her throat, she eased closer to him again, touching his face and frowning with concern.

"Are you hurt?" she asked softly as if he were a small, frightened child. His usual air of aggressive dominance, his standoffish energy, had all evaporated as he sat in the dirt.

He shook his head in response.

Edeyn quickly realized she would need to guide him for the time being, though she herself did not understand what was going on. Carefully, she took his hands in each of her own and stood, prompting him to stand with her.

With searching eyes, Palan looked upon the fallen temple. Edeyn placed one hand against the small of his back, guiding him as they began walking down the campus path, now broken and uneven as the earth quaked.

"We won't find anything in there," she said as they walked.

Blessedly, Palan allowed her to direct him as they made their way out of the campus grounds and back into the city. The main streets flooded with confused residents, many still in their night clothes.

Edeyn tried to keep her eyes open as she searched mentally for Sonny's energy, but there was too much interference from the panicked crowd for her to narrow her search. With no sign of Sonny, they continued staggering through the chaotic masses toward the city gates.

Palan stumbled numerous times, requiring Edeyn's patience in spite of everything going on around them. Not knowing the outlay of the city added complications, but she trusted her intuition to lead them down the correct path. She could *feel* a tiny shimmer of light from beyond the city, and that's where she placed her focus. Concentrating on the light, she held it within her mind's eye as they wove through the throngs of people.

When they reached the gates, one door had fallen from its hinges while the body of a guard lay dead on the opposite side. There should have been a second guard but they were no where in sight. They must have abandoned their post when the pandemonium struck.

She helped Palan to the wall, propping him up against the stones so she could free herself to push open the fallen door. It was heavier than she anticipated. Edeyn was built tough and wiry, but pushing against the door took every bit of her strength to shift.

After significant effort, Edeyn stepped back. Deciding it would have to do, she slung Palan's arm around her neck and shoulders and supported him as they staggered through to the city outskirts. There was a small land bridge there, cutting off ship access from one part of the sea to the other. She led Palan and herself across the bridge and into the sparse jungle offshore, without knowing what awaited on the other side.

The atmosphere outside Oleress was not oppressive like it was surrounding Tskela, but Edeyn was unfamiliar with the wilderness here. She rested Palan against a tree as she herself sat down in the leaves.

"I have to figure out where we're going," she explained to the vacant Palan.

To Edeyn's surprise, Palan responded. His voice was quiet but certain. "I know where I'm going. Without you."

Edeyn frowned. "What do you mean?"

Palan stared at her as if she were stupid. "I'm going home," he stated.

She shook her head slowly. "Oh... I don't see how?"

Palan's face contorted into a shape that did not in any way resemble a smile. "You're free to go," he said.

Edeyn's heart hammered faster. She forced herself to breathe slowly, keeping her voice calm in response. This was a choice she hadn't stopped to consider before. Did she need to go further when Nova was missing? She had only ever intended to help him re-claim his ship. But now she was left with only

Palan, and there would be no love lost between them should they part ways.

Something was not right. Edeyn *sensed* Palan was hiding something from her. She searched his energy, but didn't turn up anything useful. Why did she feel so strongly about following Palan? She quietly considered her motivations as it dawned on her she still held onto hope she would see Nova again.

Visions of the drowning still haunted her, but she hadn't had any new revelations since then. Her *knowing* had gone silent. The absence of Nova's energy unnerved her. He was almost certainly dead, but part of her didn't want to accept it.

"You may need help," Edeyn said, although she knew Palan would want her help less than anyone.

Palan stood quickly. "I never need help," he said.

"I thought you didn't have a home anymore," Edeyn said with a frown.

Palan gave her a withering look as his fists clenched tightly at his sides. Edeyn shrank back, falling silent.

She looked back at the city, wondering if Sonny were still alive. Her emotions swelled within her as she swallowed the lump in her throat. She floundered, uncertain what her next purpose would be now. In the end, she helped no one, and she had no home of her own to return to. For a brief time, she felt like she had a purpose. Now she understood that purpose was falsely constructed.

Edeyn stood again, feeling a mixture of pity and disgust as she looked at Palan's hardened expression. She'd had a lifetime of loneliness and rejection, meeting continuous difficulties, yet she'd never adopted the same resentment she saw within Palan.

She understood the man wouldn't care if she were to share her story. He would still believe his own grief was worse. Part of her wanted to share her vulnerabilities with him, so he would understand she knew what he was going through. But she also knew it wouldn't make an impact on him. He was too closed off.

"All right," Edeyn said, doing her best to hide her inner pain from Palan. If he wanted to go on alone, she would let him.

"Good," Palan said. He lifted his face to the sky and sniffed, catching the *scent* he needed to track. Glancing at Edeyn once more, his expression softened for a brief moment. "Fare thee well, Edeyn."

Edeyn nodded, unable to speak for fear she would begin to cry. Palan nodded in return before storming down the shoreline. She watched him until he disappeared into the darkness of the trees.

Unable to hold them back any longer, hot tears fell across her cheeks as she stood frozen in place. Edeyn wasn't ready to be alone again. Although she knew she could do just fine without anyone by her side, although she had done so for years until that point, she found herself feeling stifled by the sudden silence of her thoughts. No one else's energy to pick up but her own. It was familiar yet unwelcome and desolate.

She sat down again in the leaves and wept without restraint.

Chapter Thirty-One
THE DROWNED

Nova held Melly's hand as they wandered through the wide-open markets of Oleress. He and the child stayed silent as they moved along the carts, both of them dazed.

Nova winced at the pain piercing his temples; Now that he had his *sight* back in full force, he found the vibrant colors of the marketplace dizzying. Every crack in the painted pottery, every stitch on the embroidered fabrics hanging from shop stalls, fought for prominence in Nova's *perception*. He hoped he would adjust quickly to the return of his *sense*.

It had been so long since they had an opportunity to bathe it was starting to show. The grunge of Nova's worn-out shirt rubbed against his skin and the salt of the sea was now crusted into his hair, leaving it crispy and disheveled. The same was true for Melly. Her hair was a tangled, fraying mess, and her clothes were smeared with dirt.

After all they'd been through, Nova was thankful they were alive at all, regardless of the state of their appearance. They had survived. That was enough for the time being.

Although he was uncertain what his next move should be, Nova's rumbling stomach alerted him to the most pressing problem: food. To say they were famished would not do the aches of hunger justice. He imagined how much worse it must feel to Melly.

A tug on his sleeve drew Nova's attention to the child. He glanced down at her to see her pointing wordlessly at the market.

"Excuse me," a voice called. With a slow blink, Nova registered a woman standing behind a stall and waving to get his attention. He held onto the small translation stone he picked up in the Tskelan fortress, ready to put it to use.

The woman smiled as they shuffled across the busy market to approach her. Dressed in a pink shirt tucked into high-waisted, black trousers decorated with belts, she squatted to Melly's level. "Hello, sweetheart," she said gently, holding out an open palm. Melly eyed her with suspicion and gripped Nova tighter, digging her fingernails hard into his arm.

"Can we help you?" Nova asked, eyeing the shopkeeper warily. He was surprised at the sound of his own voice, hoarse, and whispery. He realized neither he nor Melly had spoken in days.

The woman shielded her eyes with her hand as she looked at Nova. "I was actually wondering if I could help you, my dears. You look like you've been through a fight."

Nova nodded as he glanced at Melly who held onto his arm with a death grip. "In a manner of speaking," he said.

The woman's expression moved to one of pity. "Have you any money?" she asked.

"We do not. The girl has not eaten in days."

"And neither have you, I'm guessing." The woman nodded as she assessed the two travelers with her eyes, pressing her lips together in a thin line. "If you follow me, I would be happy to get you two cleaned up. A free meal. It's on me," she said and then added, "I'm Corsa, by the way."

"Corsa," Nova repeated the name. "We cannot repay you."

"I expect no payment at all. I help where I can. Come," she said, holding out her hand to Melly.

Melly glanced up at Nova, asking silent permission, and he nodded in response. The child finally loosened her grip on his arm and cautiously accepted Corsa's hand.

Corsa took her time leading them through the market and down the road. They turned several corners and Nova couldn't keep track of where they were. At the best of times, he was terrible with direction, but in an unfamiliar place he was far too overwhelmed to remember landmarks or focus on details to retrace their steps later.

After guiding them through the busy streets, the generous woman produced a keyring. Out of dozens of keys, the shopkeeper selected the right one quickly, as if she'd memorized its position on the ring. Pushing open the hefty wooden door, Corsa ushered them inside to what appeared to be a cozy inn.

Within moments, Nova found himself and Melly seated at a table tucked away by a staircase. It seemed to Nova that Corsa only had to snap her fingers and food appeared. A hearty stew with steaming mugs of tea were just what they needed. Thankfully, Corsa allowed the two to eat without much conversation. When he finished, Nova sat back and allowed himself to take in their surroundings with more awareness. Finally, he smiled at Corsa who sat waiting silently across the table.

"Feeling better?" she asked, returning his smile.

Nova nodded. He hadn't realized how famished he was up until that point. Melly seemed to feel the same. She curled up on the bench beside him, closing her eyes. Nova placed a gentle hand on her head until she fell asleep.

"What brought you to Oleress?" Corsa asked, gaze landing on the sleeping child.

Nova hesitated, not sure how to explain his story or how much was safe to convey. In the past, Nova gave everyone the benefit of the doubt, assuming they had the best intentions. He always offered information freely and openly. Now he was uncertain who he could trust apart from himself. His trust was disintegrating more and more after Asayouga's destruction. Corsa seemed kind, but he didn't want to risk being wrong.

Finally, he decided on a vague version of the truth. "We are a long way from home. Trying to find our way back."

"Where is your home?" Corsa asked.

Nova's voice caught in his throat as he recalled the home he would never see again. "Gone," he rasped.

Corsa nodded, saying nothing. She seemed to be waiting for Nova to reveal more. When he didn't, she rose from her seat. "Wait here," she said. She disappeared into the back rooms before reappearing with an assistant. They each carried stacks of clothing and a package of provisions.

"I've only guessed at your sizes," Corsa said as she and her assistant set the items down on the table. "When you're ready, you can use the room on the top floor at the end of the hall. You're welcome to spend the night." She placed a key on top of the pile and smiled at Melly before making her way to the kitchen.

Nova carried Melly up to the rooms and laid her down on the bed before retrieving the bundled items. He looked through the supplies, satisfied they contained an abundance of anything they could have needed. After Melly's nap, Nova spent the afternoon getting them both cleaned up. Bathing felt divine after so much time away from civilization. The clothing they'd been given was soft and smelled faintly of lavender and peppermint.

After changing and eating again, Nova and Melly fell asleep long before sunset.

The inn provided deep respite for the worn travelers. Nova longed to stay in place for a period of time without running all across an island. Now that he and Melly were safe, he wished they could stay in that space forever. If not forever, then at least long enough for some semblance of peace to settle in. He was grateful for the pause.

Although Corsa assured him they could stay as long as they needed, Nova would not allow them to overstay their welcome.

The next day, Nova took Melly on a stroll through campus. They wandered at a leisurely pace, both enjoying the freedom of the open air. Butterflies fluttered near the path and Melly chased them. She grew more excited as she exclaimed at flowers they'd never seen on Asayouga.

Nova froze as a woman approached them. For a split second, he thought it was Edeyn. He had a strong urge to run to her before realizing his mistake. She wore the face of a stranger. His heart sank in disappointment, though he smiled and nodded to her as she passed by.

Rattled from his mistaken recognition, he took Melly's hand once more and continued exploring. He focused on the breeze ruffling his hair and calmed himself as best he could. Eventually, they returned to the inn.

Just as Nova wondered whether he would ever stop seeing Edeyn in places she was not, a piercing headache stopped him in his tracks. Images swirled in his mind, unbidden:

He stood on a cobblestone path winding around a fountain. In front of him, he held a candle, but he did not recognize the hands as his own. A long, white robe gently brushed the tops of his boots as he walked. He was seeing through someone else's eyes. Across the garden, he caught a glimpse of Palan, looking dazed and confused as he staggered out of a long hallway.

The *vision* left Nova as quickly as it came. He halted, steadying himself against a wall as he recovered from the onslaught of images. He recalled the first and only other time he'd experienced a similar phenomenon during their captivity in Tskela. Was it Edeyn again? Had he just seen through her eyes?

Nova slowly recovered his composure as the force of the unusual *vision* faded. He looked at Melly sadly, feeling more alone than ever. His protectiveness over the child pressed him to remain focused on a plan.

They stayed at Corsa's inn another week, enjoying the relaxed pace of life it afforded them. Corsa made sure they received three full meals every day.

On the eighth night, Nova woke suddenly as the inn shook around them. He bolted upright, bracing himself against the mattress, confused as furniture and décor rattled. He squinted in the darkness, briefly disoriented as he grabbed a light globe from the nightstand and rushed to the creaking window.

He unlatched the window and leaned out, holding the light globe high to get a clear view. Focusing his *sight* on the chaos erupting in the streets below, Nova watched in horror as pavement split and cracked, debris flying everywhere.

People stumbled from their homes, looking to the sky. A bright light exploded above them and Nova watched, slack jawed, as a rocket shot into space. The spacecraft resembled his own, but much larger, its construction far more polished.

When he came to his senses, Nova roused Melly who, somehow, remained asleep despite all the rumbling and screaming. He understood her exhaustion. The child sat up, bewildered, letting out a worried moan like a question as she looked to Nova for help.

"I know, angel," he told her. "We're going to get out of here, ok?"

She nodded, waiting as Nova hurriedly gathered their scattered belongings from around the room. He secured their satchel of provisions before reaching his hand to the child who gripped it tightly in response. They made their way down the quaking staircase to the main level where some of the patrons hid behind the bar or under tables as debris rained down around them.

Nova's focus narrowed on Corsa who braced herself in the kitchen doorway. "What's going on?" he called, raising his voice above the roar of the upheaval.

Corsa shook her head and shouted back, "I don't know! Earthquake?"

A server ran in, breathless from outside. She grabbed hold of the bar counter to steady herself and burst out with news. "They launched a rocket. Did you see it? Like the one they saw crashing into the wilds."

Nova exchanged glances with Corsa. A humming stirred in his chest as if his body suddenly reconnected to his creation. His ship had to be close by. Had the Oleressans already found it? Nova was afraid to ask.

"A rocket caused all this?" Corsa said, her voice puzzled.

"I don't know, but everyone's talking about it. It flew straight out of the ground when the quaking started!"

Nova stopped listening, his mind racing with possibilities. His ship. His way home. He knew in his soul that his spaceship was close.

"We have to go," Nova gasped.

Corsa nodded. She struggled against the rocking foundation to move to a locked cupboard. Turning a key in the lock, she opened the door to reveal a stack of weapons. She tossed Nova an energy pistol. "You might need that," she said, then added, "Get the child to safety. Go north. Follow the shoreline until you come to the mountain pass."

Nova caught the pistol and hurried to secure it to his waist belt as he listened to the rest of Corsa's instructions, trying to memorize every detail while staying aware of the dangers around them.

"Nova! I'm scared," Melly said in a small voice.

"We're going to get safe, sweetheart," he said as he swept Melly up into his arms. "Now, hang on." The child nuzzled her face against his neck and Nova darted out of the inn, doing his best to protect Melly's head as they flew through the doorway into the city quaking around them.

Chapter Thirty-Two

Aftermath

Edeyn continued crying long after Palan disappeared from her sight. She was surprised to find she had any sort of attachment to him at all after everything that occurred on their journey. The man hated her. She sniffled as she reflected on all the wounds of the past, all the times she had hoped to be accepted and wasn't. Maybe she wasn't so much attached to Palan as she was to the idea of having someone accept her for who she was.

It hit her that the reason she felt connected to Nova was because he did accept her. Edeyn's sobs worsened again, the tears flowing freely. She'd known Nova for such a short time, but she felt truly, deeply seen in his presence. And now he was gone from her life, perhaps permanently.

Even though she'd seen a clear vision of Nova and Melly drowning, she still held onto a dim hope they would be reunited. It started to sink in that she may never know if Nova felt as strongly connected to her as she did to him. She wondered if she'd invented it all in her head out of desperation to feel loved and accepted.

Living alone and fending for herself for so long meant Edeyn didn't always trust her own thoughts. She always had the *visions* and *knowing* but sometimes her secret awareness kept her from being able to discern what was real and what only existed in her mind. No one apart from herself could verify her *visions* as true which made it difficult for her to remain grounded.

Edeyn rose slowly, her legs cramped from sitting on the ground for so long. She disliked crying. It was disquieting. Normally, she remained stoic. With a steady, unshakeable ache in her chest, she returned to the city of Oleress, dragging her feet like weights the whole way.

She shrugged her way back through the collapsed gate and made her way like a ghost through the city streets. As she neared the campus, the terrain became much more difficult to cross as all the stone pavement had lifted up, broken chunks colliding and falling apart the closer she got to the launch site.

It was difficult to determine where exactly the library was—or had been. Edeyn stopped frequently to check her surroundings, gazing at the stars occasionally as if she would be able to find guidance there.

Her head hammered. All the commotion had taken a heavy toll on her body. Edeyn clambered over a pile of smashed stone pillars, standing on top and scanning for clues. The magic normally keeping the streetlights lit seemed to have shattered when the lanterns all blew apart.

She could still see the collapsed temple in the distance. From there she thought she could locate the library. The likelihood of finding Sonny seemed slim. Most people scattered as soon as the quake began. If she was still there, Edeyn worried she might not find her alive.

Without warning, a *vision* shoved its way into Edeyn's mind. Scene after scene flooded her.

She heard the heaving gasp of someone fighting for air, felt their chest tightening. Cold water surrounded her, then a burst of sunlight, then water again. Edeyn grasped her own chest at the force of the *vision*.

Nova's face flashed in her mind's eye. Wet clothing clung to his skin as he cradled a small child in a rowboat. He sputtered and coughed, but he was breathing.

"Edeyn?" a voice asked, startling her back to the present. She blinked in confusion, searching for the speaker. When her sight landed on the short woman standing at the base of her lookout perch, she lit up with a smile. There was Sonny, her pack slung over her shoulder, appearing almost entirely unscathed in spite of the earthquake.

"You're here!" Edeyn exclaimed. She stumbled as she tried, too quickly, to get down from the rubble pile. The two women collided in a hug and Edeyn wept again as Sonny held her.

"I'm here," Sonny repeated quietly, stroking Edeyn's hair.

A wave of warmth flowed through Edeyn as they embraced. She pulled away reluctantly, placing her palms against Sonny's face, speechless as their eyes connected.

"How are—" Edeyn started, breaking the silence. She meant to ask how Sonny was alive and unscathed but she couldn't find the words.

Sonny reached up, gently taking Edeyn's hands in her own, lowering their arms together. "I've become quite good at surviving library-related disasters," she said.

Edeyn belted out a laugh, caught off guard by the comment.

Sonny glanced over her shoulder at the ruins, then back at Edeyn. "Where's Palan?"

Edeyn stepped back again and dropped her gaze. "I don't know. We parted ways. He said he wanted to go home."

Sonny tilted her head and frowned. "He said he wanted to go home?"

Edeyn nodded, confirming her own words.

"I wonder how he planned to do that—?" Sonny mused aloud.

"I don't know. But he didn't want my help finding the ship anymore. The whole purpose of my joining you was to help you find your ship," Edeyn explained.

Sonny made a low humming noise before patting Edeyn's arm in a comforting gesture. "We should perhaps see what we can do to help here. There's work to be done once the citizens assemble. Not everything here was destroyed."

"We?" Edeyn questioned in disbelief. She had always liked Sonny but she did not expect her to want to stay together now that the purpose of her guidance had been made redundant.

"Yes. You and I. I'm sure I can be of use with my *touch*," Sonny said.

"You... you want me to stay with you?" Edeyn asked in a mixture of confusion and hope.

"Of course," Sonny said. "Neither you or I have any home to return to. Why not stay and help these folks rebuild theirs?"

Edeyn smiled and tears flowed again, this time with relief. She was a little embarrassed to cry in front of anyone else, but she knew Sonny wouldn't hold her tears against her.

"Come," Sonny said, grabbing Edeyn's hand, taking the lead. She guided Edeyn through the bewildered crowd into the city square. From there she led them to a quieter street corner under an awning and made a space for them to rest. Edeyn stared vacantly as she stood, barely able to absorb their surroundings. There were many others doing the same. Across the street, she could easily see the city square. People seemed to be making their way to the open space after some of the initial confusion died down.

Edeyn turned to Sonny. As she crouched to help her friend unload items from her pack, she froze again. *Pain pierced her temples as the feeling of cold, dark water surrounded her once more.*

She gasped for air, eyes suddenly clearing to see sky above. Nova's face appeared clearly in her mind's eye. This time she saw him holding hands with the curly haired child, walking along city streets.

Edeyn stumbled back, blinking in confusion as the *vision* released her abruptly. Sonny's concerned face appeared above her.

She felt a gentle touch on her shoulder flooding her body with warmth and calm again. Her breathing slowed peacefully as she accepted Sonny's healing *touch*. Pushing herself up from the pavement, she gingerly propped herself against her palms pressed flat to the earth.

"You need to eat something," Sonny suggested.

Edeyn shook her head firmly. "No, no, it's not that. It's some… it's something else," she said. She squeezed her eyes shut, wishing she could see more details of the *vision*, but none appeared.

"Eat. Tell me. But eat," Sonny urged as she handed Edeyn a satchel of dried fruit.

Edeyn forced herself to chew but she could barely taste the food, too focused on searching her mind for more details from her *vision*. "It's Nova," she hesitated.

"Another vision?" Sonny asked, prompting her to continue.

"I think they're alive," Edeyn responded. Her throat constricted with emotion. "They're alive," she choked out again through sobs before whispering one final time, "They're alive."

Sonny sat back and stared off into the distance, nodding slowly. "Where did you *see* them?"

"I don't know," Edeyn replied, unable to stop the flow of tears. "The *vision* was so quick. There was water, like I saw before. But they came up for air. At first, I saw them in a boat, and then I saw them holding hands walking along paved stone."

She stood abruptly, spinning as she scanned the crowd before dashing across the street, her heart racing.

"What's wrong?" Sonny inquired when she caught up to her, moments later.

"I can't explain it," Edeyn said, shaking her head. "He's here. I can *sense* him. I *feel* his presence." She raced forward again before turning herself in circles, certain Nova's face would light with recognition as he emerged from the crowd. Despite the overwhelming feeling that he was nearby, Edeyn couldn't see him. "I know he's here," she said, weakly.

Nova's face flashed once more in her vision and she saw him smile. Words floated to her ears sounding both far away and as close as a whisper. "Follow," he breathed.

She saw footsteps in the sand along the beach, a flash of stars, two constellations in particular—the Castle and the Knight. Nova and Melly held hands. There was a flash of footprints in the sand again, then shining, black metal panels covering the dented hull of a spaceship. Energy hummed along the ship's surface and seemed to transfer into Edeyn's body.

Finally, Edeyn looked back at Sonny, "I don't understand," she said. "It's like he's standing right next to me, but I can't see him anywhere. I... think I *see* his spaceship."

Sonny sucked in her lip, appearing thoughtful. "What did you say Palan said before he left?"

"He wanted to go home," Edeyn replied without thinking.

The two women stared at each other as realization dawned on them both.

"Palan has no home," Sonny said, voicing their thoughts.

"He knows where the ship is. He's going to take Nova's ship," Edeyn exclaimed.

Sonny hiked her pack up properly onto her back. "We need to find the ship," she said. "Quickly."

"But Nova..." Edeyn said, hesitating.

"You said you felt his energy. You *know* he's alive. Try again. You'll find him," Sonny said confidently.

Edeyn tried to push past the rising feeling of despair within her. "I *don't* know," she said. She was not confident in pinpointing Nova in such a crowded space. The plethora of energies within the city was overwhelming even when she was not fully focusing on it.

She allowed her *sense* to search, feeling along the sides of buildings, bumping into people along the streets. She knew she'd recognize Nova's energy immediately if she encountered it. There was a feeling that accompanied it unlike any other she ever come across. It was as if her soul and his were somehow connected through multiple lifetimes.

Just as Edeyn was about to give up, the same *vision* repeated. This time, she was ready to examine every detail that presented itself.

Seeing through his eyes, Edeyn followed the beach holding Melly's hand. They wandered into the sparse trees beyond Oleress. A steady hum connected her heartbeat to his. It was like a magnet, drawing Nova closer to it. A flash of dark metal in front of the sheer front of the mountains. It had to be Nova's spaceship, calling him back towards it. Nova's words were clearer this time, insistent.

"He says to follow the beach," she told Sonny.

If Sonny were skeptical about the information, she didn't reveal it in her expression. "All right then. We'd better get going."

Edeyn smiled as her heart raced. She was still deeply afraid, but the thought of seeing Nova's face again reignited a fiery hope. She grabbed Sonny's hand, holding tightly as they made their way out of the city.

Chapter Thirty-Three
WRECKAGE

As Nova and Melly approached the mountains, the terrain grew more difficult to traverse. Slowly but surely, they pressed onward in the direction Corsa gave them. Their destination was a small city called Grey Rock. Nova knew of it from books and maps about the isles, but he would never have known how to find it without Corsa's support. He followed her vague instructions with more faith than certainty. All she told them as they fled Oleress was to stay along the shoreline.

After a while, Melly resisted walking any further. He had to carry her on his back, impeding their progress. She was clearly not interested in complying with more travel after all the chaos they already endured.

A flutter in his chest stopped Nova in his tracks. He trudged over to lean against a tree where he could catch his breath. The little girl slid to the ground as he pressed his palm against the rough tree bark to regain his stamina.

"Just for a moment, sweetheart," Nova said, his heart rate speeding after the exertion. He pressed a hand against his chest, willing his body to calm down before he lost consciousness. He gulped water from his canteen, refreshed despite its unpleasant, warm temperature.

A hum of electricity surged through his nerves as his heart fluttered again. It was as if his body were a live energy weapon.

"What's wrong?" Melly asked, grabbing Nova's fingers with both her small hands.

Nova forced a smile in return. Though puzzled, he didn't want to alarm Melly who had already lost more than she ever should have. "I'm ok, dove. I just need to catch my breath. We've been walking a long time and you're getting so big!"

Melly stared at him, her large eyes woeful but trusting. Following Nova's instruction, she sat, leaning against the tree trunk.

A sudden tug in the middle of Nova's chest sent him to his knees as all the air left his lungs. Panic rose within him, briefly tormented by the memory of nearly drowning. He doubled over, unable to fully stifle a groan. Nova slid to the ground against the solid tree trunk as he grasped his chest in pain.

Melly crawled up to him and ducked under his arm. Kneeling tall, she placed her hands on Nova's face. "What's wrong?" she asked again, insistent.

Nova struggled to answer with words. A *vision* flashed in his mind. It wasn't like when he used his *sight*. There was nothing he could *see* physically with his eyes. Instead, a picture floated into his mind like a dream.

It was his ship, half buried in leaves. He saw the mountains rising above it in the background, and the spacecraft with its flickering lights, externally intact but badly damaged. The image faded as quickly as it arrived, but it was enough.

Nova rose again suddenly, shielding his eyes with his palm, scanning the distance ahead of them with his enhanced *sight*. He *saw* a wooden sign at the foot of a narrow mountain pass. The spaceship would be partially hidden from view as long as Sonny's *touch* illusions were still in place after the crash.

She had left an energetic signature on both the ship and on Nova. It was meant to act as a homing beacon, designed to pulsate when Nova neared the vessel, provided that part of the ship had not been damaged. Nova had felt its activation in Oleress but it was far stronger now.

A loud cry escaped Melly, startling Nova. He could see she was distressed with his sudden change in demeanor. The fluttering in his chest pulsed again, but now that he understood what was causing it, it didn't weaken him as it had the first time.

"Don't worry, my dear," he reassured. "We might just be a lot closer to home than we thought."

Grey Rock could wait a little longer. If Nova could feel his spaceship nearby, he wanted to find it. He only hoped it would still be undisturbed wherever it had landed.

"No home," Melly said quietly.

Nova pressed his lips together tightly. Her words reminded him how much he himself missed his home, and he imagined how much more difficult it must be for a little one.

"I know. Not Asayouga. It won't be like that again. But we might just find a piece of it soon if we keep going," Nova said.

Melly shook her head in refusal.

"Do you remember the spaceship?" Nova asked as he crouched down to Melly's eye level. Of course she would remember flying into space. It wasn't something anyone could forget. But so many events had unfolded since then, he himself could barely remember everything that happened. It must have been incredibly confusing for a child.

"It's gone," she said simply.

"We thought it was but maybe not," Nova said. "When your dad and I built that ship, we created it so I could find it again if we ever lost it." Nova pointed to his chest. "I can feel it right now. In here."

Melly frowned and stared at Nova's chest. "You can feel it?"

"Yes," Nova replied. It's sending a signal to my body. I can tell it's nearby. Do you remember playing Seek and Find with Uncle Fenwick?"

Melly's face lit up in recognition and she giggled. "He likes to hide in the tall grass."

Nova smiled. "Sometimes it was hard to find him. What happened then?"

"My dad helped me!" Melly said.

Nova nodded in response. "Yes. How did he help you?" He could clearly picture the scene on the grassy hill where they'd built the ship.

"He told me 'warmer' and 'colder,'" Melly answered.

"Exactly. It's just like that. The ship makes my heart flutter. It tells me when I'm getting hotter or colder, and I can feel that we're getting warmer now."

Melly stood up and ran ahead as if she could hunt down the ship herself. She looked perplexed as she turned back to Nova. "I don't see it," she said, sounding doubtful.

"I know," Nova responded. "But we will find it. It might be hard to *see*, even with my extra *sight*. Can you *hear* anything? Remember how the ship hummed?"

Melly tilted her head as if to *listen* more intently. "I'm not sure. The ocean is loud. Are you sure you can find it?" she asked.

Nova was not at all certain he could recover the ship, but he didn't want to let the child know. "We will do our best," he responded, which was the closest he could come to the truth without upsetting her.

"Ok," Melly agreed.

Nova sat down again and invited Melly to join him. "Let's rest first, eh? I'm getting hungry," he said.

"Me too," Melly said as she joined him. She dug into his pack and pulled out small, wrapped food rations.

Nova found himself missing hot food more than ever. He was grateful for the pre-packaged items they had, but it wasn't as satisfying as sitting down to a freshly cooked meal.

After they consumed their meal and rested, Nova gathered the few belongings they had once more. He knelt down, allowing Melly to scramble up onto his back. As he stood, he hoisted the child higher, tucking her legs securely under his arms.

"Comfy?" he asked.

Melly leaned her head against the back of Nova's neck, hugging him close. She didn't respond with words, though she had already spoken more than she had in a long time. Nova accepted her gesture as agreement and he resumed their trek once more.

It soon became too rocky to follow the shoreline closely and Nova found himself staggering in places as the terrain grew steeper. The extra pattering within his chest, close to his heart, became more and more pronounced. He did his best to adjust to the feeling.

The pulsing rhythm of the ship's beacon became steadier as they got closer. The sun lowered on the horizon, illuminating the sky with bright colors. They wouldn't have much time left to explore. As daylight faded, Nova found a small copse of trees to use for temporary shelter.

He let Melly down from his back, instructing her to look for sticks for a campfire while he worked to protect the space with his flimsy *sight* illusions. He pulled a veil of light around them, using his *sight* to camouflage them against the backdrop of trees. Although imperfect given his limited skills, the illusion would help prevent immediate detection.

For a brief moment, Nova reflected on how far he'd come since Asayouga. He had limited survival skills before leaving their homeland. Now he easily gathered nearby stones, laying them out in a circle around their sleeping space. Once the circle was complete, he used his energy to create a wall of deflection, using the rocks and sticks as elements to connect the illusory *vision* together.

It was far from perfect, but it would buy them time should anyone stumble across them in the night. Nova kept a watchful eye on Melly as he worked. Once he set up their camp, he called her in.

Excited, she ran to him with a handful of sticks.

He smiled as he examined what she'd brought, proud she had learned what to look for and also saddened the circumstances made her learning necessary.

After building their fire, Nova helped Melly settle in for the night. He tucked her in with a blanket, grateful they had more than when they escaped captivity in Tskela. He kissed Melly's forehead and sat next to her as she fell asleep.

Only then did he lean back to stare up at the stars as they became more visible in the darkening sky. He could still see the Knight and the Castle. He could still find Nayeli's star.

"At least I can see you again from here," Nova whispered to the speck of light.

"I could always see you, my love," was the reply Nova heard in his mind, but he was surprised to find the voice sounded like a mixture of both Nayeli's and Edeyn's. A wave of peace washed over him at the remembrance of Edeyn's melodious cadence. He fell asleep with a smile on his face.

Chapter Thirty-Four

PALAN

Palan wiped sweat from his forehead as he plowed through the jungle to the mountains. The trees grew sparser as he approached the steep face of rock. He traveled at a quick pace, refusing to slow down. There was no time to waste if he wanted to find Nova's ship before Fenwick did.

He chewed his lip as he reflected on the spaceship in Oleress. Palan wondered how the white stone city obtained the technology, and if the Tskelans believed it was he who double crossed them.

Palan passed the point of no return long ago. Though he never intended it, he alone was now responsible for the destruction of *two* cities. Guilt weighed heavily on his mind as he reflected on the catastrophic consequences of his actions. It was too much to bear.

Now that his daughter—the only person he still cared for—was gone, Palan saw no reason to continue pretending he wasn't a villain. In Asayouga, he justified selling knowledge to the Tskelans, reminding himself the money would allow him to provide for Sapphira, perhaps atoning for the mistakes he'd made in their relationship while also supporting their child.

Palan believed he could control which information he fed to Tskela and it would be enough. But when they discovered he'd held back the keys that would have led to the development of space travel, they retaliated. His home and everyone he loved were gone because of his decisions. He thought he could gain the benefits of sharing details with Tskela without betraying Asayouga. He failed.

Oleress, too, was devastated by Palan's actions, though he never could have known the research facility was filled with traps. Still, if he hadn't been so intent on following Fenwick, he might have avoided setting off a small earthquake.

Perhaps Tskela would accept him back if he had something useful to offer them. Maybe he could somehow redeem himself by proving his loyalty. But he needed real leverage, and for that he needed Nova's spaceship. A complete blueprint of the ship, proof that it could launch, might be enough for Palan to regain favor.

Although Oleress was much closer than Tskela, Palan couldn't picture himself staying there after he'd destroyed it. What if someone realized he was the one who set off the traps? He couldn't afford another lethal mistake.

Aside from himself, only Fen remained who knew the truth behind Asayouga's destruction. Palan found himself growling softly in his throat once more at the thought of Fen. He was supposed to be dead. He wasn't supposed to be a problem anymore.

But there he was, just like a cat with nine lives, still stalking Palan for his crimes. If Fen found the spaceship first, Palan knew he could never redeem himself.

He'd been calculating the ship's trajectory ever since their crash landing on the beach. By his estimation, he knew he had to be close now.

Navigating by the stars was second nature after a lifetime of work and study. He could rely on their placements even if he could not rely on the company of those around him. It was good to be free of Edeyn, at least. He could hardly bear to look at her since her *vision* of Melly and Nova's deaths.

He'd never meant to be the catalyst to so much destruction. His heartbreak over Sapphira was bad enough. His own ego had gotten in the way of their relationship.

Palan owed Sapphira so much. She never deserved the way he'd treated her. He knew he was never much of a father to Melly, but he loved his child. *Their* child. The guilt he felt over his daughter's death threatened to choke him.

Palan had done everything he could to provide a better life for Melly and her mother. Now they were both casualties instead, while he lived on, routinely responsible for the decimation of cities, of more lives than he could count.

Asayouga. Sapphira. Melvene. Oleress. Nova. Nayeli. The names repeated in his head. So many souls lost. His choices killed them all.

The only person apart from himself who knew the extent of his treachery was Fenwick. If only Fen had died properly at Chickadee River, Palan could have atoned for his mistakes without facing the wrath of others.

Palan leaned forward as he trudged up a steep incline. The mountain's terrain was far more challenging than he expected. He halted to take a swig of water from the canteen he still carried with him. The vessel was enchanted with *touch* magic to filter salty sea water—a gift as he trekked across the unfamiliar island alone.

Road markers indicated a village ahead, but Palan didn't want to detour too far from the shoreline.

As his breathing slowed to a regular pace, a shimmer of faint blue fabric sticking out of the sand caught Palan's eye. He nudged the dirt aside with his boot, uncovering a small hair ribbon. As he knelt to pick it up, the *scent* of straw and Melly's beloved old rag doll flooded his perception. His gut twisted in agony at a sudden memory of his daughter.

~~~

Palan pushed open the front door. After a long day on Observation Point, he'd decided not to go out for a drink that evening. He was trying to make better choices. Heavy feelings were his usual downfall for bad habits—drinking, carousing, gambling. But that day he wasn't looking to escape. He wanted to show up as a father, as if he lived there and could be part of Melly's life as often as he wished.

The truth was, seeing Sapphira's disapproval every time he showed up at her door created far too much shame within him to endure on a daily basis. He resented her inability to move on for the sake of their child. Yet he knew he owed her something. *The least he could do was provide her with monetary stability.*

That night was different. That night, he wanted to face his shame, even if it were painful.

Melly sat on her mother's lap, giggling. As soon as she saw Palan, she squealed with delight, colliding with his legs as she ran into him.

Palan avoided Sapphira's gaze and instead smiled down at Melly, patting her head. He crouched to the child's level and presented her with a rag doll, perfectly crafted in her likeness. He had custom ordered it for her.

Her delighted squeals made Palan smile, a fleeting glimmer of belonging filling his heart. Her joy could not erase his past, the memories of his own thoughtless words and actions that haunted him hourly. But it helped him forget for a moment.

~~~

Palan pushed aside a wave of grief. If he allowed himself to weep, he would never stop. It would consume him entirely. How could he have failed at the one task he vowed never to falter in—providing for Melly; protecting her as long as he lived? He had once more failed to deliver on his promises. Palan knew there was nothing redeemable left within him. He hurled the dirt-caked hair ribbon as far from him as he could.

In lieu of redemption, Palan hoped he could bargain his way into something passing for a life. An existence of hard labor, perhaps. All he needed was the ship. That would be his leverage to remain within Tskela.

If it went wrong, they would kill him. A fate which he knew he deserved. But if it went well, he could devote himself to work which might atone in some small way for his actions. It was the only thing left to do, apart from walking into the sea to drown himself.

The thought did tempt him. But then he would certainly die a traitor, and if there was any way to absolve himself of that title, he had to at least try. If he didn't make it in time, at least the sea would not fail him.

Palan continued. He made an educated guess at where the ship might be, based on what little he could pick up of its *scent*. Pinpointing it exactly was more complicated, and he knew he might not be able to see it immediately with the camouflage Nova and Sonny had given it.

Uncovering its precise location would be a true test of his tracking skills. The amulet would provide him with some ability to *see* beyond the illusions as well, but the crew provided little cloaking when it came to the spaceship's *scent*. Palan counted on this one advantage.

In order for his *scent* to be useful, it needed a link—a *whiff* of the item so he could follow its trail. Palan was well-acquainted with the ship's *scent* after taking part in its construction. He couldn't forget it easily. It would be harder for others gifted with the *scent* to find the crashed vessel without a link.

The specially-crafted metal scent *wafted* occasionally to his awareness. Palan pulled the amulet into his grasp and closed his eyes to concentrate on all the *senses* rushing in at once. The world around him came alive. He *heard* every creature living in the jungle, the ocean life layered beneath the waves, even the shifting clouds. But there was nothing that would help him locate the ship. He opened his eyes again, scanning with his enhanced *sight,* but it revealed nothing further.

Palan sighed in frustration. He considered waiting for nightfall so he could use the stars to navigate more acutely, but he didn't have time to lose.

While he debated his next move, the sound of distant voices reached his ears. He grasped his amulet as he focused on the *sound* energy within it so that he could *hear* more clearly.

Palan scurried behind some trees, pressing his belly to the ground so as not to risk being seen. He grasped the stone again and focused.

"What's wrong?" asked a little voice.

The voice was familiar. Palan felt hot prickles across his body as he recognized it as his daughter's. Quickly, he dismissed the thought. Melly drowned, he reminded himself. She wasn't coming back. He must have imagined the resemblance to her voice.

Another voice answered, but it was muffled by ocean waves and wind. Palan couldn't make out a distinct answer let alone who the voice belonged to from his distance.

There was silence. Hearing nothing more, he released the stone from his grasp and sat back. More than anything, he wished the child's voice really was Melly's. But he knew it couldn't be true. He chewed the inside of his lip as he contemplated what to do next. If there were travelers nearby, he definitely couldn't wait for nightfall. The longer he lingered in one spot, the greater the chance there was of him being seen, or of Fenwick finding the ship ahead of him.

Resolved, Palan stood to continue his search. He focused once more on the one ability he knew he could rely on, especially as it was enhanced further with the stone.

"Come on, Palan. Where is that ship," he asked himself out loud. He waited as the many *scents* of the beach, air, sand, sea, foliage and animals sorted themselves out in his mind.

At last, he could pinpoint it. The unmistakable *scent* of metal panels Palan himself helped to design stood apart from the natural surroundings. He followed the *whiff*, pausing frequently to confirm he remained on the right track.

It was slow progress, but at least it was progress. As the sun sank below the horizon, Palan knew he was closer than ever. At one point, he thought he caught Melly's *scent* again. There had always been a soft, distinct aroma to her hair.

"You're imagining things," Palan told himself, shoving the thought aside. He needed to concentrate on finding the ship.

As night descended, stars appeared. Palan paused to examine the sky. He pulled out a knife to carve calculations into the side of a fallen tree, glancing up repeatedly to reorientate himself. He had to be close. The *scent* grew stronger and the alignment of the constellations reassured him he was still on the trail.

Melly's *scent* reached him again, this time feeling too real to dismiss. Palan allowed his mind to be distracted for a moment. He leaned against a tree and sniffed the air, this time filtering out the metal and searching instead for his daughter's signature.

Palan froze. Not only did he locate Melly's *scent* easily, he found Nova's as well. They were still together. And alive. He grabbed the pendant in a hurry, listening again for their voices. Their words were more distinct this time and there was no mistaking them. He would never forget the sound of his daughter's laugh as long as he lived.

He shoved his hand between his teeth and bit down hard, fighting off tears as relief flooded through him. Palan hated how vulnerable and exposed he felt when crying. But how could he not? His child was alive, and close by!

The power of his relief quickly transformed to rage. Edeyn lied. Had she fabricated the drowning completely? Palan's mind raced, considering all the other possible ways she could have betrayed him. He needed no convincing: He had been fooled by an actress. It wouldn't be the first time, though Edeyn seemed to him to be a cut above in her convincing masquerade. Infuriated, Palan balled his fists, digging his nails into his palms.

At the sound of a twig snap, Palan whirled around. He squinted into the darkness while clambering for the amulet. He curled his fingers once more around the stone and called upon the *touch* for a light to guide him.

As he held out his palm, filled with a luminous orb, a flash caught in Palan's peripheral vision. Any trepidation he felt at the sudden noise vanished as he smiled, realizing what had reflected the light. It was the shining, black metal of Nova's spaceship.

Chapter Thirty-Five
OF SPIES AND LIES

Edeyn and Sonny kept a brisk pace on their journey to Grey Rock. Sonny searched for Nova's and Melly's energy with her *touch* as best she could, hoping she would get a hint of them before long.

Edeyn's *visions* confirmed they were both still alive, but she couldn't tell Sonny details about where they'd find them. She tried to get Edeyn to describe the constellations she saw in her vision, but since Edeyn knew very little about astronomy, it was difficult for her to describe. Sonny did her best to estimate based on what she told her.

Sonny allowed Edeyn to take the lead, as she knew her travel companion understood the terrain much better. She had never been much of a traveler. Instead, she preferred collecting knowledge, and organizing information—quiet, solitary activities that didn't involve much trekking through the wilderness.

But Sonny could also hold her own when she needed to. The challenge now was helping Edeyn focus on reuniting them with Nova while staying alert to signs of Palan who she suspected would re-appear at an inconvenient moment.

With her *senses* on full alert, Sonny quietly searched the background for signs of Palan's energetic signature. He often kept his emotions walled away which meant there was a lot of intensity kept close to his body. Sonny had never found it a challenge to locate that intensity. He changed the atmosphere of a building just by being in it.

Some people lit up a room with their presence, but Palan did the opposite. He seemed entirely unaware of himself and the effect he had on others.

It was a beautiful day. Sonny enjoyed basking in the warm, refreshing air drifting in the open water. "How far away did you say this village was?" she asked.

Edeyn made a noise indicating Sonny's voice startled her. "I'm sorry, what did you say?" she said, sounding distant.

Sonny patiently repeated her question.

"Oh," Edeyn said. "Well... I'm not sure they're in the village."

"But that's the direction we are taking," Sonny prompted.

"Yes. It's a full day's journey. We will need to stop somewhere to rest for the night," Edeyn responded.

Sonny nodded. She hoped they would find the ship before Palan did. In general, she didn't like to reveal how much information she knew. She knew far more about who the man really was than anyone else did but she kept it to herself. People could be unpredictable. It seemed safer to hold onto secrets as much as possible.

As she reflected on Palan, her mind drifted to old memories about how he treated those he claimed to love most.

~~~

Sonny pushed a mug of tea into Sapphira's trembling hands and watched her from across the table, keeping quiet to hold space for the other woman's grief.

"I don't know what I'm going to do," she said through stifled tears. Her eyes met Sonny's in a silent plea for hopeful news.

With a wan smile, Sonny patted her friend's hand. "One step at a time, my dear. For now, drink your tea." Sonny always used her touch to bring out the healing properties in food and drinks. The tea would not cure Sapphira's problem, but it would help calm her enough to make a plan.

"I don't know any of the steps. I can't do this myself! If I was going to do this, I was supposed to have help. You know he won't help me," Sapphira said, her voice strained with worry.

Sonny could not tell her she was wrong. She wasn't sure Sapphira ever told him about the pregnancy, and she didn't want to appear unsupportive by asking. It wouldn't have changed anything. Palan thrived off attention and thrills. He'd acted on his own impulses and his choices weren't Sapphira's fault.

Sapphira was beautiful. Her light blue eyes combined with her dark hair were striking to everyone who saw her. But Sapphira had nothing Palan wanted, nothing that could elevate his status or make him proud to show off. Sonny knew he wouldn't sacrifice his time to help with an infant. He would consider his work more important.

Sonny was very glad she'd never cared about the opinions of others. It seemed like a heavy burden to have to consider everyone else's views about herself, when none of them understood her the way she understood herself.

She'd never understood the games people seemed to play for power, wealth and status. Sonny loved her books. She loved to learn and consider other perspectives and she never thought the information she knew, in any way, gave her more power than anyone else. She couldn't relate to people like Palan who used every bit of knowledge in an insatiable quest for status.

Palan was objectively attractive: he was tall, his features were pleasant and he had that slow, sneaky smile that hid a thousand secrets. Though Sonny was not attracted to men, she could appreciate Palan's aesthetics, but his arrogant energy made her wary of him.

Logically, she understood why Sapphira fell for him, though Sonny could not directly relate to the feelings herself.

"What if he runs away when I tell him?" Sapphira asked, breaking down into sobs.

Sonny thought he probably would. Palan wasn't likely to handle the news well at all. Out loud she encouraged Sapphira to drink her tea. "There's no point dwelling on what-ifs. You will have support, even if it isn't from him," she said before patting Sapphira's hand again. "Please, drink some tea. It will help."

With shaking hands and tears streaming down her face, Sapphira lifted the mug to her lips and sipped. The two women were silent as she took steady, even gulps of the fruity herbal mixture.

"When she is here—" Sapphira started.

"She?" Sonny interrupted, overcome with curiosity.

Sapphira smiled a watery smile as she answered. "That's just what I feel. Her name will be Melvene."

"A lovely name," Sonny agreed. She waited for Sapphira to add to her statement.

"It was my great grandmother's name. She was a strong woman—"

Sonny nodded again, waiting, again, for Sapphira to finish her thought.

"When she's here, will you please make sure she's looked after if... if anything should happen to me?" Sapphira asked. She chewed her lip as she looked at Sonny. "I know that's a huge thing to ask of you..."

Sonny leaned back in her chair, stunned as she contemplated the unexpected question. She'd never been great at hiding her strong emotions. "Of course! I will do my best. But nothing will happen to you, I'm sure," she stammered.

"Maybe Palan would but—" Sapphira began and trailed off.

"In case he doesn't, I will," Sonny reassured her. She drummed her fingers against the tabletop for a moment before adding, "And even if he does, I will keep watch over her as best I can."

"Thank you," Sapphira said. "That helps. A lot." She smiled at Sonny and resumed drinking her tea in silence.

~~~

The memory faded and Sonny returned to her vigilant search for Palan. Her neck and shoulders grew stiff with the tension of continuous alert. With only the sound of their own breathing taking up space between them, Edeyn and Sonny trekked in relative silence.

She felt instinctively protective of Edeyn. Even though she knew the woman could easily take care of herself and her own needs, there was a gentle innocence about her. She always seemed to believe the best in people, even Palan.

Sonny found Edeyn's strength admirable. Even after Palan cast her aside in Oleress, she didn't let it stop her from taking action.

It could not have been easy for Edeyn to keep her unusual *sense* a secret for so long. Sonny empathized; she was no stranger to the weight of keeping secrets. She understood the fear of being found out, the underlying trepidation at the prospect of being rejected just for being who she was. She imagined Edeyn carried a similar burden.

They marched through a small cluster of trees onto the rocky shoreline. The terrain grew more treacherous the closer they got to the mountains.

Edeyn halted abruptly. She chewed her lip as she scanned the horizon. "We're going to have to return to the main road. Getting over all of this safely will take ages," she explained.

"Of course," Sonny agreed, "Should we head back to the road?"

Edeyn nodded. They hadn't gone far before Edeyn gasped, holding up her hand for Sonny to wait.

"What is it?" She asked warily. Sonny shielded her eyes with her palm once more, surveying the horizon, but she couldn't see what Edeyn saw.

Edeyn's eyes widened in fear as she looked back at Sonny. "I can't tell. I *saw*... something. But I don't think it's happened yet. We need to hurry."

"What did you see?" Sonny asked.

"I *saw* the ship but—" Edeyn hesitated. She hurried down the road ahead as she continued, "There's no time. We need to find Nova quickly. It may already be too late."

Sonny tried her best to keep up with her but she was running out of stamina. Her legs were not as long as Edeyn's and after a lifetime of indoor living, she was not conditioned for long distance journeys on foot. Her frustration grew until she could no longer stifle it.

"Please, you must tell me what you *saw*," Sonny said, as she trudged uphill, attempting to match Edeyn's pace.

Edeyn did not pause or slow her steps. "It's too hard to explain," she said. "Even I don't really understand what it was."

"*Who* did you see?" Sonny asked, the question bursting out of her more forcefully than she had intended.

Edeyn shook her head. "I'm not sure. It was so quick. It was all in shadows, really. I don't know. I think Nova may be in danger if we don't reach him in time."

Sonny pressed her lips into a thin line as she thought about Palan. "Lead on, then," she said, though her direction was unnecessary.

The journey continued in a blur. Sonny's steps slowed eventually as the muscles in her legs grew fatigued from the rapid walking and climbing. She clutched her side as pain twisted her belly.

Unable to continue, Sonny grasped Edeyn's bicep, silently urging her to wait for her to catch her breath. As she sucked in the cool, evening breeze, a familiar energy washed over her in a warm wave.

"They're close," Sonny huffed through uneven breaths.

"Nova?" Edeyn asked, her voice catching in her throat with obvious excitement.

Sonny closed her eyes to focus on each presence she felt. Darkness had already begun to fall, and she would soon need to rely on her *touch* to provide a light source to help guide them. It was doubly important to be precise in their movements now.

She did *sense* Nova and Melly. The child seemed frightened while Nova's energy felt determined. But she *sensed* other energy ahead. They were not alone.

The beacon of the spaceship also warmed Sonny's breast as the beacon within her activated. "Nova is ahead," Sonny commented, "But be cautious. I don't think they're the only people nearby."

Both Edeyn and Sonny quieted their movements as much as they could, trying their best to make progress as the darkness deepened.

Sonny careened forward as her foot snagged on a protruding tree stump. She felt the wind knocked out of her as she landed face first in the dirt.

Edeyn's scream seemed to pierce Sonny's soul. She sat up in time to see a bolt of light streaking through the darkening sky ahead. The unmistakable hiss of an energy pistol blasted into a nearby tree, igniting a small fire that extinguished itself seconds later.

Sonny felt the familiar presence looming over her before she saw who it was. She squinted through the darkness at a familiar face.

"Oh, thank the stars!" Sonny exclaimed, breathless with relief as she recognized Nova.

"Sonny! It's really you!" Nova replied. He half wept and half laughed as he fell on top of Sonny, hugging her and clinging to her hair.

She smiled as she patted Nova's head. "I missed you too," she said.

Nova offered his hand to Sonny when he stood again. She grasped it firmly, using it to steady herself as she rose to her feet. As she swiped at her clothes to clear away the accumulated dirt and foliage she was interrupted by a squeeze around her legs.

Sonny's smile widened as she lifted Melly onto her hip and held her close. "Hello, baby. You're safe," she whispered to the child who whimpered and clung to her.

Sonny turned to speak to Nova again but stopped short when she saw him standing, frozen, his fingers at his side, staring into the darkness. She followed his gaze to Edeyn who stared back, equally frozen in place.

Chapter Thirty-Six

REUNION

Edeyn's heart was in her throat. She rubbed her eyes, hardly daring to believe what she saw clearly in front of her. After witnessing so much of his journey through her *visions*, the actual reality of Nova in front of her felt like a dream. Simultaneously elated to see him and terrified she might be hallucinating, Edeyn resisted the urge to run into his arms.

Nova moved first. He raced to Edeyn and cupped her face in his hands, pressing his nose against hers.

Edeyn's eyes filled with tears as she succumbed to her emotions. She grabbed Nova's face and kissed him deeply. Or he kissed her. She couldn't tell as their lips pressed hungrily together. Nova's hands trailed along her back and waist as she clung to his hair as if her life depended on it.

Her spine tingled as Nova caressed her through every kiss. Finally, she leaned her forehead against Nova's chin, tangling her fingers in his hair as they gazed into each other's eyes. Edeyn imagined if she looked away, she would lose him again, and she didn't think she could handle going through it a second time. It had been a heavy journey to begin with.

"I saw you drown," she whispered at last, dropping her gaze.

Nova's eyebrows raised in surprise. "Well..." he said, trailing off.

"Well?" she prompted him to continue.

"We almost did," he responded softly, smiling as he gently rubbed the small of Edeyn's back.

He didn't ask how she'd known. Edeyn was not accustomed to being believed immediately. People were often suspicious or even angry when she revealed what she knew, so she always kept her *knowings* to herself. But Nova believed her. And he didn't seem frightened at all.

Neither of them pulled away, holding each other in the perfect stillness of their reunion. It amazed Edeyn to realize Nova must have missed her just as much as she missed him. She wondered if Nova thought of her as unceasingly as she thought of him, too.

In a way, she felt connected to his energy since the moment they met. It never seemed to leave her, even when she was not consciously thinking of him. Perhaps it was possible he had experienced the same.

Edeyn embraced Nova and nuzzled her face against his neck. "I'm glad you didn't. I thought I'd lost you," she said.

"I thought so too," Nova responded, "And I couldn't stand it."

"Your ship is nearby, if my *visions* have been correct," Edeyn offered.

Nova smoothed Edeyn's hair with his hands. "I can feel it," he affirmed.

Edeyn looked up at him, full of curiosity. She knew Nova didn't *sense* things the same way she did and she wondered what his words meant. Was he having *visions* too?

Apparently reading Edeyn's unspoken question, Nova gently detached himself from her and opened his shirt, tracing his finger along a tattoo above his heart.

Edeyn examined the small, inky image before pressing her palm against it. "It's beautiful," she said, though she still didn't fully understand how it connected to Nova's words.

"Sonny created it with her *touch*. It warms when I'm near the ship. It's very close, though I haven't *seen* it yet with my eyes. Perhaps in the morning," Nova explained.

Edeyn glanced over her shoulder at Sonny who smiled in acknowledgment. She grabbed Nova's hand and pulled him to sit in the grass before gesturing to Sonny and Melly.

The four of them settled onto the ground where moments of silence passed as they basked in the glow of their reunion. Eventually, words spilled out, tripping over each other as they all tried to speak at once.

Even Melly participated in the sharing of stories as she held onto Sonny without letting go. Sonny didn't seem to mind.

Eventually, Edeyn's eyes grew heavy with exhaustion. As Nova laid back, Edeyn rested her head against his shoulder and held her arm around him closely, feeling safe calm at last.

As she succumbed to sleep, images filtered into her dreams.

She saw a flash of shining, black metal peeking out from beneath the underbrush of the jungle. Two shadows rose tall against the mountain behind them. She couldn't make out who the human forms belonged to, instead seeing only darkened silhouettes. Their shapes stretched taller and taller before zooming toward each other.

When they collided, a spark of fire rose from the middle and the jungle lit with flames. She floated safely above the blaze but watched as flames stretched their molten fingers closer and closer to Nova, asleep on the ground.

A blast of gunfire jolted Edeyn from her sleep. She leapt to her feet, hand automatically moving to her weapons before remembering most of them were missing.

Nova stood beside her, confused as he emerged from his own slumber and regained connection with the waking world.

Edeyn turned to him, eyes wide with fear. "You heard that too? I can't have been imagining it," she said, still half in the dream world.

"You weren't," Nova said and then shrugged as he added, "I mean you weren't or we both were. I heard it too."

"Me too," Sonny said. She joined Edeyn at her side, holding Melly's hand as the child cried softly.

Another flash of light streaked visibly through the trees. Nova unholstered his energy weapon and plowed forward. "Follow," he said, voice steely with determination.

Before following his instructions, Edeyn turned to Sonny. "Maybe you should stay here. Guard Melly," she said. Just then, her head throbbed as a sudden *vision* of a tall man with tousled, black hair and a desperate grin pointed a weapon at her. The image was short-lived but it was enough. She knew who was ahead and a cold chill ran through her.

Sonny nodded and pressed her mouth into a thin line. "I will watch her for now. But if there's trouble—" she started.

Edeyn patted Sonny's forearm and nodded. "You'll help if you need to. Just keep the little one safe. She has seen more than enough."

"We all have," Sonny said with a sigh as she held Melly's head against her side protectively.

Nova waited for her, though he stood on alert.

Edeyn's chest tightened, remembering all they had endured on their journey. Would she ever be able to rest? She nodded as she solidified her resolve. There was little choice but to respond to the gunfire.

Nova held up his hand, gesturing for her to wait. She scowled in confusion.

"I'll go first. Just stay close," he told her as he led them into the darkness.

Edeyn—used to taking charge of situations herself—allowed Nova to lead the way. Following someone else's directions was foreign to her, though she trusted Nova who could *see* better in the dark. Additionally, his connection to the spaceship would bring them where they wanted to go.

An unfamiliar, glowing warmth settled into her belly which she identified as safety. It was unusual for her to trust other people, but it felt good to be able to.

In the past, Edeyn put too much blind faith in others even when they treated her poorly. Palan never trusted her, yet she believed she would win him over with her kindness in time. Nova and Sonny's easy acceptance made her realize she didn't need to convince Palan to change his mind. She didn't need his approval.

She followed Nova deeper into the jungle, sticking close to him as the darkness grew thicker. His footsteps were nearly silent.

They communicated without words. Nova glanced back at her, then pointed straight ahead into the darkness. Drawing his pistol slowly, he waved for Edeyn to do the same.

Edeyn took her cue, drawing her single glaive, acutely aware of her other missing armaments. She was grateful to have Nova's support. Just being near him fueled her confidence.

Nova crouched, half crawling and half walking. Though her knees ached from the awkward position, Edeyn followed suit. All she could see in front of her was Nova's neck and back, all she could hear were the soft sounds of his breathing combined with the night life of the jungle in the background.

After a time, they halted again. There, camouflaged in the foliage, was a black, shadowy outline of machinery. Edeyn gazed at it as the moonlight glistened off its shiny, mirrored surface.

"Wow," she whispered, unable to prevent herself.

The spaceship looked as if it had chosen its landing site intentionally so it could blend in with its surroundings. Edeyn gripped her weapon tightly at her side as they crept closer to the grounded vessel.

Edeyn stared in awe at the craftsmanship. This was the ship she'd seen streaking out of the sky, so long ago now. It was similar in appearance to the Oleress rocket, but crafted with care and not nearly as large. It had been created with a loving purpose, after all. That in itself was bound to influence the way it looked.

She watched as Nova touched his hand to the hull, lowering his head and closing his eyes. Edeyn's chest tightened as she *sensed* Nova's flood of emotions. Fragments of his thoughts entered her mind, unbidden.

"I can't believe it's here. After all this time," Nova whispered.

Edeyn smiled at him in silent support. Her body reacted to whatever emotions swirled within him. The ship felt like home, to Nova. She allowed his thoughts of belonging and reunification to settle peacefully within her. She, who had never known what home felt like, felt it now.

Nova crept around the side of the ship, tracing his fingertips along the hull as they traveled. He pressed his hand to a nearly invisible panel and it hissed in response as the ship came alive with lights, the door swishing open to reveal the interior.

The craft had not landed upright and it was difficult to climb onto the lopsided platform. Edeyn gazed in open-mouthed wonder at all the equipment buzzing and glowing with life. She had never seen anything like it before.

"There you are," said a slow, drawling voice.

The chill running through Edeyn's spine alerted her to who spoke even before she turned to confirm. She steadied herself against the wall.

Palan!" Nova gasped.

Palan returned no warmth in his reply. "You're alive," he said.

"You're here!" Nova exclaimed.

Palan tilted his head as he shot a cold glance at Edeyn. "I thought you were dead, Nova," he said.

Nova shook his head. "Nearly! It's a long story," he replied.

Tension gripped Edeyn's throat as the two friends spoke. Anticipating trouble, her body reacted warily to every word that passed between them. She watched Palan closely.

"I'm sure it is," Palan said. His voice remained low and even.

Edeyn regained her composure as she remembered the gunfire that had led them to the crash site late at night.

"Is everything all right, Palan?" she asked. There were no signs of weapon fire around the spaceship.

"I wonder what you'll tell them," said a raspy voice.

Edeyn whirled to see an unfamiliar figure emerging from one of the inner chambers. He held his side, his breathing rattling as he spoke.

"Fenwick?!" Nova shouted.

Chapter Thirty-Seven
ROSES FOR PASSION

"Nova," Fenwick said, his voice barely above a whisper as he struggled to breathe. "It's a pleasure to see you again."

Registering the pain his friend was in, Nova ran to his side, pulling himself closer to Fenwick. A blast of energy snapped at the metal in front of his feet. He halted, both confused and alarmed. Who was shooting?

He frowned in confusion at the sight of Palan leaning solidly against the hull of the ship, weapons gripped in each hand, aiming squarely at Nova's face.

"I would suggest leaving him alone, if you know what's good for you," Palan said, each word measured and cold.

Fenwick groaned as he fell to his knees.

Nova planted his feet wide apart, his gaze shifting back and forth between Fenwick and Palan. He could barely believe Fen was not only alive but had somehow located their spaceship. His mind searched for a logical explanation. He assumed Fenwick was dead back on Asayouga. He wanted to rush to his friend's side.

"He's hurt!" Nova pleaded with Palan, eyes wild as they searched his friend's face. He couldn't wrap his head around what was happening.

"And you're dead," Palan sneered. "At least you were supposed to be, according to that—" Palan paused a moment before spitting the last words "—that THING."

"What?" Nova asked. His heart sank as he looked to Edeyn who crouched on the opposite end of the chamber, her weapon propped in a defensive posture.

"No, Nova, no that's not what I said," Edeyn started.

"You wanted me dead?"

"Of course not!"

Palan's mouth twisted into a distorted smile. "She wanted me to believe you were dead. And my daughter. Where is she, by the way?"

"I didn't *want* you to believe he was dead," Edeyn shrieked.

Nova frowned. He trusted Edeyn, but he'd known Palan longer. His stomach dropped like a stone. Why would Edeyn have lied about his death or Melly's for that matter? What kind of monster would intentionally lead a father to believe his child perished if it weren't true?

Palan shot a bolt of light just past Edeyn's head.

"You lying little bitch," Palan hissed at Edeyn. "Where is Melvene?"

Nova rasped, "She's back at camp with Sonny. She's alive, Palan." He noticed how strangely distant he felt from the rest of his body. It was as if his mouth had responded without his mind's permission. His face was numb.

"Explain yourself," Palan said, refusing to lower his weapon away from Edeyn.

"I don't know what to explain," Edeyn whispered. "I *saw* them drown. Later, I *saw* them living. I was wrong."

"What an apology," Palan replied, tone dripping sarcasm.

"Hold on," Nova said. He had been inching closer to Fen, careful not to alarm Palan. When Palan's attention snapped back to him, he halted.

"She lied to me. Told me my child drowned," Palan said as he advanced closer to Edeyn. "I don't believe she deserves to live."

"Palan!" Nova gasped, desperate to resolve the misunderstanding. He couldn't bear to watch another person he loved die. "She saw us drown because we very nearly did!"

Palan narrowed his eyes at Nova without lowering his weapon. Nova seized the moment to explain, "When we escaped Tskela, I jumped from a window. We ran to the boats. They nearly captured us there and with Melly in my arms it was—it was nearly the end of us both." It was difficult to recall the full event. He remembered flashes of memory, bits and pieces of the flight but not the entire puzzle.

For a moment, Nova thought he'd gotten through to his friend. A shadowy look passed in Palan's eyes and the moment vanished.

"She is not to be trusted," Palan said under his breath.

"Why do you insist I'm lying?" Edeyn asked, voice filled with rage. She stood tall, gripping her glaive, poised to strike. "All I've ever done is speak truth to people who never wanted to hear it. I've never been believed. And I didn't really care. But I would *never* have told you a lie like that. Never. I didn't want them to be dead! Why do you insist that I'm lying?!" Her voice began to shake as her volume increased.

"Because *he* is a liar," came a weak reply.

Nova noticed Fen had propped himself in the doorway with his boots pressed against the frame. His face was pale from blood loss.

"I should have killed you when I had the chance," Palan snapped.

A barely audible chuckle escaped Fen's lips. "You always have been missing chances. You'll never get another one with me," he said.

"What has Palan lied about?" Nova asked, frowning, still not able to untangle the situation completely.

"Asayouga, for starters" Fen said with a pained grimace.

"What?" Nova asked. He looked at Palan quizzically. "What does he mean?"

"Who knows. Fen's a traitor," Palan spat.

"But what does he mean?" Nova insisted, unable to form other words to ask a more coherent question. For a brief moment Nova thought of Sonny and wished she were there to help Fenwick before he faded away for good.

"Why don't you ask him about the Rose Network," Palan said with a sneer.

Nova looked back to Fen who was clearly in no shape to answer anything complicated. A sudden memory of Nayeli crafting a vial of perfume, specifically designed for Fenwick, strongly *scented* with roses, came to mind which brought Nova further confusion. Was that the Rose Network?

But there was too much missing. He didn't have all the information. He recalled how Nayeli shared her work with him. She was helping Fen to attract his lover. The *scent* was uniquely crafted, designed to be alluring to a special someone. She kissed Nova's cheek, satisfied that she'd helped Fen. Fen was often around them, helping in their home far beyond working hours. Nova wasn't sure why he recalled the moment now when it had seemed so insignificant at the time, so unworthy of committing to memory.

Palan's words successfully planted doubts in Nova's mind. Why had Nayeli designed the *scent* so specifically? What if Fen stuck so close to them because he had feelings for her?

"What Rose Network?" Nova asked when he regained his ability to speak.

Fen pulled in a long, labored breath to respond. "It's how I found out—" he paused again, struggling to breathe. "–found out..." he slumped forward and moaned in pain.

Nova launched himself to Fen's side, pulling the man's arm around his neck to support him. "You have to let us get help, Palan! He'll die!"

"You want to save the man who was secretly screwing your beloved wife? The one you devoted all of our time and resources to reuniting with by building this accursed ship and stranding us in the middle of the after realms?" Palan said, voice dripping acid.

Nova froze in immediate disbelief. He could not accept that Nayeli would deceive him. He felt Fenwick's trembling body clinging to him for support. It was plain to see his friend was fading quickly. "Nayeli wouldn't do that to me," Nova insisted, though the seeds of doubt took root.

Palan laughed. "You are so naïve," he said with obvious disdain.

"He is not," Edeyn declared.

Palan chuckled without glancing at her, keeping his attention locked on Nova and Fen. "You just believe everything everyone says to you. You never think about anything in reality," he said. "It's pathetic."

"I loved Nayeli. She was my dearest friend. But it wasn't her I wanted to be with," Fen said, voice fading, barely above a whisper, but Nova heard him.

Nova held the hand of his lifelong friend and looked deep into his green eyes now filled with pain. "Then who?"

Fen drew in a series of labored breaths. "Palan… I only ever loved… Palan."

The room fell silent. Nova's thoughts raced, replaying the memory of Nayeli as she crafted the rose perfume. She must have known and kept Fen's secret safe. Nova's heart warmed with pride as he remembered how genuine Nayeli had been.

Palan appeared stunned, though he did not lower his weapon. "You're lying. You're always lying. You were always talking to Nayeli!" Palan shouted, breaking the silence.

Fen managed a quiet laugh before he replied, "Oh, Palan. We were only ever talking about *you*. I only wanted *you*... the roses... for passion. Your *scent*..." Fen's chest heaved as he strained to breathe. "But you... betrayed us all."

Palan gripped his weapon more tightly, adjusting his stance. His face twisted in a mixture of fury and confusion.

"What does he mean, Palan? What is the Rose Network?" Nova asked. His mind raced as it tried to piece together the things he had noticed but never paid close attention to over the years. Moments of the way Fen gazed at Palan. He knew Palan had trusted Fenwick, once. He wondered what changed.

Palan snorted. "That's just his little make-believe game where he spies on people and shares their secrets."

"A game?" Nova asked, perplexed.

"You are free to go," Palan snapped, redirecting the conversation. "But he stays. He stays," Palan repeated, staring coldly at Fenwick.

The sudden clang of heavy boots against the metal platform of the ship suddenly drew their attention.

"They may be free," said the strong, confident voice belonging to Sonny. "But you won't be. Ever again." She stood wide, feet planted firmly as she held both her pistols pointed at Palan.

"Drop your weapons, Palan," Sonny said.

Chapter Thirty-Eight

Drop Your Weapons

Frozen with indecision, Palan gripped his pistol tightly in his fist. "What are you doing here," he hissed through gritted teeth.

"Hopefully talking some sense into you," Sonny replied.

"Get out! The ship is mine now," Palan insisted, his voice crackling against his wishes, betraying his inner terror. He couldn't maintain command of the situation if they realized he was afraid. He needed to silence Fenwick before it was too late, and Fen appeared altogether too alive for his liking.

Sonny fired a shot at Palan's boot and he danced to avoid it.

There were too many against him; Palan couldn't decide where to point his pistol. He fired at Sonny, narrowly missing her head. A sizzle rose from her hair where the energy singed it. She leapt out the doorway and Palan pursued, abandoning Nova, Fen, and Edeyn behind him.

Palan knew he would overtake Sonny in no time. She couldn't run quickly. Torn between chasing her down and returning to silence Fenwick before he could recount all of Palan's egregious mistakes, he lagged behind nonetheless.

Suddenly, a blow landed with a resounding crack against the back of Palan's head, dropping him to his knees. He folded, the impact jostling his pistol free from his grip. It landed with a thud in the grass beside him.

As he reached to retrieve the weapon, the rod of Edeyn's glaive pressed against his throat. Instinctively, he gripped with both his hands, fighting to topple her. He underestimated her strength once more. For one so small and wiry, she maintained a remarkably solid stance. Palan could not move her.

Though he could no longer see Sonny, the strength of her *scent* was strong. She was close. He would still be able to find her if he could only free himself from Edeyn's grip.

Palan maintained his hold on the glaive, refusing to succumb to unconsciousness from the unrelenting pressure against his windpipe.

"It was you all along," Edeyn hissed against Palan's ear.

He had never heard her voice betray so much anger. Palan felt a tingle of fear run down his spine at how steadfast and resolute she sounded. He'd never trusted Edeyn, but he also hadn't anticipated she might kill him.

The world around him dimmed. He wouldn't be able to withstand the pressure much longer. He threw all his remaining force into a sudden thrust against the weapon, ducking as he did so, successfully sending Edeyn hurtling over his head.

She landed on her feet and spun to face him again. Palan scrambled up, fumbling to regain his pistol. He shook as he aimed at Edeyn.

"I don't know what you're talking about," Palan shouted, gasping from exertion.

"I thought you hated me because of my gifts. A lot of people do," Edeyn said, "But you were just afraid I'd read your thoughts and expose your lies. The *whole* time, you were the reason their home was destroyed! You're a coward."

Palan huffed. Pulling the trigger would end the fight and any possibility of Edeyn exposing everything she could read from his thoughts. He fixed his sites on the space between Edeyn's eyes.

"Daddy," a small voice cried.

The precious sound broke Palan's resolve. Blinking slowly, he turned his head toward his daughter. "Melly," he said in soft disbelief.

She ran to him, hurling her whole weight at his legs, embracing them in a tight squeeze.

The moment's hesitation was too long. Palan collapsed before he heard the loud crack of a branch against his skull.

~~~

A sharp scream rang out from beyond the walls of the ship, ripping through the air in pure agony. Nova frowned as he cradled Fenwick's head in his lap. The man's breathing had become shallow and his consciousness seemed to be fading. Nova couldn't leave him there to die alone.

Although his body was tense with the urge to run into the night to protect Edeyn and Sonny, he forced himself to wait. They could take care of themselves.

Images of Nayeli's lifeless body on the forest floor outside a desolate Asayouga plunged to the forefront of Nova's mind. She, too, had been able to take care of herself. And it wasn't enough. Panic rose within him as if he were living those horrible moments all over again.

"She loved you," Fen rasped, barely intelligible.

"What?" Nova asked as he blinked away the flashback and looked at Fenwick's face.

"Nayeli," Fen said.

"Of course she loved me," Nova said as he re-focused his attention on his dying friend. He noticed how dry his mouth had become.

A burst of activity in the doorway pulled Nova's attention away from further questions.

Palan's body thunked along the metal plates as Edeyn dragged him in, her muscles bulging with effort. She propped him next to a wall and secured him to a panel. Finally, she leaned against the hull and slunk to the ground, breathing heavily from exertion.

Sonny carried Melly inside, cradling the child close to her chest. She locked eyes with Nova, surveying him and Fen.

"Ok, little one," she whispered to the top of Melly's head. You stay here with your dad. He's going to want to see you when he wakes up," she said. She carefully deposited Melly on the ground next to her father before hauling herself across the inclined deck of the ship.

She knelt before Fen and Nova, placing one palm against Fen's forehead and another against his chest. She closed her eyes, breathing slowly and deeply.

Palan let out an angry moan drawing everyone's attention. Melly threw her arms around her father's neck.

Palan embraced his daughter while staring over the top of her head at Nova and Fen. "Holding the one who betrayed you," he sneered. "That's precious."

"What does he mean, Fen," Nova asked quietly, afraid of the answer.

"Only that I figured out his secrets," Fen replied, his voice cutting in and out as he grew weaker.

"There is nothing I can do for him," Sonny said, interjecting. "He's already fading. I haven't the strength to pull him back." She looked into Nova's eyes with a silent apology.

"I didn't want it to be him. I should have ended him when I knew," Fen whispered. His eyes fluttering to a close. "But... I loved him...I'm sorry."

Nova grasped Fen's hands in his own. "There's nothing for you to be sorry for, my friend," he said, reassuring him. He didn't fully understand everything, but he couldn't allow Fen to pass without knowing he was forgiven. Nova could find answers to his questions later.

A wisp of a smile crossed Fen's face, indicating Nova's words comforted him in his final moments.

Nova held him reverently until the last of his breath escaped his lungs and the rattling of his labored breathing ended.

There was a long silence. Palan stared but didn't speak.

"Goodbye, Fenwick," Sonny whispered. She kissed the top of Fen's head before wiping her tear-filled eyes with her sleeve. When she looked up, her whole demeanor changed. "Fen betrayed no one. The only traitor here is Palan."

Nova almost missed hearing her, she spoke so quietly.

"You know nothing," Palan snapped.

Sonny's voice grew stronger as she replied, "That's what most people assume. You all forget about the *touch* because you assume it's only for healing, for fixing all the things the rest of you break. When I heal, I dive deep into feelings, pull the energy to the surface and put it back where it should be. But I feel *everything* deeply. Not just physical wounds. I can feel your deception, too." She never broke eye contact with Palan as she spoke.

Nove swallowed hard against the lump in his throat, not daring to interrupt her. Sonny had more answers than he would have guessed.

"It is Palan who is responsible for Nayeli's death," Sonny declared.

Nova's stomach lurched. Palan and Fen had been with him on Observation Point when the city was ransacked. How could Palan be responsible? His mind revolted against the idea that either of them could have had anything to do with the death of his beloved. It had surely been an accident, the result of a struggle fighting back against the unknown assailants.

Sonny patted Nova's shoulder.

"How would you have any idea at all who attacked Asayouga," Palan sputtered.

Nova's breath caught in his chest. "What are you saying?" he said, barely able to force the words from his lips.

With a sigh, Sonny rose to her feet. "You know deep down, Nova. Palan gave away your research to Tskela. Fen should have turned him in if he knew but... he didn't."

"I don't understand," Nova stammered.

Sonny shook her head sadly at Fen's lifeless body. "It's too much," she whispered before trudging her way back out to the jungle where the sky was now lightening with the approaching dawn.

"Nova," Palan started, sounding desperate.

"What happened to Nayeli?" Nova demanded.

"She was never supposed to die," Palan said, his voice cracking, betraying both fear and regret. "I had no way of knowing they would attack us. I had no way of knowing she would die. Please believe me, Nova."

Nova's heart felt as heavy as a stone. "I don't."

Chapter Thirty-Nine
REPAIRS

Nova stretched as he sat up in his bed, grateful to have a comfortable, steady place to sleep after their long journey. Grey Rock had proven to be a restful place to wind up. Out the window, he could see sunlight filtering through the clouds, the sky already bright blue in the daylight.

He swung his legs off the bed and rubbed his face with his hands before beginning his morning routine. After he dressed, he made his way down the winding staircase to the front room where he helped himself to fresh fruit and baked goods. The townsfolk had given them a surprisingly warm welcome. Sonny offered her services in exchange for a place the group could stay while they repaired their ship.

Nova bit into a juicy apple and smiled at the sight of Edeyn sitting at her favorite table near the front windows. Dust particles floated in the air, illuminated by sunlight streaming through the window like a halo around her. He joined her, sliding into his chair across from her.

She maintained her focus on a large sheet of paper filled with drawings and schematics for their ship. "Good morning," she said without glancing away from the paperwork.

He and Edeyn had made alternating trips to and from Oleress with supplies for the spaceship. Nova was surprised at first to see how quickly Edeyn learned the information she needed to. She had been more than willing to help Nova with rebuilding, seeming to bask in the glow of acceptance as part of his work and world.

Sonny's loud footsteps from her uneven gait announced her presence for her. She scraped a chair away from the table and plopped down heavily before struggling to bring the chair back to the table. Nova reached over to help but she batted him away.

"Has my contact been helpful in Oleress?" she asked.

After Fenwick's passing, Sonny revealed the mystery of the Rose Network, and her role within it. She was an analyst, constantly learning intelligence and investigating data patterns to find connections no one else could. It turned out, she had worldwide connections with other libraries in the Network.

"Very," Edeyn answered for both of them. "They're going to help us with nutrition rations."

"You're that close to relaunching?" Sonny asked, raising an eyebrow in surprise.

Nova nodded the affirmative. "We really are." He felt a flutter of excitement rising within him as he realized how true the statement was.

Oleress was still in shambles. The trap Palan activated was an emergency failsafe in case enemies were to intrude and discover their research facility. In essence, that was exactly what happened, although Palan had not intended for there to be such dire consequences. Whoever designed the trap overlooked the extent of the damage it could cause.

Although Sonny already established trust through her contact there, they all chipped in with rebuilding efforts in exchange for access to materials and resources needed to rebuild Nova's ship.

Everything would be set in perfect order before Nova soared into space a second time. This time, he would be taking the trip solo.

Nova grasped Edeyn's hand and she looked up, startled. Her expression softened when her eyes met Nova's.

"Are you ready for another journey?" Nova asked.

"Let's get going," Edeyn responded as she quickly rolled her parchment, wrapping leather bands around it to secure it closed. She rose from the table.

Nova helped her pack her papers into her bag. "The carriage is ready," he said.

"You two have fun," Sonny remarked.

"Thanks," Edeyn said in a cheerful voice.

Nova wanted to hold Edeyn's hand as they walked, but he knew she preferred to have her hands free, so he refrained as they made their way down the road to the small, two-seater vehicle.

They dropped into their respective seats and secured themselves before programming the destination's coordinates into the front panel. The vehicle began to tick and hum in a pleasant rhythm as it transported them through the town and down the road to Oleress.

The trips back and forth were made much more convenient with a vehicle to travel in.

"This might be one of our last trips," Edeyn remarked as they relaxed in the seats.

Nova hummed an acknowledgment. He was staring through the open sunroof, squinting at the sky as he often did, still trying to make out stars in the daylight. It comforted him to find Nayeli's star even if it was faded behind the dazzling blue of midmorning.

"We'll be there soon," Edeyn announced after some time passed.

Nova pulled his attention back to Edeyn. "Yeah," Nova replied. He smiled, grateful for the ease of her presence. He'd missed her during their separation. Despite only knowing each other a short time, there was a mutual understanding between them, as if they'd been friends for years.

The vehicle parked itself in the outskirts. They always walked through the city gates together on their trips to Oleress. After spending the day at the research center assisting with rebuilding, they would haul carts of supplies back to the vehicle to carry back to the spaceship. The daily visits kept them busy from morning until late at night.

"Do you want to see how Melly is doing today?" Edeyn asked as they re-entered the city.

Repair crews were hard at work fixing the roads and buildings that had fallen into varying states of disrepair after the upheaval.

Nova sighed with a pang of guilt as he considered saying no. Leaving Melly behind for so long was one thought that made him doubt whether they should really attempt the rocket launch again. He wouldn't be gone forever, but he didn't want the child to feel abandoned yet again.

But seeing Melly also meant seeing *him*. Nova could hardly stand to be in Palan's presence after everything. Maybe some day Nova would find it within himself to forgive the man for his betrayal, but for now the best he could muster was to be grateful Melly could remain with her father. He may not deserve to be alive, but Melly deserved to have her family.

Edeyn gently squeezed Nova's bicep. "We don't have to," she said reassuringly.

"No," Nova said. "We should." If everything went well that day, they could be done with supply runs and ready to put the finishing touches onto the ship.

"Ok," Edeyn agreed without pressing him further.

They carried on to the research center in comfortable silence. As soon as they arrived, Ayah greeted them and lead them to the workshop as she did each day.

"Let's see the schematics again," she said as she touched a wall panel, enlivening the ceiling lights one by one across the room.

Edeyn unrolled her parchment onto the table, placing heavy stones on each corner to ensure the edges remained flattened.

Ayah examined the paper for a few moments before turning to Nova. "Will you need help assembling anything on your end?" she asked.

"No. I'll take care of it," Nova said. Although an extra technician would have sped up the work process, Nova was too strongly protective of his work to allow anyone new near it.

He was still bitter after learning how Palan betrayed Asayouga. All along, Palan had been stealing his research plans and selling the information to Tskela for his own gain. He claimed it was to help support his daughter and Sapphira. Nova learned Palan tried to give the Tskelans false leads, but when they found out he was stringing them along, it ended in catastrophe.

Nova believed Palan's intentions were to elevate his status and help his daughter, but ultimately, he couldn't maintain his double life. Nova could understand his motivations; Sapphira and Melvene were undoubtedly important to Palan, but his ego had gotten in the way.

Eventually, Tskela became aware of Palan's duplicity and invaded the city, taking all the information they could while leaving no possibility for Asayouga to continue developing its own technology.

Sonny explained that the Rose Network was a community of intelligence agents. She and Fen were both a part of it. Fen found out about Palan's actions but, not wanting to betray the man he loved—in spite of Palan not reciprocating the feelings—he'd kept the knowledge to himself until it was too late.

Nova wished they'd been able to save Fen. He only ever told Nayeli about his secret love for Palan. It was a testament to how trustworthy she was. She loved everyone and wanted everyone else to feel loved as well. It made Nova miss her all the more. So far, he hadn't found a star for Fenwick's soul, but he hoped one would appear somewhere near Nayeli's. He hoped his fallen friend would find peace in his new form.

Working on the ship now felt sacred to Nova. He couldn't allow just anyone to go near it. He trusted Edeyn and Sonny, but there would always be part of him that remained on high alert, looking for subtle signs of treachery.

"All right. Your ration supply order should arrive in a few days. We will clear you for launch as soon as you give the go ahead," Ayah said with a grin. She held out her hand to shake Nova's. "Congratulations!"

Nova felt a tingle of excitement. He couldn't wait for the quiet majesty of the stars. Nova and Edeyn went over the supply list once more to be certain nothing was missed. Once the food supplies arrived, they would be ready to launch.

After verifying the details, they departed the research center and walked along the city streets toward the school.

Palan sat on the curb outside the building, bouncing a ball back and forth with Melly. Melly's face looked joyful, while Palan's expression remained blank.

"Nova!" Melly squealed, tossing the ball before running to Nova.

He grabbed her in a bear hug and twirled her in the air. "Hey, sweetheart," he said. "How are you doing?"

"Happy!" Melly chirped.

Palan picked up the wayward ball and stood stiffly on the curb while Nova and Melly talked. Nova glanced his way but couldn't bring himself to speak to the man. Every time he saw Palan's face, flashes of Nayeli fighting off assailants invaded his mind. It was too painful knowing how deeply his former friend had betrayed them all. Knowing he was responsible for so much death sickened Nova.

Nova was glad Palan would not be accompanying him into space when he re-launched. If the first launch were successful, Palan would have lived next to the souls of people he unwittingly sold into death. Now Palan would, instead, remain in

Oleress with his daughter. As much as Nova hated the man, he was glad the little girl wouldn't lose another family member. He hoped she never learned of her father's treachery.

It warmed Nova's heart to see Melly doing well. He set her on the ground in front of him and crouched to her eye level, placing his hands on her arms. "I might not see you again for a long time after this," he said, fighting the urge to cry as he tucked a lock of curly hair behind her ear.

To his surprise, Melly simply hugged him in response. "It's ok, Uncle Nova," she said. "You need to go home."

Nova embraced the little girl one last time, shedding a few tears he could not hold back. He lifted Melly's hand gently and kissed her fingertips. "I'll see you again, angel," he said.

"Bye, Nova," she said before running to Palan's side. She clung to her father's leg and waved.

"Good luck, Nova," Palan said huskily.

Without looking at him, Nova managed a curt nod in reply. He turned his back before he could lose his resolve. Instead, he smiled at Edeyn. It was time they returned to Grey Rock.

Chapter Forty

The Soul from the Supernova

"I'll miss you," Nova said.

Sonny laughed and hugged him tight. Nova felt his spine crack under the pressure of her embrace.

"You won't miss me whatsoever. You're going exactly where you've always belonged," Sonny replied.

Nova chuckled. He would miss her, but there was so much to look forward to in the outer sphere. Not knowing when he would return to see them again was a daunting thought.

He bit his lip as he took Edeyn's hands in his. Leaving her on the ground was the hardest decision they had made together. They built communication systems to maintain contact. It seemed wise to have someone on Kelmundy who knew how the spaceship worked, in case he needed to make another emergency landing.

But Edeyn felt as much like home as Nayeli always did. Nova was left torn between his soul's two mates.

Tears welled in Edeyn's eyes and she raised herself on tip toes, leaning in to kiss Nova. "Until we meet again," she whispered.

"My heart is always open to yours," Nova replied. Even if their communication systems failed, he was certain he would still feel Edeyn with him, just as he had when they were separated in Tskela.

Nova tromped up the gangway into the ship. He gave Edeyn and Sonny a salute before activating the shuttle doors. They swished closed, leaving him alone, surrounded by humming consoles and lights.

There was no urgency in Nova's launch this time. Every piece of equipment was perfectly calibrated. The supply rooms were packed to the brim, filled with everything he would need for a prolonged stay in space.

With the help of the research facility in Oleress they were able to upgrade much of their technology. He agreed to exchange data with them when he returned, in exchange for their support through the rebuilding efforts. He could stay in the stars as long as he had supplies.

"Ready?" Edeyn's voice crackled through a panel near the central core.

Nova grinned as he pressed the button to respond. "Ready as I'll ever be."

"I'll activate the launch sequence from here," Edeyn said.

Nova drew in a deep breath, closing his eyes as he thought of how Fen would once again miss the spaceship launch. He hoped he would see his friend sparkling in the heavens near the Asayougan constellation.

"Proceed," Nova breathed.

The engine swirled with full power, and metal thrummed beneath Nova's feet. A countdown echoed throughout the ship's interior. Nova strapped himself securely into his launch seat, ready for a successful take off this time around.

Edeyn's voice broke through above the sound of the launch countdown. "Nova...?"

"Yes?" Nova queried.

"Good luck... please come home."

Nova smiled as he soaked in her words. "I will always come home."

The countdown ended and the rocket soared. The world streaked past the windows too quickly for Nova to discern details, even with his enhanced *sight*. Instead, he closed his eyes, allowing himself to experience the full sensation of the launch.

As the ship emerged into the darkness of space, everything fell quiet. Nova released the security belt and rose from his seat. Pressing both palms to the windows, he stared in awe at the void. He couldn't have fathomed what this moment would feel like.

"Wow," he whispered in reverence.

Panels beeped and whirred around him. Nova examined the telemetry screen before inputting a complicated equation that would orient the ship in his chosen direction. He then peered through one of the many scopes they installed and found her: Nayeli's soul star.

A sudden *vision* flowed to Nova's mind. *His fingers interlaced with Edeyn's. Peace flowed between them as she rested her head against his shoulder.* "You're still here," Nova thought.

"*Always.*"

Even in the profound silence of the spaceship, he held his new home in his heart. Nova would never be far from the ones he loved.

Acknowledgements

I wrote the first draft to this little adventure in 2008. It was incredibly bumpy and missing any sort of plot. None of the characters had any depth. I abandoned the story for the next 15 years until 2023, when I finally picked it up and gave it the love and attention it deserved.

The Soul from the Supernova is a story that's close to my heart as it carries so many threads from my life in the real world. But it wouldn't have been possible to finish this book without some key individuals. First, I must thank my editor, Jaz (@thestorymaestro). Through her gentle questions in the margins of my manuscript, I strengthened the storyline and tightened up the prose. I learned so much about structure through her work and without her, this book would never have been in any sort of shape to bring to all of you.

Then there's my second editor/beta reader, Skylar. Sky and I formed a friendship purely by accident through a gaming

Discord server hosted by a mutual friend. A recent university graduate with an English degree and a love of fantastical tales, Skylar agreed to help me proofread and copyedit this book. She also provided valuable beta reading comments and for her, I am very grateful. Not only did she help with all of the above, but she also has been putting together my author newsletter for me these past few months! I always wanted to connect with my readers through a more direct mode, and I couldn't seem to organize myself to do it alone. Thank you again, Skylar, for your willingness to help put my ideas together and bring a dream to life.

Next, I must acknowledge my friend and fellow author, B.J.J Lierz. Without her kindness in saving me from a cover artist scam, this book wouldn't even have a book cover. I wanted a hand-painted, whimsical design but the person I originally commissioned gave me something more nightmarish. B.J.J swooped in to help without a second thought. In the end, she seemingly read my mind and translated it to a book cover. Saying thank you doesn't feel like enough in her case. So, I strongly suggest you go look up her incredible book, Soul S ifter!

Finally, to 2008 Angela: You got us here. Thank you...or me? Well, thank you to all the versions of myself.